AFTER THE WATER BROOKS

a novel

Erica Dansereau

Identifiers: Library of Congress Control Number: 2023915974 | ISBN 979-8-9858237-4-5 (paperback) | ISBN 979-8-9858237-6-9 (hardcover) | ISBN 979-8-9858237-5-2 (e-book)

This is a work of fiction. Any references to historical events, real people, real publications, or real places are used fictitiously. Other names, dialogue, characters, and events are products of the author's imagination. Any resemblance to actual persons, living or dead, is purely coincidental.

Cover design by Brittany Howard
Author photo by Walkyria Whitlock
Cover images: Canva

www.ericadansereau.com

To Patrick—my Claude. I love you.

And to Gram,
Always on my mind, always in my heart.

"As the hart panteth after the water brooks, so panteth my soul
after thee, O God."
Psalm 42:1

AFTER THE WATER BROOKS

1

1981
Goldfield, Nevada

THE DUST THAT danced in the wind tasted of home—or rather, what remained of it. I took a step toward Claude and slipped my hand into his, the calloused ridges and soft pockets a welcomed condolence.

"They told me how bad it was, but I didn't believe them," he murmured. He stepped toward the charred grounds, the foundation of his childhood home the only thing still intact. Our arms stretched between us until I let go of his hand and wrapped my cardigan tightly around myself.

I wasn't ready yet to get any closer. The scene threatened to bring me to my knees, and like this old home, I felt the urge to crumble. The destruction was too much—the soot, the ash, the reminders of . . . My mind drifted to my father.

At the thought of him, I stiffened, my back as rigid and delicate as the spines of a Joshua tree, teetering between two extremes. This fire had nothing, and yet everything, to do with losing my father. My brain clung to his memory now, not caring that my heart was incapable of bearing such a burden. My head spun. I wouldn't allow myself to think of him yet. I simply, physically, couldn't.

He is not here. Was not here. The reminder didn't help much because, to my exhausted soul, he might as well have been. Casting a feeble glance over my shoulder at our parked Dodge Dart, I swallowed the clumping dust in my throat.

It was a mercy, I knew. As much devastation as was before us, we had much to be thankful for. The fire had started when Ginny and Leonard were grocery shopping in Tonopah. They made it home in time to watch a lifetime's worth of memories burn. Flames licked away every ding in the walls caused by three boys wrestling and every carefully measured height mark on the backside of the hall closet door until no trace of the family remained.

Claude stepped into the ruins. My breathing hitched. The man was always more sentimental than me. I'd always been the one afraid of holding on too tightly to anything for fear of losing it. But this . . . This hurt more than I thought it would. We'd been away from Goldfield for a good number of years, after all. We'd moved away and moved on, but a hometown never really leaves you.

I pulled myself together enough to join Claude.

"We'll never be able to come back here again," he said as I walked over soot and ash to stand at his side. "This house . . . the memories . . . I can't believe it's all *gone.*"

"I know," I whispered back and realized my hand had crept to my throat. I swallowed against the disbelief. "Our memories still remain, though. No flame can consume those. They're untouchable; ours to keep."

He nodded and licked his lips. His untucked plaid shirt

flapped in the wind, and he used a knuckle to wipe the single tear that snaked down his cheek.

"This fire brought your parents out to us. We get to enjoy them now in their later years. If it hadn't been for this, you know they never would have left," I reminded him, tilting my head to watch his face.

He softened slightly. "You're right."

It was true; they had been set on staying here until their dying day. When we'd left for Colorado, chasing a new opportunity and searching for somewhere to settle down with our growing family, we'd tried to convince them to join us. But Ginny and Len loved this land, and I couldn't blame them. Parts of me still ached for the desert.

Claude moved into what had been the kitchen. "Can you imagine if they hadn't been gone that day? Mom . . . she couldn't have . . ."

As her age increased, Ginny's arthritis made it hard for her to move quickly. I couldn't bear the thought of what he was insinuating.

He tilted his head to the sky and peered at the endless blue above. "Mom always complained about not having enough natural light in here."

If I wasn't so sad, I might have laughed. "Too bad it took the roof collapsing to make her dream come true."

Claude swept a hand over the charred remnants of a barely distinguishable cabinet. "The Lord is good, even in the wreckage. He's here, shielding us from the furnace." He wiped his soot-stained hands on the pants I'd freshly pressed only hours ago in a hotel room.

Looking at the ruins around us, some would be apt to deny the evidence of God's presence here. But what Claude said was true. He and I knew from experience that the Lord could be found in the most desolate and broken places.

I moved toward the brothers' old bedroom. The roof remained in part, as did the blackened studs of the walls. Stooping next to a heap of ash, I used a broken scrap of wood to poke through the pile, half-hoping in vain to uncover an unscathed piece of the past. But I knew it was of no use. There was nothing salvageable here except for the memories and, of course, God's grace.

I tossed the piece of wood into the ash and turned to leave, but something caught my eye at the outer edge of the rubble.

"Fly!" I called to him, the nickname still as fresh as when we were kids. I took hold of the wood scrap again and stretched across the pile, using the wood as an arm, swiping at the small object and moving it closer until I could reach down and grab it.

It was covered in grime, and I blew at the debris until the shiny glint of the pocketknife flashed in the sun. "Honey! Come look at this."

A smile crept onto Claude's face as I handed it over. He ran his sooty fingers along the side. "This was Cliff's," he said. "Wait a second . . ."

He paused for a moment and tilted his head to the side as though puzzled. He held out the knife and pointed to the engraved initials on the gold exterior.

"J.H.?" I questioned. "You're sure this was Cliff's?"

In the sheen of his eyes, I saw something click into place.

"John." His smile grew. "Man, I never did know his last name. I'm going to have to ask Dad."

"As in Big John?"

Claude nodded. "On the trip he made here just after Vern passed, Big John gifted me his Bible and, to Cliff, his pocketknife."

Big John. My memories of him were scarce and far away now, though a big presence like his was not easily forgotten. In fact, his presence carried on to this day in the form of the Bible that still sat on our coffee table at our home in the Rockies, well-loved all these years later.

Claude blinked back tears and slid the knife into his pocket. A sudden gust of wind whipped through the remains and sent ash dancing across the ground. Once again, my mind darted to our car—to the other set of ashes that sat motionless and settled, awaiting their release.

This trip was one of goodbyes.

I was tired of goodbyes.

How much sweeter were hellos? How deeply did I long for the inflating feeling of looking into a face for the first time rather than struggling to conjure up the image of a loved one last seen. I knew deep down that hard goodbyes were the evidence of a life well lived. The grief of those left behind said a lot about the person who left.

Even so, that sweetness aside, I was terribly tired of goodbyes.

"Come on." Claude placed his hand on my back and guided me out of the Fisher family home to the remains of my own childhood home next door—the home Claude had renovated when we were barely old enough to call ourselves adults. The home that brought healing. The home that welcomed our first two children into the world.

The wind had carried flames to it, and it bore the scars as proof. It stood stronger in comparison to Ginny and Leonard's home but was entirely inaccessible. The door was blocked, and the whole place posed the threat of collapse if we were stupid enough to try getting inside.

I'd made peace with leaving our first home when we sold it years ago. I'd taken everything I'd needed, everything I'd wanted. Never did I imagine it would be crushed like this, though. A dwelling once full of brokenness, restored by the healing poured out from our Maker's good hands, was now destroyed. It had served a good purpose, had run its course and been the face of redemption.

I took one long, sad look at our home before I had to turn away. This desert was the safe haven to which we could always return. But so much had changed, as time had a way of doing. The years had blown by; the land had changed. I was no stranger to aging, too. Wrinkles fanned from the corners of my eyes, and my skin sagged in places once taut. Tomorrow would mark one more year on this earth for me. In the relentless desert wind, I felt the scooping and hollowing of my bones, the youth of a woman drying up, the giving over to age, and the ever-increasing closeness of more goodbyes on the horizon.

I left Claude gazing at the two former Fisher homes and went to the car. It wasn't long before he joined me, and we drove to the cemetery on our way out of town. The cemetery was divided into sections. We drove down the rocky road that led to the back corner and parked. To continue down the road would lead us to the area where the town's founders were buried and where the tombstone that read "UNKNOWN MAN DIED EATING LIBRARY PASTE" stood.

But we wouldn't be visiting that section today. There was only one person who brought us to this desert burial ground. We walked through the gate and among the headstones. Some were beautifully decorated, while others were untouched and unreadable. At Vern's grave, we both kneeled. A lizard scurried across Vern's name plaque and disappeared into the scrub. A small wooden cross stood beside the headstone, weathered now from thirty-six years in the elements.

Claude's body hardened beside me. I knew he still felt the unfairness of losing Vern to my father's inebriated mistake despite coming to terms with the tragedy over time. But Claude was the last remaining of three brothers, and it was a lonely title to carry.

"Your brothers would have been so proud to see the life

you've led," I said. "They always were proud of you. No matter the teasing in childhood, they sure adored you."

He looked away and reached for my hand, squeezing it as a thank you. I watched him swallow the creeping sadness away and look back at the grave, giving a curt nod toward the one who rested beneath.

The wind whipped again and fingered itself right into the place that hurt. This was an ending of sorts. With Claude's parents now permanently displaced, what reason aside from nostalgia would we have to visit Goldfield? To return to the hills that bore sole witness to my mother leaving in the dead of night. To visit the dust that had carried our laughter in its grains and the dirt that had soaked up our tears.

I took one last look at Vern's grave. He would be the only Fisher to be buried here, for Cliff was on a hillside overlooking the Pacific Ocean, his remains flown from an unforgiving war overseas and laid to rest under a white wooden cross. The lineage of the Fishers and Ralphs here in Goldfield was over.

I despised this sudden finality—the feeling as though someone had shut and locked this portion of our lives away forever. I felt the guttural ache of life's surprises, felt the air growing stale inside, trapped, like one final breath needed to escape.

Just like the urn that waited for me in the car.

2

1945. 36 years earlier . . .
Tonopah, Nevada

THE WIND RATTLED Peggy's car and howled through the slit of the rolled-down window where cigarette fumes escaped into the desert air. Sitting in the passenger seat, Kitty angled her body away and hugged her arms around herself. Even miles away from Goldfield, she still felt Claude's warmth.

A tear slid down her cheek against her will, and she ground her teeth. If her aunt saw her crying over *those people* again, there was no telling what she might do. Kitty took a slow breath, careful not to reveal her fragile state, and watched the sagebrush tick by like tally marks drawn on her heart.

How many individual sagebrush bushes separated her now from the only true family she'd ever known? The miles were plenty—twenty-six too many, to be precise. But it might as well have been more. She'd told Fly not to tell her goodbye. The words carried too much weight, too much pain to hear them out loud, but the dark clouds brewing in her belly told her that goodbyes would be all she ever knew.

To the mother who left without a trace, *goodbye.*

To the alcoholic father now in jail, *goodbye.*

To the almost-brother in the grave, *goodbye.*

To the neighbors who'd become family, *goodbye.*

And to the boy who made her feel things she didn't quite understand . . .

Goodbye.

"I wasn't planning for any of this, you know that," Peggy said as they neared Tonopah, as though anyone could have planned for the events that had transpired over the previous few days. "But I'll fix you some sort of room. It'll be nicer than your daddy's jail cell, at the very least."

A lump built in Kitty's throat as she turned to watch her aunt. Peggy's features hardly budged; her colored lips remained flat, her eyes squinting at the road ahead. The cold remark left but a small stain on what remained of Kitty's shredded heart.

Claude had been convinced that this tragedy-born separation was only a minor hiccup in the road. She had felt the heat of his hope in the final words he'd spoken at the threshold of her home, in the way he'd hugged her like he'd meant it. But in the embrace of Claude's mother, Ginny, she had felt the weight of loss, of apology, as though Ginny's reality told a different story than Claude's.

Kitty wanted to hold on, to believe in a possibility that could be bigger than the devastation she saw before them. But the light she'd basked in all her life, the light of the Fisher family next door, had been snuffed out and the rug of security ripped from under her feet. The fact that she had let herself believe for her fourteen years of life that she belonged in a family such as theirs was almost laughable to her now as she sat beside the aunt who felt like a stranger, and she wondered about the fate that seemed reserved for someone such as her.

3

Lia

1937
Galia, Oregon

RAIN SPLATTERS AGAINST the window, and the hairs on my neck prickle at the sound of the baby crying. Except, as I push away from my melancholic window seat perch, I realize the house is as quiet as ever, and the baby—can I still call her a baby—is fast asleep.

My heart refuses to settle, but will it ever in this big house? We've been here from California for over a year, and still, I struggle to feel at home. Though, when have I ever felt such a feeling?

I decide to make myself some tea. The lavender kind that Dr. Bruce told Tenn would calm my nerves. Young motherhood stress aside, even a pungent tea will do nothing to soothe a broken heart. This much I know for sure. But still, I put on the kettle and wait, drifting back to the window to watch the rain saturate my garden and the meadow beyond. It's soothing.

My heart leaps from its cage at the sound of the hissing kettle, the whistle piercing through my skin and stirring up my heart again. I imagine the baby crying once more, which only pricks tears of my own.

The clock tells me Tenn won't be home for another hour at the least. I don't want to be alone anymore. I steep the tea and look around our home, searching and hoping for a cluttered corner, a dust bunny, anything to reveal itself as needing to be done. But the chores have been finished; I did them at four this morning when I couldn't sleep. Dinner has already been prepped, and the garden needs no watering in this rain.

You do too much, they all say. *You must learn to relax, to go slow.* But they don't know that keeping my hands busy is the only way to forget. Because I live to forget and hope that my body will adapt to a new set of memories. Tenn worries for me. If he were home, he'd insist I sleep when the baby sleeps. But sleep is the worst part. Letting my mind go still on purpose. What a horror!

Oh, how he loves me far more than I'm worth. And I love him, this is true. But the days without him are long, and I could do with more to fill my arms, maybe another hobby, a child, a friend or two.

I sip my tea and watch the rain slow to a drizzle and eventually to nothing at all. It's a shame the clouds threaten to part, and the sun dares to peek through the thick curtains of clouds that have felt all day like a sad and needed hug.

The doorbell chimes, as though God is delivering to me my innermost thoughts. Is He there? Does He listen to nuisances like me? But as desperate as I am for a distraction, something builds in my chest, the heavy-laden pull of dread at odds with the sparrow-like flutter of hope. *What if it's . . .*

The bell chimes again, and this time, it wakes the baby. She wails from her crib down the hall, and I spring into action.

"One minute!" I holler as I pass the entryway to retrieve my distraught toddler. She is standing, holding onto the crib rails. Hot tears snake down her cheeks. But she soothes instantly in my arms as I lift her from the bed. The smell of her sweaty head brings a smile to my face. With her resting snugly on my shoulder, I move to answer the door.

It's only Edward, the milk delivery man. He greets me kindly and lifts the box full of milk bottles from the porch. I open the door wider for him to enter.

"My boots are a bit muddy." He hesitates. "Let me—"

"Nonsense. The floors are due for mopping anyway. Come in," I insist and lead him through the house to the kitchen. "How hard is it to maintain a few milk cows, Edward?"

He shoots me a puzzled look. "Why do you ask?"

"Oh, I'm thinking of broaching the idea to Tenn."

"Don't you have your hands full enough?" He sets the box of milk onto the counter, and his eyes shift to the sleepy body in my arms.

Not nearly full enough, I think to myself.

I force out a light laugh and say, "You're only frightened of losing my business."

He smiles. "Well, what good would a milkman be if all of his customers started supplying their own milk? What good would my milk cows be if everyone got one of their own?"

My thoughts run cynical. What good is any of this? I wrap my arms tighter around my daughter and curse myself for living under such a dark cloud. *You have a good life, Lia. Why can't you accept what's here before you?*

I realize Edward is waiting for my reply. "You present a fair point. I suppose the milk cow idea shall be laid to rest among the other failed ideas in my brain."

"You have many?"

"A whole graveyard full." The words come out heavier than

I anticipate, so I laugh and wave my hand as though it were a frivolous joke.

"Well, I'm sure your next idea will take root and grow into something quite beautiful, much like yourself and your sweet little girl there."

"I appreciate that, Edward."

He tips his hat. "Onto my next delivery," he says, moving out of the kitchen. "Say, since the owning cattle idea isn't going to pan out, why don't you and Tenn come out to the farm sometime when your little one gets a smidge older? I'll show you around and let her try to milk one if she'd like."

I follow him to the front door. "I'm sure she'll get a kick out of that. Thank you."

We bid one another goodbye, and I am again alone in my too-big, too-quiet house. Though, I do have my daughter, who now lifts her head from my shoulder and offers the most adorable sleepy smile. I know that she deserves the best version of me, not the one who wants to curl into a ball and cry herself into oblivion. She is my joy. And I know deep down that she wouldn't be here if I hadn't done what I did.

I close my eyes against the pain, and she holds my cheeks between her tiny hands, squishing them together like a fish. She laughs, and suddenly I'm glad the sun has come out, and my daughter is awake.

For now, all feels right in the world.

4

1981
Galia, Oregon

WE DROVE UNTIL the desert became a distant memory, and endless forests led us to the expanse of the Pacific coast. A charming fishing town, Galia had the light touch of tourism, but the place radiated more with the easy delight of simplicity than with the bustle of neighboring cities with their river harbors and budding wealth. Our nephew Rand had suggested the location because it was yet untouched by commercial greed, boasting instead of its jagged cliffs and timbered land that rushed the coastline just like the waves that rushed the shore.

We checked into our hotel and got the spiel from a woman named Donna, the owner of Cape Galia Inn and a lifelong resident. She told us about the shops that punctuated the town's charisma. The two cafes. The few boutiques. The bookstore. The souvenir shop that doubled as a bike rental. The saltwater taffy stand on the pier. The grocery market next to the bait and tackle.

Donna led us up a flight of stairs carpeted in pastel teal and delivered us to our room for the week. A queen-sized bed took up most of the space, its mustard yellow quilt a bright ray of sunshine in a room otherwise drowning in a frenzy of blue.

Claude deposited our luggage near the desk in the corner. After driving all day, his face looked exhausted, but he managed to scrub the lines away in a single smile as I made my way to the window.

I leaned against the frame and paid no mind to the passersby on the street below; my gaze instead fixed itself on the sliver of the ocean that could be seen from our room. The relief I'd promised myself, the unbridled sense of freedom that I thought would come with the brine in the air, fell short, nearly as nonexistent as the Fisher family home in Goldfield.

Claude came up behind me and planted a kiss on my cheek. "Okay, birthday girl. What's on the docket for tonight?"

For better or for worse, this trip was full of reminders. Reminders of what we'd lost, what we'd gained . . . and the inevitable goodbyes that continued to come with age.

"Birthday *girl*?" I cringed. "More like birthday dinosaur. As a middle-aged woman, I hardly qualify as being called 'girl' anymore."

"Dinosaur? Sweetheart, fifty hardly makes you a dinosaur."

"Oh, yeah? Then what does it make me?" I turned to face him.

"Old enough that perhaps we should avoid perusing that antique shop we saw on our way into town. Someone there might slap a price tag on you." The skin around his eyes crinkled at the corners as he laughed. "But definitely not a dinosaur."

In spite of myself, I laughed too. "Make jokes while you can. You're not far behind me, you know. And dare I mention that you have more threads of gray in your hair now than do I?"

"Hey, I'm still in the first half of my life for another two months."

"That's only *if* we make it to one hundred."

"Well, if we do, you'll have bragging rights for beating me there."

Fifty felt monumental, but this birthday was laced in melancholy and tinged with grief. All of my prime years were behind me, my four babies raised and out of the house, the eldest of them now raising a family of her own, the youngest entering her freshman year of college. And no matter how natural it felt to see my children grown, I hadn't yet found my footing with the concept of growing old. It was like someone had turned the dial and switched radio stations mid-jitterbug. I could still hear music playing, but my feet didn't yet know the new dance they were called to perform—the one that involved me offering help as a grandmother, finally accepting a bowling club invitation, and staving off hokey greeting cards that declared me "over the hill." The scales were already tipped in that direction; this birthday only solidified that fact.

"Do you think Claire will start walking while we're away?" I asked. "I'd hate to miss that."

"We'll be home in a week."

"A lot can change in one week, Claude. She's teetering on the edge of taking her first steps. Maybe we shouldn't have come all the way out here, so far from home. And what about your mother?"

"What about her? Maisy is taking excellent care of her."

"Yes, but what if—"

"Kitty." He placed one hand on my shoulder and held my chin with the other, directing my attention to his face. "You're the woman who so selflessly takes care of everyone else, but it's time for you to take care of yourself."

My fingers twitched, and I wished I had something to keep them busy.

"Sweetheart," he said gently. "I know you have something

difficult to do while we're here, but let's try to make the most of this time together. This is our first solo trip together in years. Plus, it's your birthday. Your life is a beautiful thing to celebrate."

I relaxed into my husband's chest and tucked my head beneath his chin. "We've been talking about a parents-only vacation for what feels like a lifetime, and now that we're finally on one, here I am wishing it away." I pressed into him more. "I'm sorry."

"You have nothing to be sorry for." He kissed the crown of my head and released me. "I love you."

"I love you too."

"So, what do you say? Can we go celebrate the birthday girl now?" His eyes danced with mischief as he held up my beige cardigan. I looped my arms into the sleeves.

"As long as you stop calling me that."

"If you prefer *birthday bat*, I can use that instead."

I stamped my foot. "Fly Fisher, I am not above tattling to your mother for picking on me."

"If I'm lucky, she won't have her hearing aids in when you call," he quipped as he grabbed our room key from the table, and we walked out the door.

"I'll be sure to tell her *that*, too."

Cape Galia Inn bore the marks of a chic hoarder. The overwhelming amount of macrame and shells somehow exuded charm instead of lunacy, though I felt sorry for the employee in charge of dusting every surface. The place smelled of brine, vanilla, and old books, which was fitting, considering the main level boasted bookshelves that stretched from floor to ceiling, stuffed to the brim with novels. I imagined plucking one from the shelf and sinking into one of the plush, albeit mismatched, chairs for an afternoon. Maybe my fifties would lend the time for me to read for pleasure.

"Mr. and Mrs. Fisher!"

We turned toward the front desk, where Donna waved cheerfully. Her ratted blonde hair remained high and unmoving in spite of her bubbly hello.

"How's your room? Do you need anything?"

"So far, so good," Claude answered. "Though maybe you could point us to a nice dinner spot. Where can we find the best seafood in town?"

She whipped out a map. "You're in luck. We have some of the best seafood restaurants around, all serving daily fresh catches. I highly recommend Oceana on the corner of Anita and Caspian, or, if you're looking for dinner with a view, then The Salty Nook on the pier."

"Whatever the birth—" Claude shut his mouth and gave me an apologetic glance before Donna pounced.

"Birthday? Wait." She gasped and looked at me. "Mrs. Fisher, it's your birthday? What number are you celebrating? Twenty-seven?" She winked theatrically.

"Double that, and you'll be close," I said, forcing my voice to match her cheer.

She jotted down walking directions as though the pier was hard to find and sent us with a handwritten note for the owner of The Salty Nook. *"Todd: Free dessert for this sweet couple on me. – D."*

The pier was one-half mile away, nestled in a spray of beaches between protruding cliffs and ragged rocks. The late summer evening was kind to us as we strolled toward the shore. We were unencumbered tonight, but all I could think about was home. Was everyone alright? Had Maisy remembered Ginny's meds? Was Leonard bored? What about my grandbaby, Claire? Had she taken her first steps?

The sun peeked out from behind a curtain of clouds, and Claude slipped his hand into mine. The warmth of his palm pulled me back to the present. Why did I find it so difficult to focus on what was in front of me and let God deal with the rest?

We reached the pier. The wooden walkway was knotted under our feet as we moved past a worse-for-wear gift shop and the saltwater taffy stand, wave watchers and fishermen. Heavy with salt, the breeze escorted us to the end of the pier where a window-clad, octagonal-shaped restaurant stood, weathered and patient as though waiting for our very arrival.

The sign above the door read: The Salty Nook. EST. 1935. I drew in a humbling breath. I was older than this worn building. Was I as aged, too? The exterior walls ached for a new paint job, the existing yellow peeling and cracking under the constant ocean spray. My stomach moved in tandem with the waves undulating under our feet as a kinship formed between this rundown building and myself. We were both weary and wishing for better days.

A bell chimed overhead as we entered through the door. The hostess, a youthful gal with a shaggy red bob, showed us to a booth with a beautiful view of the Pacific. The clouds had moved, and now the sun basked us with its light and glared off the metal napkin dispenser. I moved it to the side and turned my attention back to the ocean, where swells careened and receded.

"How imminent would divorce be if I told the waitress it's your birthday?"

I resisted the urge to smile as I rolled my eyes at Claude. "I read an article in a magazine the other day that said fifty percent of marriages end in divorce. So, the odds aren't really in your favor, are they?" I raised my brows and flattened my lips for good effect.

"Thirty-one years is a decent run." Claude shrugged, and as the waitress approached to take our order, he whispered, "I'm feeling lucky, though. Think I'll take my chances."

My mouth fell open. *He wouldn't dare. Would he?*

He cleared his throat. "Excuse me, miss. I just wanted to let you know"—his sparkling eyes darted briefly to me—"it's a special day for us."

"Oh, is that right?" The waitress pulled out the pencil tucked behind her ear. "Out celebrating a birthday? Anniversary?"

A thrill zinged through me. For over thirty years, I'd had the privilege of loving this man as my husband, and beyond that, a lifetime worth of friendship. In spite of all our years and hard seasons in life, he still managed to thrill me. Secretly, I hoped for him to tell her, if only so I could razz him about it afterward. Though, if they made me suffer through some humiliating song and dance, like last year at the Mexican restaurant when the waiter slapped a sombrero on my head and got the entire fully packed restaurant involved, I might keel over at an early death of fifty. Thankfully, The Salty Nook wasn't teeming with patrons, and a sombrero was nowhere in sight.

"We're celebrating life," he replied.

The waitress smiled. "How thoughtful."

"You just get sweeter with age, don't you?" I murmured only for him to hear.

"And you, more beautiful," he whispered back. Then, with a wink, he said to the waitress, "Oh, and it's her birthday."

His mouth twisted into a wry smile. I kept a level face as the waitress wished me a happy birthday and took our order. Only when she bustled back to the kitchen did I reach over and swat his arm.

"What? Your life is worth celebrating. I'd shout it from the edge of the pier for all the world to hear if you'd let me."

"At this point, go ahead." I laughed and, in a moment of spontaneity, shouted to the uncrowded restaurant, "It's my birthday!"

He looked at me then like he did when we were young, and I couldn't fight the laugh that bubbled up from my chest. "She's only trying to get free dessert!" he hollered.

I covered my burning face with my hands, smiling into my palms all the while. Claude reached across the table and pulled my hands away.

"What?" I asked.

"I meant what I said earlier."

"About the dessert?"

He laughed. "No. Donna from the hotel gave us a slip for that. I meant what I said about you getting more beautiful."

To be called beautiful was one thing, but it was something else entirely to be called beautiful and know how truthfully the word was meant. My heart stirred, though I couldn't help but consider the building we were in with its weathered walls and battered edges, the structure that had faced stormy gales and sweeping waves. Was I as resilient? As sturdy? Was *this* the face of beauty?

The thought of all we'd weathered together brought a tinge of sadness to the moment. Claude's warm eyes, more crinkled now than ever at the corners, roamed over my features, but in the puckering of his brow, I detected the telltale sign of worry. Before I could change the way I wore my heart on my sleeve, he asked, "What's the matter?"

My eyes flicked away to the expanse of the ocean unfurling for what looked like forever. There was a plethora of metaphors for the infinite pool beneath us, but in spite of the glorious looming of eternity that gave me hope, the moments between now and then were too finite. I could only answer Claude with a shrug as words proved elusive.

If he really wanted an answer, I could take him to the shore after dinner, scoop up handfuls of sand, and declare that time was running through my hands in the same manner. It was an age-old adage, a cliché. But clichés were only popular because they are true no matter how trite or overdone.

The only problem was that time wasn't the only thing slipping from my grasp but the very people I loved too.

"It's your dad," Claude said softly.

A moment later, I clarified, "It's everything."

"Do you know when . . ." He let his question drop. "Sorry, I didn't mean to bring that up. Not today."

But it was too late, the unfinished question hanging in the air as an unwelcome presence.

Did I know when I would be ready to let go? A good portion of my life had been spent at odds with my father. A game carried out like the one the tides play. Me standing on the shore of our relationship, in a state of constant yearning, reaching, and hoping for his full attention and affection. Him, never quite reaching where I stood in the sand, always receding into the depths of a stingier desire.

But then, by the grace of God, came healing. Years where we learned how to love one another, how to let down our walls and allow the past to be redeemed. They were sweet years, though cut too short in a sick form of poetic justice as his life was taken by a drunk driver. Thirty-some years, he'd managed to stay sober, clean up, and learn to love his daughter and his grandbabies.

My mind brings me back in time to the days of him crawling on the floor, pretending to be a bucking bronco with Lorraine, Al, Gloria, and Hazel riding on his back. He'd humored them in ways he'd never poured himself out into me. In all the ways I'd been robbed of a parent's love, he made up for as a grandpa, never missing a ballgame, birthday party, or graduation.

He'd made up for lost time—time that was prematurely stunted. After the severity of the crash, cremation had been our only option. Only the week before his death, he'd divulged to me that one of his aging wishes was to visit the coast. He didn't care where; the ocean was an anomaly he'd never before seen. But he didn't live long enough to see it.

In the great expanse of Heaven, I knew the ocean would sorely pale in comparison to the treasure there. But the least I could do, the only sendoff that felt in the slightest like closure, was to bring his ashes to the place he'd longed to see.

I finally brought my eyes back to Claude. "I'm not ready to do it yet. But I'll let you know when I am," I murmured. "Not today."

5

1945
Goldfield, Nevada

HOPE WAS A dangerous thing. It was a phantom loose end, always dangling around, inviting her to grab hold, but she feared that pulling on the cord would only unravel her more, that everything would come crashing down even more than it already had.

The truth, as Kitty saw it, was quite near unswallowable. It was a desert without springs. A highway with a dead end. A drawstring pulled tight around her lungs. She needed to accept it—had to. But maybe one day, she would breathe again. Maybe one day, all of this would make sense. Maybe one day . . . There she went toying with hope again, allowing it to seep into the cracks of her brokenness.

No.

Something clattered in the kitchen, and Kitty drew the sheet over her head to drown out Peggy's grumbling. A week had slogged by like a foggy nightmare that wouldn't let up its grip. Kitty held her breath, waited, and hoped for Aunt Peggy to leave the house. Bitterness hung around Peggy like a cloud, and Kitty longed for reprieve from the suffocation.

Her new school had been kind enough. She was new blood. Fresh, interesting. Not that she wanted the attention, but the setting was a distraction from everything else. But the weekend now suspended her in time, providing no distractions nor diversions from the truth or from Peggy's contempt for life.

The bedroom door opened suddenly, and Kitty jumped.

"If you'd been up at a decent time, I would have offered to set your hair. That messy ponytail isn't doin' you any favors. You're a young woman now, you know."

Kitty bit her tongue. She'd learned over the last week arguing back only made the problem worse. But she couldn't help wondering if her looks were so bad.

"Well," Peggy said when Kitty didn't respond. "No more lollygagging in bed. Get ready."

"Where are we going?" It was Sunday. Where could Peggy possibly be dragging her to? A flame flickered in her heart, but she knew better than to feed the fire.

"Church. Hurry up. I don't like being late."

"Church?" The idea was as foreign to her as Peggy was, as preposterous as picturing her aunt—who she'd learned from classmates used to work at the local brothel—on the interior side of the stained glass. "I don't go to church." Sure, she'd gone a few times in her youth with Claude's family, but never more than that.

"Well." Peggy smacked her lips. "I didn't either until my husband blew to bits. Let's go."

She said the words so plainly, as though the explosion that claimed her husband's life had been nothing out of the ordinary. But Kitty had learned over the week that her aunt's hardness had deep roots. Roots that ran into territory that made Kitty even more uncomfortable and sad than she already was.

"Can I please stay here?"

Peggy's eyes narrowed to slits. "You realize you have a lot to be grateful for?"

Kitty's chest constricted, and she could hardly believe her ears. "Grateful? Grateful for what?"

"This new life you get to build."

"A life I didn't ask for! I don't want to be here. I want to be *home*."

"Your daddy was leaving you to rot in the desert. You didn't deserve to be there, at the mercy of folks next door, like a sad little mutt. I'm here to help you move on from this . . . start you've had in life. Who knows where we'll go."

Go? As in leave? Again? Kitty's heart throbbed in her chest. Everything had changed in the blink of an eye. Her father's drunken mistake had claimed the life of her neighbor, her friend, her practical older brother. It had led to the appearance of an estranged Peggy, coming in from out of town to save the day while her father decayed in jail. It had wrenched her heart out to leave the Fisher family, to leave the best friend she'd had all her life . . . And now Peggy was telling her to be grateful?

Fury built inside her heart, but it was only when she heard Peggy shut the bedroom door that Kitty felt safe enough to let it out. Once she ran out of tears and breath, Kitty finally rose to make sense of the mess she was.

She brushed her shoulder-length hair and teeth, careful not to meet her own gaze in the mirror. She slipped into the cotton dress that Ginny had only recently mended and still smelled of home. That is, the Fishers' house next door to her own . . . miles away in Goldfield.

They made it on time. The service slipped by, slow as a leaky faucet drip, and Kitty might not have minded it so badly if it weren't for the theatrics of Peggy's waterworks the whole time. It was clear to Kitty that Peggy's heart needed mending, but it was hard to offer her compassion when all she'd been met with was calloused nonchalance.

After church, they walked home. Soon after, Peggy left, this time allowing Kitty to stay behind. Kitty couldn't decide, though, if this was for the better. Her thoughts were loud, but the emptiness of the house was louder.

A knock at the front door brought her to a grating halt. Blood coursed through her veins like shards of ice through a straw. Visitors at the door lately had only been bad news. First, the sheriff on Ginny and Leonard's doorstep informing them that Vern had been struck by a car—the real kicker being that Kitty's father, Jeb, had been the one behind the wheel. Next, her aunt budging into her life to whisk her away like she had every right. And finally, Claude at her doorstep to say goodbye.

The knock came with a bit more *umph* now. Did she have the right to answer her aunt's door? Maybe it was a new friend from school, like Bethany or Georgianne. They'd been quite welcoming to her all week. She adjusted the bobby pin that scooped her hair away from her face and walked cautiously to the front door. On tiptoes, she pressed one eye to the peephole in time to catch a nervous hand rake through honey brown hair and the soft pleading of kind, hazel eyes willing the door to open on the other side. She couldn't rip it open fast enough-to tumble into the arms of the truest friend she'd ever known—Claude "Fly" Fisher.

6

Lia

1937
Galia, Oregon

I AM A fraud, living a fraudulent life, trapped blissfully within the pages of an enchanted storybook. It's written with a happily-ever-after. Man meets a woman in distress, woos her, and provides her a life of luxury in a mansion manor amid depression and war. The ease of my life is one to adore, and it's even complete with a perfect child and the promise of more in the future.

But this is no fairytale, for the fair maiden of a fairytale can't be bent on destruction. The ease that her hero promised forsaken as she chooses to bear her burdens on her own. The seamstress fired; now, the maiden's fingertips are pricked and rough from sewing hems and garments. The maid fired, too; the house now kept by the exhaustive labor of an already tired woman. The gardener dismissed; the weeds pulled and foliage tended to by her calloused hands and dirty nails.

The grit is what I was born for. The grit is what I deserve. How foolish to think I could ever escape my destiny.

How many women would dream of such a life? There were many, I assure you, that sought after Tenn's hand. But somehow, for some reason, his eye caught my brooding lump of tears at a table in the back of a restaurant in Los Angeles. I had just finished my shift. My feet were sore and blistered from the shoes I'd worn, and I wasn't yet prepared to walk the many miles to my rundown apartment.

My friend, the chef, had given me a small batch of French fries, and I'd sat in a booth watching the escapades of the wealthy and carefree, marveling at the way they danced together. The merriment of it choked me. I'd traveled so long, so far, had taken risks that didn't feel like risks at the time, all to drop it like a grenade. And as the band played a tune that was supposed to be joyful, I became weepy instead and felt the full effects of the explosion on my face.

I don't know how long he'd been there, but when I dared lift my tear-streaked face from the folded crook of my arm, Tenn was sitting across from me. Patiently watching. Waiting. I wiped my eyes and felt my cheeks burn.

"I . . . I'm sorry. You must need this table." I grabbed my purse and moved to slide out of the booth, but he reached a long arm across the table to stop me.

"No. I saw a sad girl and thought she might need some help. Are you alright?"

I pinned my shoulders back and said, "Yes. Quite." As well as I deserved, anyway.

Just then, my chef friend poked his head through the double doors to the kitchen and said, "No, she ain't. This one's not been alright since she came to join us last year."

"You have a party to return to." I nodded my head in the

general direction from which the stranger had come. "Those women are giving me dirty looks."

His smile fell flat, and he said, "Those women are only after my money."

"You sure it's not your good looks?"

"Ah." He grunted, and even under the dim lighting, I thought I detected a flush on his cheeks. "Positive."

"So, your money, huh? You're not pinching pennies like the rest of us are still reeling from the Depression, then?"

A smugness clouded his eyes. "I come from a line of good businessmen. I don't know what else to say."

Instantly, I knew I did not want to know him.

"Well, mister . . . ?"

"Please, call me Tenn."

"Tenn, it was a pleasure to meet you this evening, and I appreciate your concern for me. But I really must be on my way out the door." I rose and scooped up my belongings from the booth, then snatched one last French fry.

"You're traveling alone in the dark at such an hour?"

"Nonsense. I'm meeting my husband just outside." My lie made me wince, and it cut to a deeper place than I'd prepared for.

He smiled. "As long as you're taken care of."

I tried to smile in return, but what did he care about me? I was a stranger, a literal nobody to him until mere minutes ago. He hadn't even learned my name. But for whatever reason, he held my gaze and bore into me with his thoughtful, light eyes. Was he trying to figure me out? He wasn't used to being turned down, I assumed. But I wasn't a mouse for him to catch, nor a contender in the contest for his heart. Because I was Lia, a young woman with regret stitched into my flesh and a heart so swollen it could burst at any moment.

I was not a woman worth knowing, that much was for sure.

My secret filled the space that should've been open for someone else. There wasn't room for three. Three is a crowd.

I'd walked out of the restaurant and into the dead of night. I leaned against a lamppost for a moment to give aid to my tender feet. From my purse, I withdrew two napkins I'd swiped from the restaurant and stuffed them into my battered Cuban heels for padding. And then, I rested my head against the cool metal of the post, building my stamina for the long, lonely walk home.

I'd only hobbled half a block when I heard the jogging steps of someone behind me. Whirling around, I found Tenn chasing after me, his face in a pinch.

"Thought you said your husband was waiting right outside," he panted.

I narrowed my eyes. "What are you doing, following me? I'm meeting him down the street."

"Where?"

He wasn't going to relent. I gave him the runaround a few more times before he blew out a puff of air and said, "You are a tenacious woman, but will you give up your ruse?"

I pressed a hand to my chest. "And what *ruse* is that?" I said it as a dare. *If you have me all figured out, then pray tell, what is my hidden secret? Which would you like first? The darkest? The saddest? The one that will make you the angriest?*

"You have no ride home," he stated.

Oh, the simplest. Sure.

"You caught me. No ride."

"My driver"—he turned and pointed toward the town car waiting up the road—"can take you."

"That's really kind, but I'm not interested."

"In me? Or a ride home?" His brows bunched closer together. Under the glow of the streetlights, he looked young. Not much older than me. A square jaw, a sharp nose, and light hair that seemed to glisten under the lights.

I opened my mouth, but he held up his hand.

"Consider it, please," he said.

"Consider you or a ride home?"

A smile played on his lips. "Just a ride home. Consider me off the table."

The blister on my heel begged me to accept. Was there truly any harm in receiving a ride? After a moment, I said, "That would be lovely. Thank you, Tenn."

The next day, I received flowers at my apartment. Well, I didn't actually receive the flowers. They were stolen from my stoop, with the only remnants of their existence being the fallen petals left on the ground and a card that read: *Dinner, The Rift. 6:00 p.m.? —Tenn*

The last thing I needed was someone falling for me. The other last thing I needed was someone caring for me out of pity, like one would a hurt animal. I was no helpless, needy puppy. I was a beast, a monster. Savage and feral. Selfish. But scared all the same. Acting out of necessity, out of fear, out of what I'd thought was survival but now viewed as stupidity.

But as I looked at the card, a tear fell. I thought I'd cried them all dry, but as I watched it splatter onto the concrete, I realized I'd only dammed them up. I didn't want to get to know Tenn. Didn't want him to see the sides of me that were ashamed. No one ever had to, I decided that day. The secret that burned in my chest, the searing shape of all that I left behind, would remain mine and mine forever.

My stomach had growled just then, and I flicked the card as I held it between my thumb and forefinger. "Fine, Tenn. I'll go, but it's only on account of my stomach never knowing when it will get its next meal."

Survival, I told myself.

But it was selfishness; I know that now. Stringing on a man who had no business being entangled with such a woman. I didn't know he would fall so in love. I didn't know I would either. I certainly didn't think I was capable of such a feeling again. Never knew that love could surmount the anguish that had taken residence in my being. And then when our little girl came, and I felt her kick in my stomach, when I heard her cries and felt her in my arms . . . I couldn't help but wonder at the fact that she wouldn't be in existence if it wasn't for my choices.

That thought both swells my heart and crushes it still. How can one make sense of heads or tails here?

The truth is, I don't know how to start or end. I don't know how to admit to Tenn that what I've done is punishable by jail, that he has lived a lie in our love for all our years together, that in one simple sentence, I could change his entire world. But keeping it inside is threatening to unravel me.

My secret has room enough to run around this big estate and taunt me. The words in my heart need a space to breathe, a page of their own on which to exist. My suffering needs a place to take form.

I gather my stationery and bring it to my bedroom as the baby naps. I will write. It feels like the only logical solution for the time being. I sit and begin. First, about the day I met Tenn because it's fresh on my mind.

Every single letter I pen showcases the disfigurement of my heart; in every curve, I feel the twist of a knife. In every straightway, I'm reminded of my cowardice; in every dotting of i's and crossing of t's, of the time that has passed, the finality of it all.

But I have to give my heart a chance to breathe. I must. Or else, I fear that this secret might eat me alive.

7

1981
Galia, Oregon

CLAUDE GROANED. HIS eyes sagged with exhaustion after he'd been up all night, pale as the moon, hugging the toilet bowl with what I could only assume was food poisoning.

"Honey, I can't leave you here to suffer alone all day," I protested as I dabbed his forehead with a cool cloth.

"We didn't drive hundreds of miles for you to sit in a hotel room and stare at your sick husband. I'll be fine." His smile, though weak, was earnest. "I'll make your day miserable if you just sit here and stare at me. And I'll do it on purpose."

I snorted. "Come on."

He grabbed the cloth from my hand and nodded toward the door. "Go. Really. The worst of it has passed, I think. Maybe you can find a store while you're out and bring back some ginger ale and crackers."

His eyes pressed me to acquiesce, and after a long moment, I sighed. "Okay, fine." The thought of exploring this little town on such a sunny day did lift my spirits. "But I'll only be gone a few hours, and if you need anything, call down to the front desk."

"Sweetheart." He warmed my cheek with his hand. "Worry about you for just one day, okay? Shop, sightsee, get one of those bear feet you like so much."

"Bear claws, Claude."

"Feet, paws, claws, whatever. Just go." He dabbed his head with the washcloth. "See? I'm perfectly capable."

I glanced at the open window and felt a twinge of guilt for wanting to explore beyond the confines of our room. As if reading my thoughts, Claude nudged me.

"Kitty. Go."

"You're sure—"

"Go."

"Okay, okay." I still hovered over him.

"Go!"

"I'm going!" I grabbed the room key and dropped it into my purse, then slipped into my loafers and dragged my feet to the door. "How about I—"

"Go?"

"Yes." I couldn't help but laugh. "That's just what I was going to say."

"I love you, Kit," he said with a tired smile. "I'd kiss you goodbye, but . . ."

"No explanation needed. I love you too." I blew him a kiss and latched the door softly behind me. I leaned into it, pressing my ear to the teal painted wood, listening for any sign of him retching all over again.

"I can see your shoes under the crack," he hollered.

A grin broke loose on my face. Busted. "Goodbye, honey."

Downstairs, I stopped at the front desk and informed Donna of Claude's condition and that he'd be calling in the case of an emergency or a dire need, and then I set out through the propped-opened doors of the Cape Galia Inn.

I came to a halt on the sidewalk outside. I didn't know which way to go, and quite honestly, I didn't know how to venture out without Claude's hand in mine, a child tugging at my pant leg, or a companion of some sort. It occurred to me then that I no longer knew how to be alone, how to exist in solitude simply as myself.

Drawing in a deep breath, I turned up the street and chanced a glance through the bright sun to the second story of the hotel as I walked. I half expected to see Claude watching me from our window, ensuring I made good on my promise to leave. There was no sight of him in the windows above, but if there was, I knew he'd be shooing me along, encouraging me to make the most of my time.

I went in the opposite direction of the ocean, toward the businesses that convened within the town's center. What tourism Galia attracted during the summer months had waned with the ushering in of September. Summer still clung to the air, though, and the few shops in town displayed the last of their seasonal items.

Outside a clothing shop called The Coastal Bee, I trailed my hand across the outfits hanging from an outdoor sales rack. The fabrics burst with bright colors and fashion styles far beyond my years. I lifted an obnoxious rainbow-striped blouse by the hanger. *Doesn't Hazel have something just like this?*

For a moment, I thought about buying it. I could imagine my children's reactions if I was to return from this trip decked out in neon and cutoffs. Maybe I could get a perm while I'm here, too. Move over straight-legged denim jeans and soft, feathered hair; it's Mid-Life Crisis' time to shine.

I looked up to see a teenage girl skipping down the stairs from the shop. "That top is totally rad," she said as she passed.

I carefully rehung the blouse and left The Coastal Bee. As I continued to walk up the street, I found a bakery called The Screaming Peach. Through the propped-open door, the smell of pastries hit me before I even saw them. I went inside.

"Can I help you?" the man behind the counter asked.

I approached without taking my eyes from the bakery case. There, in the center row, were two bear claws. I ordered them both, along with a black coffee, then found an open table on the patio outside under the rare clear blue sky.

"Alright, this first one is for you, Claude," I said out loud and promptly took my first bite of the cinnamon-sweet goodness. I took turns taking bites and sipping my coffee, and when I'd devoured the whole pastry, I picked up the second and said, "And this one's for me."

My belly ached with happiness by the time I was through. I returned my plate and coffee mug to the counter inside and continued on my quest to nowhere. A lightness—save for the two bear claws weighing down my stomach—buoyed me, and I turned the corner only to run smack into an elderly woman.

I gasped and reached for her, and she embraced me instantly with a slight shake in her arms. She wore a floral-patterned silk nightgown that touched her ankles. Her eyes bore the anguish of worry, though they still seemed to smile as she looked into mine.

"Hello," I greeted her. "Sorry about our collision. Are you alright?"

She didn't answer. I looked beyond her, over her shoulder, but the street behind was empty with no trace of a companion. "Are you . . . alone?" I asked.

No response.

"Are you lost?"

Still nothing. I tried again. "My name's Kitty."

Her brows squished together as she studied me. A look of concern clouded her face. I glanced around, but there was still no one in sight. We stood outside of a brick commercial building with two separate entries. One was unmarked with a *For Sale by Liam Boxworth Realty* sign taped to the inside window. The other had a sign hanging above the door: Bluebird Books.

I clasped the woman's soft, wrinkled hands in mine. "Come in here with me, dearie. We'll figure out where you belong."

The woman happily accompanied me through the heavy wooden door into the dark, cavern-like interior, where the musty smell of new and old books greeted us with vigor. As we walked together, I noticed she wore mismatched house slippers. The V's that were already worn between my brows deepened. This poor woman. Lost and alone, albeit in a state of seeming incognizance.

The store was quieter than any library I'd set foot inside, and there was no soul in sight, only books upon books stuffed into rows of shelves arranged at odd angles.

"What's your name?" I whispered to the woman on my arm.

She remained resolute. Was she mute? Hard of hearing? Had she lost the cognitive ability to understand my words?

"That's okay," I said. "I'm sure we will figure this out."

Suddenly, she leaned her head near mine and, in a secretive voice coated in velvet and butter, said, "I'm looking for my baby."

My brows shot toward the ceiling. "Your baby?"

She chewed her bottom lip, and her eyes darted away. My heart grieved for this dear woman, for a life so far away that she was slipping into the past. I squeezed her hand gently.

"We'll find your baby," I assured her. "Not to worry."

We walked slowly through the store, one small shuffle-of-a-step at a time, until we found the shopkeeper at the back of the building, sitting in a folding chair with his feet kicked up on the desk, a novel in front of his face. The desk was cluttered with mounds of books surrounding the register.

"Excuse me?"

His eyes peeked from behind the pages, then darted back for a few more beats. I figured it must've been a riveting scene and couldn't blame him. Stopping mid-paragraph was practically a sin for book lovers everywhere. Finally, he slipped a bookmark inside and set the novel on the desk.

"Finding everything okay?" he asked.

"Well," I laughed lightly. "I'm finding more than I bargained for this morning, actually. I would love to use a telephone and help this lovely woman find her way home."

"Is she lost?" He leaned forward and rested his elbows on the desk.

"It appears that way. Do you have a phone here I could use?"

"Yes, of course." From behind a stack of books, he presented a landline, lifted the receiver, and handed the phone to me. I fussed for a moment with the tangled, spiral cord and awkwardly leaned over the desk before deciding to simply walk around to the other side to dial the police.

As respectfully as possible, I informed the dispatcher about the situation. Interestingly enough, she relayed to me that a local retirement home had reported a resident as missing and potentially endangered. By the description I gave the dispatcher, she seemed to believe that this woman was, in fact, the missing resident. Regardless, officers would be on their way shortly, she said.

I hung up the phone and walked back around the desk, touching the elderly woman gently on the arm. "Someone is coming to pick you up soon." I smiled reassuringly at her.

"What exactly did they say?" the shopkeeper asked as he tucked the landline behind the stack of books from where it originated.

I kept my voice down and answered, "If she is who they think, then she's a missing resident from someplace called

Thimbleberry Cottage."

His face twisted. "That's a good five miles from here."

Shock coursed through me. "Five miles?" I glanced at the woman. She picked up a glass figurine from the desk and held it in her shaky palm. She'd walked five miles today? In mismatched house slippers, no less? It was by God's grace that she'd remained unharmed thus far.

"The police are notifying her kin, and they should both be here soon."

Suddenly, the woman set the small figurine on the desk and reached toward the man. "I didn't get your name," she said sharply, in a voice that sounded as though she were accusing him of something.

He shot me a look of concern and cleared his throat. "Nicholas."

The woman's eyes clouded. Her smile drooped. "Are you the one who's taken my baby?"

Nicholas' mouth went agape. He tilted his head. "Your baby? No . . . ?"

"Are you hiding something?" She leaned across the desk, her eyes now on fire. She pressed a hand firmly on the desktop. "Where'd Kitty go?"

Wide-eyed and panicked, he pointed. She followed his finger and rediscovered me standing at her side. I lifted a hand in a calm wave.

"I'm right here, honey," I soothed, unsure what had spiked this sudden shift in mood. "Don't worry. I won't leave you until you're with your family. How about we head to the front of the store to wait?"

She inched a step closer to me, and I took her hand for reassurance. I guided her back through the shop and to the front entrance just as two police officers opened the door from outside. The woman instantly dropped my hand and reached for the nearest officer.

"Have you found my baby?"

The officer's face softened. "Don't worry, ma'am. Your baby is safe and resting at home."

Relief emanated from the woman in waves. Her tense shoulders dropped, and she wiped mist from her eyes.

"God bless you," she said weakly. "Thank you."

The officer tipped his hat to her. "My pleasure. You must be Maggy Monroe."

She offered no confirmation or denial. The other officer regarded me now for a quick statement. The door opened again a minute later, and in came a slender woman with sleek blonde hair and white-framed sunglasses. She ripped the glasses from her face and threw her arms around Maggy.

"Mom! Thank goodness you're okay! Where on earth have you been?" She asked the question as though not truly expecting an answer. She turned to me. "Are you the one who found her?"

I nodded.

The woman wrapped her arms around me without hesitation, and when she pulled away, tears brimmed in her eyes.

"You are a Godsend!" she proclaimed. "Thank you. We've been worried sick all day!"

"I'm so glad she's okay."

The woman sighed and tucked her sunglasses on top of her head. "I've been making myself ill thinking of the worst possible scenarios. Can you imagine losing your mother like that? Just *poof* she's gone with no one having a clue where she went!"

I swallowed hard and smiled. Actually, I *could* imagine . . . I've pondered that question for nearly fifty years now, though under entirely different circumstances.

"That must have been a nightmare," I said earnestly, for I could only imagine the anguish I'd feel if my stand-in mother-turned-mother-in-law ever went missing.

"A total nightmare, alright. She lives right in the forest, you know. At Thimbleberry Cottage."

I shook my head. "I'm not from around here. I don't know the place."

"Oh. Well, there are so many trees and streams of water around the place. My husband and I have been frantically searching the woods all morning." Her words tumbled out in one long breath. She inhaled sharply. "I'm Joy, by the way."

"I'm Kitty."

"Oh—"

One of the officers tapped her on the shoulder, putting an end to our conversation.

"If you could just sign this stating that this woman is your mother and that you will be escorting her to the appropriate accommodations, we'll be on our way, and you're free to take her home," he said and handed her the form.

I looked around and noted that Nicholas, the shopkeeper, was nowhere to be found. He was probably at his post, shoes kicked up on the desk, nose in a book, staying out of this ordeal so as not to be accused of stealing an elderly woman's child again. Maggy stood to the side, a vacant expression on her face as she stared at a shelf of books labeled as popular fiction.

I moved over to her, and she startled when I touched her arm. Her frightened expression faded as she laid eyes on me.

"It was lovely meeting you today, Maggy Monroe."

She smiled and looked beyond me to her daughter, who bid the police goodbye.

Joy strode over to us and clucked her tongue. "Oh, Mom," she said with exhaustion. "What a wild day. Let's get out of here."

The three of us walked outside, and when we stepped onto the sidewalk, Maggy clutched my hand so hard I feared my bones would break. For a waiflike woman, she had impeccable strength. Joy's orange Chevette was parked on the curbside, and she opened the front door and gestured for her mother to climb in.

But Maggy did not move, blink, or drop my hand.

"Okay, Maggy," I prompted kindly. "I fear it's time to say goodbye." I tried withdrawing my hand from her grasp, but her grip remained solid.

"Mom!" Joy laughed and held out her hand. "Your little excursion is over. We need to let Kitty be on her way now."

Maggy didn't budge.

"Maybe we could stop for a soda on the way," Joy tried.

Still nothing.

I gave Maggy's hand a squeeze and stepped toward the car. "Come on, Mags." I tugged lightly. "Do you mind being called Mags?"

Maggy didn't answer, but she did follow me a few steps in the right direction, though she angled for the back door rather than the front.

"She never liked the nickname Mags," Joy said, answering on her behalf. "She's always just been Maggy. But then again, in her later years, she's been full of surprises, so who knows. Maybe Mags will finally stick."

"Alright, *Mags*." I addressed my new friend as I opened the back door with my free hand. "It seems like you'd prefer to sit in the back?"

She lifted our clasped-together hands and said, "You first, dear."

"Oh, Mom." Joy put her hands on her hips and shook her head.

The two women stared off in a contest of who was more stubborn, mother or daughter. Finally, I said, "I don't exactly have anything of importance to do at the moment. I'd be happy to ride along if it means returning her happily and safely to her home."

"I can't ask you to do that," Joy said.

"I'm offering."

"Don't tell me you're as tenacious as the rest of us."

A laugh escaped me. "You can ask my husband whether or not that's true. But really, I don't mind."

"Are you sure? My mother seems so taken with you for some reason."

"Of course," I said. I slid into the backseat and patted the spot beside me, welcoming Maggy to join. She finally sat down too. Joy buckled her in and shut the door.

Maggy smiled at me as Joy walked around the car and took her place behind the wheel. She glanced at the two of us in the back seat and said, "Life is one big adventure, isn't it?"

8

1945
Goldfield, Nevada

SHE WISHED FOR wings that could take her away. To a place where pain didn't exist. Where darkness, once and for all, would be swallowed up. To a place where the static in her mind dissolved. Where she never again had to break the heart of her truest love.

On the schoolyard in Tonopah, Claude licked his lips, his eyes wild with worry as he waited for her to come to her senses. He'd skipped school in Goldfield and stolen a car, all to make sure she was okay. A web of emotion spun and tangled in her stomach. She didn't know how to make sense of the recent turn in their friendship, the spark that flared between them now. Their tragic world, however, held no room for budding romance, and the impulse to wrap her arms around his neck and cling to him was stunted, clipped like the wings she never really had. Her place had been made clear.

Good things were unreachable. The sentiment settled in her heart, like pebbles sinking into place at the bottom of a stream. The sooner the truth took hold, the sooner she could numb herself to it. Because it was only a matter of time before Peggy whisked them away to someplace else. Peggy had already told Kitty they'd capitalize on the first opportunity out of the *"godforsaken desert."* It didn't matter what reassurance the Fishers gave her; Kitty's fate was sealed.

"You shouldn't be here." She knew what Claude showing up to her school could mean for everyone involved, not to mention the state of their already broken hearts.

"Why?"

Wasn't it obvious to him? "Because it makes it harder," she pleaded. Just the sight of him standing before her, his heart on the line, nearly brought her to her knees. "There's no changing this separation. You're there, and I'm here—"

He took a small step, his jaw hardening with determination. "We're both right here, right now."

"You know what I mean. Peggy is bound and determined to get out of here. Remember what you said about ending up facedown here in this desert dirt? As soon as she hears from my dad—what will he care—that she has permission, we're gone, Fly."

Speaking the words out loud took a piece of life from her. Claude's eyes widened, and she knew the truth would only make him more determined to figure this out.

"You have to fight this, Kitty. Call your dad and—"

"And what? I'm at the mercy of people who have never truly put me first a day in their lives. You think they'll listen to me? That what I have to say matters? It's so easy for you to tell me what to do when you aren't the one living it."

She had no say in her life and no more strength to hold onto the hope that enticed and tricked her. For the first time, it felt as though Fly didn't understand. For the first time, she realized that she truly was alone.

"You told me to come back for you, Kitty," he said. "To keep coming back for you. That's what I'm doing, and that's what I'll continue to do."

"Well, stop it. I shouldn't have said that," she said, knowing deep down she wouldn't take back the words even if she could. She wanted more than anything for him to save her. But it would be better for both of them to cut this off now, before she found a way to hurt him even more. She wasn't worth coming back for. She never had been for her mother, and certainly not for him. She wiped beneath her eyes with a knuckle, ashamed at the scene she was creating. "I'll always be your friend, Claude," she said. "But you really ought to go home before you get us both in a world of trouble. It's not worth it."

His face fell. "You're giving up?" His voice cracked right alongside her heart.

But it wasn't giving up. Not to her.

To her, it was saving him.

The weight of his heartache pummeled into her, and she turned, rushing for the privacy of the school before all her new schoolmates could see the tears gushing down her cheeks. Her heart pounded like a stampede, like the herd of horses that ran wild in the hills.

Lub-dub.

Goodbye.

Life used to be an adventure.

Now it was a death sentence.

9

Lia

1937
Galia, Oregon

I WISH I knew what these are. Are these letters to you or to myself? Why do I feel like penning these thoughts is the only thing keeping me sane? But I will admit that the threat of Tenn finding these letters hovers over me most of the day and night. Though sometimes I feel like getting caught would be a relief. Would it feel freeing to have this all in the open? Because this weight is crushing, and I've spent many days just wishing that one day I would wake up and not remember at all. That I would forget.

Am I wrong to want to forget?

But how could I? How could I forget you? And these demons that keep me in the past? The waves push me along, yet I remain, bobbing in open water, anchored in place. You will forever be part of me, imprinted upon my heart. Alongside is the unimaginable hurt, the kind that only I could inflict upon you.

When I was a young girl, my grandmother shared something that has stuck with me since. It was the day before she disappeared. Yes, disappeared. We didn't know until they drained the swamp what happened to her.

It wasn't the first loss I'd endured. I'd already lost my mother from a young age. Not physically; her presence hovered over me constantly until the day I left for the boarding school in Syracuse and then again when I returned before leaving home for good. But what my mother gave me in her presence, she stole from me in her actions. The coldness, the apathy, the abuse, the warmness that only came when I was a "good girl."

I hear a door open downstairs unexpectedly and set down my pen. My hands tremble.

"Tenn?" I yell from our bedroom upstairs. "Is that you?"

I tuck the pages under the mattress for the time being and scoop the baby up from the floor where she's been playing with a pen and paper of her own, practicing scribbles and obscure shapes.

When I get downstairs, I find nobody. Tenn isn't in the kitchen or his study. I do a cursory sweep of every room, only to find the house perfectly empty and still. The front door is locked. Troubled, I quickly move to the study and lock the door from inside, keeping our daughter with me as I dial Tenn's office in the city.

The secretary answers and tells me that, yes, Tenn is there and in a meeting with a client as we speak. Would I like her to interrupt them? Leave a message? I say no and thank her, then hang up the phone.

I'm jumpy and rattled and confused. I carry the baby to the window and gaze out, but there's nothing suspicious from my vantage point of the front lawn. No cars in the drive that I can see, nothing unusual amidst the spruce trees or the viburnums.

Still, I close the curtains and curl up in Tenn's favorite leather chair.

"Did you hear a loud noise?" I ask her. But she doesn't respond, only wriggles down from my lap to explore her father's office—a place she's not often allowed to be.

I don't want to live in this fear. Fear of what, I'm not even sure. Had I imagined the slamming of the door? Is my own mind playing tricks on me?

The house feels too empty, too big. Too many pockets and nooks and crannies. I'd rather it be filled with an entire family, loud and distracting and rambunctious. A grand presence.

I watch my daughter get lost in play. I glance at the clock and note that thirty minutes have already gone by with us cooped up in this room. But it's cozy in here, and quite frankly, I don't have it in my stomach to leave and be in the empty dissolve of the main house quite yet.

My sweet girl has happily found a rogue toy to play with. She catches me watching her and brings it over, unsteady on her feet. Wonder is written across her face.

"What did you find?" I say with excitement. "My little explorer."

She hugs my knee, and I lean to kiss the top of her head, then her cheek, then to blow a raspberry on her neck. Giggles erupt and fill the small space. *Yes,* I think. *This is the only sound I want to hear filling my home.* I do it again, and she giggles another round and then another, until she suddenly points and gives me a curious look.

I follow her finger to a glass paperweight sitting atop Tenn's Bible.

"Oh, this is a bit too dangerous for you, sweetheart," I say and move the weight to another shelf, out of her reach. "But perhaps you'd like to play with—" I look around and find a wooden bowl holding paper clips on the shelf. I dump out the paper clips and hand her the bowl. "Here. Try this."

She grins and carries it away. My gaze drifts back to the Bible. Grandmother is still on my mind from earlier. Growing up, she was the only one I'd ever seen reading the book. Everyone else in my family had talked about it and preached about it as though their walk with the Lord was something to be jealous of. Even my own mother harped to the five of us children about righteousness as she'd slap us across the face for being a minor inconvenience.

But I do remember Grandmother, the day before she'd been lost to us forever, sitting on the porch, glasses perched on the tip of her nose. I had been on the cusp of leaving for boarding school, which was arranged at the insistence of my affluent aunt, who worked at the school in New York. She'd secured me a scholarship to help with the costs, and try as my mother might, the offer was too good for even her to refuse.

I shake the thoughts of my mother away and search through the office for a piece of paper. I want to finish recording this memory before it drifts away forever.

When I would ask what Grandmother was reading, her response was always the same. "Oh, it's the most exciting story!" I could always expect a paraphrased, children's version of whatever Scripture she'd been immersed in.

When I asked that specific day why she liked to read her Bible for such long stints of time, she said, "I didn't always. To be quite honest, when I was a little girl like you, I thought it was boring. Stories for grown-ups, and even then, when I had grown up, I was too busy and consumed with all the daily chores that I never had time for it. It hasn't been until my older age that I've really taken the time."

"So, I should wait until I'm older to read it then?" I asked.

"I wouldn't waste another minute if I were you."

She laughed when she saw the fear in my eyes. "Oh, sweet child.

What did I say now?"

"Is it that important?" Nobody had ever told me to read the Bible before. Nobody in my family had taken the time to invest much into me at all.

She closed the book and said, "What's important is this. We're all broken, hurt, scarred, and weary—oftentimes at our own doing. We may do our best to patch up the holes, but the only thing that can make us new is the grace of a good Father and the love of His only Son."

I didn't like to think of myself as broken, but the truth was, I was more broken than I ever could have understood. And the next day, when grandmother never returned from her walk, I thought maybe she had left me. Maybe she'd realized that we were all a little too broken for her to stay.

And maybe that idea came from Mother. From the way she blamed us all for what had happened. I think she was only angry, scared even, and lashing out at those closest to her. But I wanted to shrink back, hide away, to leave, and go wherever Grandmother had gone. Anywhere would have been better than there. Thankfully, I had that chance for a few too-short years with school.

And then, back home again, I met a man. I'm sorry, Tenn, it wasn't you. He was handsome and kind and lived with a twinkle in his eye, a hope that said, "These hard times won't be hard for much longer." None of us were strangers to going without. Life, in some form or another, had nearly strangled us all. But he was optimistic, and I liked that about him.

It didn't take long for us to marry. I was young, which was of no objection to me, since it meant I could leave the house and cling to him. And it didn't take long for us to conceive. I still remember the first time I felt her kick. Bliss came first. Then came fear.

What did I know about being a mother? Let alone being a grown woman?

I ignored it. I kept thinking the ever-growing darkness would slip away as fast as it had come. I thought of Grandmother and her brokenness and how this must be part of mine—an inability to be happy. Maybe if Mother hadn't berated me during my early stages of marriage and pregnancy, I'd have felt differently. I don't know. But I wanted to run away. I knew I was undeserving of it all.

And then, my husband came along with an idea. There was big money to be made out west. We could leave and start anew.

I stop writing. My eyes warm with hot tears. I don't want the baby to see me cry. She wouldn't understand. I don't want her to ever understand this brokenness.

I reach for Tenn's Bible, which I know he dabbles in from time to time, although quietly and to himself. Whatever faith he has isn't the type to turn him into an evangelical, nor is it the type to lead him to boast. I've heard him say that religion is often a crutch, a way to make oneself feel better, a way to encourage.

But Grandmother was convinced that Christianity was something more. Not just a salve for the wounded but a magical state of transformation.

I lift the heavy book onto my lap and flip through at random. Did Grandmother hold fast to her faith as she drowned in the swamp? Had the psalms she'd uttered to herself done anything to soften her great distress? Had they even come to mind at all?

I find the Book of Psalms and scan to see if any of them jog a memory. But the book is vast, and the memories feel so far away, even now.

10

1981
Galia, Oregon

TAKING A SLEEPY road where hemlocks and spruce trees lined the pavement, draping the forest beyond with dipping boughs that promised to keep secrets, we reached the tucked away estate of Thimbleberry Cottage. Salt still clung to the air and hung heavily like a weighted blanket but gone were any ocean views. Not that it mattered much, for Thimbleberry was a vision in its own right. The frame of the single-level Tudor cottage sloped in a dramatic flair. Periwinkle blue shutters framed the front windows. Vivid green ivy grew on the majority of the facade. It belonged in the pages of a storybook.

"This is the retirement home where she lives?" I asked as I shut the car door. "It looks better suited for a fairy princess or a family of woodland creatures."

"Charming, isn't it?" Joy said from the other side of the car, where she helped Maggy to her feet. They walked around to me, and the three of us slowly made our way to the arching wooden door.

"How many people live here?"

"There are ten rooms, I think. We had a horrendous time at the first nursing home that Mom went to. It was nothing short of a nightmare."

"Why?" I asked, though unsure I wanted to hear the reason. "What happened?"

"The staff was cruel and negligent. But thankfully, Thimbleberry had an opening, and so far, it's been wonderful. She's very blessed to be here. I just hope they don't deem her above their care level now. They were a bit skeptical about accepting our plea in the first place."

My heart sank at the thought of poor Maggy, already confused and out of sorts, having to readjust at another facility.

"Would they do that because of her leaving this morning?"

"They might." She sighed. "It's not the first time she's escaped, sadly. But she's never gotten past the parking lot until today. Our next option would be a care facility with a lockdown unit for advancing dementia. The closest one is over an hour away and doesn't have the best reputation."

She fiddled with her sunglasses and tucked them into her purse, then continued, "What I've learned on this journey so far is that not everyone values elderly human life the same way." She opened her mouth again as if to say something else but refrained.

I shivered at the image my mind conjured. Cold, sterile walls. Buzzing overhead lights. Maggy sad and alone in an unfamiliar place where no one cared the way family would. It made me ache.

Please let her stay, I prayed.

The front door chimed as we walked in, and a caretaker immediately appeared from around the corner.

"Now, what do we have here?" The caretaker *tsk tsk tsk'd* at

Maggy in feigned dismay. "Girl, you are trouble! Were you looking for this?"

It was only then that I noticed she held a baby doll. It was bald and dressed in a plain pink onesie. Maggy's lips parted. She reached for the doll and brought it to her bosom. "Shh." Maggy quieted the lifeless doll while patting its bottom.

I looked at Joy. She brushed her curtain bangs from her face and offered a sad shrug. Maggy moved down the main hall, and we trailed her into the sitting room.

"She's had that doll for a year now," Joy whispered. "When we first started noticing her changing—you know, slips of the mind here and there—we didn't think much of it. Even when bigger things started happening, like forgetting to turn off the stove, getting lost when going places she's visited all her life, we none wanted to admit that something was seriously wrong. Instead, we made light of it as a family and tried to laugh it off."

I didn't know why she was divulging all of this to me, but I listened intently as we watched Maggy sit on the loveseat in the room and rock her baby doll.

"But then one day, she went into hysterics, panicking about *'her baby.'* We didn't know what she meant, of course. But she got angry. Accused us of stealing her infant. Tore the house to shreds searching for it. That was the first day we really thought Mom might be losing her mind.

"Dad brought her to the doctor a few days later, and that's when we were told she has a progressive form of dementia. The doctor suggested he buy her a baby doll to calm her paranoia. And it worked. She's hardly let that thing out of her sight since. But it didn't take long for her mind to slip to the point that Dad could no longer keep her safe or care for her alone at home."

"I'm so sorry," I said with a pit in my stomach. "She's very lucky to have a family who loves her enough to ensure she's getting the proper care she deserves."

Joy tried to smile but faltered, and I wondered what this meant. Her eyes remained trained on her mother.

"Thank you again for riding along with us," she said after a minute. "I don't know what got into my mom, but your presence seemed to soothe her. I just want to make sure she's settled, and then I'll drive you back into town."

"No problem. Thank you." I hoped Claude was faring alright.

"You seem to be a natural caregiver to the elderly. Do you have any experience?"

"Oh, nothing more than the average person." I thought of Ginny and Len and the ladies of *Wilted and Quilted*. The memory made me smile. I hadn't thought of those ladies in years. The remembrance of them warmed my heart.

"I hear you went on a wild-goose chase this morning," a cheerful, small voice quipped from behind.

We turned to see a petite, red-haired woman standing there, positioned behind her walker with a teasing grin that spread from ear to ear.

"Yes, a wild-goose chase indeed," Joy replied.

The woman tittered and shook her head, then said to me, "Are you new here? I'm Abbi."

I was startled. *Am I new here?* Certainly, I didn't look *that* far past my age . . . *Did I?*

"Well, I am new, but I'm just seeing that Maggy has ceased her goose chasing for the day."

"Oh, I see. I knew they'd been looking for help."

I let out an internal sigh of relief. She'd mistaken me for the new staff, not a resident. I almost laughed out loud.

"Something about you is so familiar. Are you sure you haven't been here before?" Abbi said with narrowed eyes. Her head poked out like a turtle stretching its neck, though the movement only brought her centimeters closer for a better look.

I smiled politely. "Nope."

Abbi lifted a wrinkled brow. "You're certain?"

"Quite." I nodded. "I've never even been to Oregon before this week."

"It's funny, actually," Joy said, looking at me with her head cocked to the side. "I thought there was something vaguely familiar about you when we first met as well."

My cheeks burned under the scrutiny. "Best I can say is I have a doppelgänger running around Galia."

"You sure you don't have a twin running around instead?" Abbi asked. "I swear I've seen you before."

"Not to my knowledge." The murkiness of my maternal lineage made my stomach pitch forward.

"Hm. You know . . . I might have a clue or two in my room." Abbi stared at me a second longer, then sighed. She looked at Joy. "It's perfect timing anyway, because I've been meaning to catch you and ask you about something I found the other day. Here, follow me." Abbi turned with her walker and receded down the hall from which she'd just come.

Joy winked at me and followed Abbi down the hall, and I remained where I stood, an out of place visitor. I thought of checking on Maggy while Joy catered to Abbi's wishes, but before I moved a single step, Abbi called over her shoulder to me.

"Hurry up, slowpoke!" A flurry of giggles sprung from her mouth. Once she saw me take my first step, a satisfied smile fell on her lips, and she turned her back to me and took off again.

The three of us made it to her room, where she instructed Joy and me to sit in the pair of floral-patterned armchairs set up in the corner. I obliged, though the chair took me by surprise as it leaned backward dramatically and spun. I yelped.

Abbi held her side as she laughed at the sight of me. "I call those my Venus flytrap chairs. That's the only reason I invited you to my room. I'd get rid of those stupid chairs if it weren't for the comedy they bring."

My mouth fell open, though I couldn't help my own laughter. And Joy couldn't help hers, too, apparently.

"You're naughty," Joy declared and carefully lowered herself into the other deathtrap of a chair. "Ruthless."

"A troublemaker through and through," I chided.

Abbi stood behind her walker and pressed her hand to her chest in shock. "You must be confusing me with someone else. Perhaps I have a doppelgänger, too."

"That's just too much trouble to even consider," Joy teased.

Abbi parked her walker next to her armoire. "Now," she said to garner our attention. Whatever reason she brought us here seemed direly important. She held onto the armoire as she moved without her walker, sliding and bracing herself as she shifted to the front side. She carefully opened the doors and pulled at a drawer to no avail.

"This darn thing is stuck again," she muttered under her breath through gritted teeth. She yanked again, and I feared she'd lose her balance. "Dadgummit."

"Can I help y—"

"No. I've got it." But the tone of her voice told me she did not.

Abbi yanked one more time with all the might left in her old body, and to all our surprise, the drawer flew out of its compartment and landed on the floor, barely missing Abbi's right foot. Abbi herself teetered, and I flew to my feet to brace her.

"Are . . . you . . . kidding me?" Abbi huffed and gripped her dyed, fire-engine red hair.

Joy was on her feet now, too, and put a hand on Abbi's shoulder as the three of us stared at the mess on the floor. It was a heap of photographs, newspaper clippings, jewelry, and miscellaneous items ranging from matchboxes to a dog leash to two pocket-sized Bibles, and that's only what I could see. The sheer number of items that had been crammed into the drawer astounded me.

Joy gasped. "Oh, don't tell me this is your whole collection of recovered things?"

"Worse. It's all my own, too." Abbi hung her head. "I'd just consolidated everything into one drawer the other day. The right side were my belongings, the left belonged to the yet-to-be-identified."

"We'll help you clean this up," I said, stooping to set the drawer right side up.

"Bah! Cleaning is what got me into this mess." She flicked her hand with annoyance. "How's that for organization?"

Joy took Abbi's arm and assisted her to the side of her bed, where Abbi sat and puckered her mouth.

"I always say 'Grow up, but don't grow old,' yet here I am. Look at what these old hands went and did." Abbi held her palms in front of her face as though they'd understand her scowl of shame.

"Seemed like a faulty drawer to me," I said. I sat on my knees and reached for a photograph sitting on top of the pile. In it, four young women dazzled in beaded, fringed cocktail dresses with strappy heels on their feet and bold lipstick accentuating their beaming smiles. I held the photo out for Abbi.

"Is one of these lively ladies you?"

A sly smile crept onto her face as she took the photo. "Look! Proof I really was once young!"

"You're still young," Joy said as she sat next to Abbi on the bedside. "At least at heart."

"Tell that to my cardiologist," Abbi retorted. She tapped the second woman in the lineup with a shaky, crooked finger. "That's me. Little Abbigail Banks. The swanky little hoofer herself."

"You danced?" I asked.

"Oh, boy, did I." Abbi laughed breezily and moved her arms in a motion reminiscent of the Charleston, making the bangles on her wrist jingle. "Nobody could keep up with me, and I don't say that to boast. I say it because it's the truth."

The woman was a spitfire; that much was obvious. Youthful despite the sagging skin that covered her aging, birdlike frame. Despite her age, however old that was, her eyes still sparkled and danced like a mischievous child.

"Abbi, what are we going to do with this mess? Would you like us to just pile it into the drawer?" Joy asked.

Abbi studied the items on the floor, the wrinkles around her eyes multiplying. The clock on her wall *tick-tick-ticked* as we waited for her direction. Time stretched, and I began counting the seconds.

. . . Thirty-seven . . . Thirty-eight . . .

"What is all of this exactly?" I broke the silence.

"It's a pile of junk, can't you see?" She tried to laugh, but this time fell short. "A life full of sparkle and whimsy, and this is all that's left." Abbi sucked in a breath. "And some of what you see isn't even mine. It's unclaimed junk I've found in recent years. Like some sort of unofficial lost and found."

I wasn't prepared for this sudden, sad turn.

"Was there something you wanted to show me?" Joy asked.

Abbi grunted. "Oh, what's it matter now? It was just a tiny little brooch. Do you wear brooches?"

Joy shook her head.

"Then I suppose all of this was for nothing." Abbi sighed. "If you ladies don't mind, just go ahead and toss it all in that sorry excuse for a drawer, and I'll sort through it when I muster the nerve again."

We cheerfully obliged but did what we could to organize the

drawer into sections rather than toss the items in at random. We began putting all the photographs in one stack, the necklaces and loose charms and earring studs in their own pile, and then the miscellaneous odds and ends in another. Abbi kept watch from her bedside and inserted smart aleck remarks as she saw fit.

I found a ladybug brooch the size of a pinky nail and set it on Abbi's bedside table. "Is that the brooch you were talking about?"

Abbi picked it up. "Yes. Isn't it cute? But the pin on the back is bent. It's no wonder it fell off."

"Look at you!" Joy gasped and held up a picture for Abbi to see.

"Oh, yes. That was the night of my first and only date with Clark Gable."

I lifted a brow. "You dated Clark Gable?"

"It may have only been for one night, but that was plenty enough for me."

I laughed and exchanged glances with Joy. "Do tell."

She flicked her wrist and shook her head. "Another time. This old body of mine is hankering for a nap, and I'll never shut up if you get me talking about that date."

Just then, a caregiver poked her head into the room. "I hate to interrupt, Miss Abbi, but your ride is here."

"Ride for what?"

"You have a doctor's appointment today," the woman said.

"Bah! That's today?" Abbi pursed her lips and hung her head. She lifted it after a moment. "I was so close to that nap, and you had to go and ruin it, didn't you?"

"Every party has a pooper, you know that," the woman replied.

"Well, you're sure the poopiest today. Am I supposed to go *now*?"

The caregiver nodded. "Do you need any help before you

go?"

Abbi shook her head. "The sooner I go, the sooner I can get back, right?" She pointed to her walker. "Hand me that, would ya?"

Joy slid it over. Abbi stood and looked at us. "Just pile the rest of it in. Thanks for your help, ladies."

Truly, I was disappointed to see her go. We bid Abbi farewell and set to finishing our task. A few random photographs and bits of paper remained scattered on the floor, and as Joy put the last of the jewelry in the drawer, I scooped the other items into a small stack and glanced through them.

An illegible address on a crumpled, yellowed paper scrap.

A bent photograph of an industrial skyline.

A handwritten receipt from a dry cleaner.

A small, folded piece of newsprint, which I unfolded with care.

My mouth went slack. I blinked. *You're tired, Kitty*, I told myself. *Or coming down with whatever illness Claude has.* I squeezed my eyes shut, but when I reopened them, the cutout from the newspaper—a dated picture I'd recognize anywhere— remained the same.

I stared at it.

At her.

At . . . me.

11

MY ENTIRE BODY bristled at the sound of my name.

"Kitty?" Joy repeated with unease. "Is everything okay? You look unwell."

I blinked. The picture blurred before my eyes. "I, uh . . ." The words wouldn't come. My tongue felt heavy and thick in my mouth. "This is . . ."

"What is it?" Joy reached out her hand. I placed the photo in her waiting palm.

"More like . . . whom," I managed to say.

Joy stared at the worn newsprint, unflinching. "Do you know her?" She raised her head to regard me, but as her eyes set on mine, they widened with dawning.

"Wait. This . . ." She looked down at the photo with its tattered edges and crease marks down the center in the shape of a cross. "How is this you?" Her forehead wrinkled as she looked back and forth between me and the picture.

"That's exactly what I'd like to know," I whispered. My hands reached for what remnants from the drawer remained on the floor, moving with a frantic flair that I couldn't squelch if I tried. I searched the last few photographs and bits of paper for an explanation, but I knew the only one who held the answers I sought was the woman who had just left.

Abbi.

"You're sure this is you?" Joy held the picture beside my face. "I mean, it sure looks like you."

"It's me."

"I'm dumbfounded," she murmured and absently patted for glasses on top of her head that weren't there. She tucked her hair behind her ears, and I felt her eyes cast a speculative glance in my direction. "Do you have family in this area? Are you sure you don't know Abbi from somewhere?"

"No. I'm positive." The wall clock ticked loudly in theatrical punctuation to my perplexed state. "Can I see that again?"

She handed me the photo, and I scoured the front and back for any written inscriptions, but there wasn't a clue to be found.

"This makes no sense."

"I guess you'll be coming back tomorrow?"

I nodded. My gut churned. As much as I wanted to stay and solve this curious mystery, it couldn't happen with Abbi at an appointment. And besides, I had an indisposed husband needing my care. I didn't have the time to wait for her to return today.

"Should we put this back now?" Joy asked, gesturing to the drawer.

I looked at all the belongings arranged inside and longed to search through them, this time with intention. But I couldn't do that without permission.

"Sure. Let's lift it together." I set the newsprint photo of me on Abbi's nightstand, and together, we hoisted the drawer back into its position inside the armoire.

Despite my confusion, something unexplainable pricked behind my eyes. But I staved off the tears, retrieved the photo from the nightstand, and placed it in the front of the drawer for my return. I shut the younger, printed version of myself away, and we left Abbi's room.

We found Maggy dozing in a chair in the sitting room. After Joy informed the staff of our departure, we stepped out of the facility that looked as though fairytales were born in its walls, and I wondered if maybe they were.

Clouds covered the sky, and the forest pressed itself around us as we walked to her car. I wished I could take my picture back to the hotel to prove the validity to Claude of the ridiculous-sounding story that I'd soon be telling him.

Who are you really, Abbigail Banks? And why do you have my photograph?

The driver's door closing snapped me from my thoughts, so I climbed into the passenger seat. Joy started the car, and as we pulled out, she asked, "Are you alright?"

"I think confused is a more fitting word." I watched Thimbleberry disappear from sight. "What's Abbi's story?"

"I don't know the whole thing, but from what I've gathered, she has a colorful background. She rubbed shoulders with the rich and famous and traveled the world. But for being an affable socialite most of her life, she appears to have nothing and no one to show for it, aside from the keepsakes and stories."

"Does she not have family still around?"

"To my knowledge, no."

I tried to occupy my wandering mind by looking out the window, but my thoughts couldn't be wretched from the newspaper cutout of my face in Abbi's drawer. No wonder she thought I looked familiar, for she had truly seen me before. I shrugged my cardigan from my shoulders, only aware now that sweat had gathered between my shoulder blades, and I cranked the window down for fresh air.

"Thank you again for everything you did today," Joy said.

"Oh, no need to thank me. I'm glad your mom is alright. She seems like a sweet woman."

"I wish you could have known her before. She was the type of person who could find joy in every circumstance. She had the best laugh. I think that's the part of her I miss the most. Some days, I still see that light in her; other days, it's like she's trapped in a dark world and can't escape."

I wanted to hug her. "It must be hard to watch her change like this."

"Dementia isn't for the weary. That's for sure," Joy murmured, somberness lacing her words. She turned a corner, and I caught sight of the ocean again for a brief moment. "To be honest, most of the family has stopped coming around to visit her."

"To visit your mother? That's so sad."

"Dad hasn't seen her in months. Says it's just too hard to not be remembered and to see her so combative."

"Combative?" I wouldn't categorize the behavior I saw today as *combative*.

Joy shrugged. "For some reason, ever since her dementia worsened and my dad would come around, my mom would get terribly upset, at times even aggressive. But yet, she also acted as though she didn't even recognize him in spite of the long, happy marriage they shared. But the disease doesn't seem to care about that, and Dad wants to remember her how she was, not how she is. But still, it breaks my heart."

My heart broke right alongside hers. How would it be if one day Claude no longer knew me? "I'm so sorry."

"It's our lot," she said lightly, though her frowning eyes betrayed her. "What more can we do? I think the hardest part is seeing them exist in separate worlds. This disease has created an uncrossable ocean between them. It's like she died to him even before her time. Like they've both died to each other, really. I know we all grieve in different ways, but he says, 'I don't know who that is, but she isn't my wife.'"

The sadness permeating Joy's words rendered me silent. "What about your siblings?" I finally asked.

"They don't come around as much as they did at first. I guess they just don't see the point." Her brows knit together, and her voice trembled with wisps of frustration and loneliness. "They're too busy to be unremembered. Everyone is bent on burying the living when they aren't even dead."

"I applaud you for looking after your mother so well. She's blessed to have a daughter who cares like you do."

"The way I see it, she cared for me when I was helpless, incontinent, and unable to communicate. The least I can do is return the favor."

The sentiment made me smile. "I couldn't agree with you more. The value of a human life doesn't decrease with age."

"I actually told that to my father. I said, 'Does the Lord look at the elderly or incapacitated and deem them void of His loving-kindness? No? Then why should you, a follower of Christ, do the opposite'?"

The truth in her words filled the car. "What did he say in response?"

She pursed her lips. "He simply told me that there are things I don't understand, and then he walked away. The only thing I don't understand is his behavior." Joy made another turn, and this time, I spotted the teal blue Cape Galia Inn just down the street. "Enough about my family. What about you? Are your parents still around?"

The question caught me off guard. I bristled. "Umm, no. My dad recently died in a car accident, actually."

Joy sucked in a sharp breath. "Oh, wow. I'm sorry to hear that. What about your mom?"

I averted my gaze and trailed the fading pines through the

window. "I, um, lost her a long time ago too." I hesitated a moment, but the next words tumbled out on their own. "She left when I was a baby."

The situation was something I'd come to terms with over the years—or so I'd thought. Admitting my orphanhood out loud now to this virtual stranger gutted me.

"Oh, honey," Joy said with a sympathetic undertone.

I waved the pity away and said, "I'm a grown woman." As though age would whisk away the desire for one's parents. "I still have my in-laws, who have honestly been parents to me my entire life."

"Really?"

"I married the boy next door." The declaration never failed to bring a smile to my face. I thought of Claude. Was he still miserable in bed? Was he wondering where I'd been all day? "Who is unfortunately quite ill right now. Our trip so far hasn't gone the way we were expecting."

"That's how it always seems to work, doesn't it? What brought you to town, by the way?"

The car came to a stop outside of the hotel, and the world came to a stop right along with it. Joy's question probed into the far spaces of my mind that I wasn't yet ready to explore. Within the week's time, though, I would have to. Ready or not.

"My father's ashes." Why was I revealing all of my secrets to this near stranger? "He wanted to see the ocean before he died but never got the chance. So, I guess it seemed right. We had a nephew visit here once, so the town came highly recommended as the perfect place."

Joy's eyes softened, and she touched my arm in a sisterly way. "Your virtue is admirable. Please let me know if you need anything while you're in town. I should give you my number." She found an old slip of paper in the center console and wrote her number on the back. "If your husband doesn't get better soon, my brother-in-law is a physician. Just give me a call if you need to have him checked or anything."

"I appreciate that, Joy. Thank you." I carefully slipped the paper into my purse and reached for the door handle.

"You plan on returning to Thimbleberry tomorrow?"

I paused. My stomach knotted. "Yes. I think a mystery of this magnitude deserves my sleuthing, don't you?"

The sun broke through the clouds as Joy laughed. She slid her oversized sunglasses back over her eyes. "I'll put it this way: If you don't ask Abbi, I will."

"Glad to know I have your backing." I opened the door and slid out of the seat. "Thanks again for the ride."

"And thank you for saving my mother. Kitty?"

"Hmm?"

"I don't mean to sound trite, but I can't help wondering if God brought you here for a reason."

Had He? I gave her a wave and shut the door. As I watched her drive away, fatigue nearly overcame me. Apparently, two bear claws and two confusing discoveries weren't enough to sustain a woman all day.

With my mind still boggled, I went inside. The front desk was empty, the lobby quiet. My feet dragged up the stairs to our room, and I yearned for a drink of cold water. Claude was sitting up in bed when I entered. A rerun of *M*A*S*H* played on the wood-paneled Zenith. Claude's face flushed when he looked away from the TV to me.

"Don't tell me you're still feverish." I dropped my purse and belongings on the entryway table, then immediately went into the bathroom and filled a cup with sink water. I chugged and refilled it twice before checking on my poor husband. His forehead was hot and clammy under the back of my hand.

"It just needs to run its course," he grumbled. "I'm so sorry."

"Sorry? You've nothing to be sorry for. I'm the one who's

sorry for leaving you to fend for yourself all day."

He pulled a tucked hand from beneath the blanket and reached for me. "Did you have a good day, I hope?"

I drew in a breath. "You'll never guess what I'm about to tell you."

12

Summer, 1946
Manhattan, Kansas

SHE DUSTED OVER her freckles, dragging the powdered brush over the faint scar on her chin, the result of a past adventure-gone-wrong with Claude. She moved the brush upward all the way to another scar near her temple. Her father probably didn't even remember giving it to her. But she remembered. The memories played like a bad movie in her head.

She could see it all, even now . . .

Through the front window, she could see Claude straddling his bike, waiting for her to join him so they could embark on their adventure. But Jeb, her drunk excuse of a father, stumbled from the kitchen just as Kitty came around the corner to fetch the small snack she'd prepared for the day. Jeb staggered and stabilized himself against the wall while Kitty tripped and nicked her forehead against the scarcely-filled bookshelf in the hall.

He mumbled something at the same time Claude hollered for her outside.

She pushed past her father and ran for the bathroom. She wet a cloth and held it to the gash. A little blood stained the rag, but thankfully, it was mostly a superficial wound. Enough, though, for someone to notice. Her hands shook as she took her brush and attempted to cover the gash with her sandy-blonde locks with no success.

If she had a pinch of makeup, maybe she could conceal it, just like she wished to conceal so many pieces of her life. She took a breath and couldn't even fool her reflection with the broken smile she attempted, her eyes as brown and sad as the whiskey that her father drank.

Claude hollered again, and she took one last glance at herself before rushing out of the bathroom and through the living room. Jeb was slumped down on the couch, one arm draped over his eyes.

"Your head alright?" he muttered, the words a jumble.

She almost stopped to give him a mouthful. But what would that matter? What would that change? He didn't care. If he did, he wouldn't continue to drink himself into oblivion.

She pushed through the screen door, happy for the dramatic smack that it made when it shut.

"Kitty!" he shouted as her feet pounded down the steps of their humble home. But she wouldn't stop or turn around. His calling for her meant nothing. It would be followed with a long nap rather than a chase down, another night of drinking rather than looking for a new job. The dance was too familiar, too routine.

She didn't want to dance that dance. She wanted to move to the beat of adventure, the rhythm she and Fly knew so well. Claude peered at her from under his ball cap as he straddled his bike. For a moment, predictability didn't seem so bad after all. She could always depend on Claude. At least she had him.

She blinked away the memory now and coated her lashes with a layer of mascara she'd found in Peggy's drawer. Maybe she didn't have to be that girl anymore. Maybe she could be a different Kitty May Ralph in this new land where the hills rolled and the grasses swayed, tall and sweeping.

Maybe this was the start of something new, as Peggy had repeated time and time again. Kitty liked the idea, though it seemed too good to be true. Not when flashes of her former life kept igniting inside of her mind. How could she really move on if she couldn't even say goodbye?

She hadn't allowed *goodbye* to be spoken when she'd moved from Goldfield to Tonopah with Peggy. Goodbyes were final, and with Claude, the finality of goodbye was too much to bear. Back then, she'd had hope. At least more than she had now over a thousand miles away. When they'd set out in Peggy's car for their move to Kansas, Kitty more as a prisoner than a copilot, she knew that too much time had passed for a formal goodbye to make sense. It went without saying now. That chapter had closed. That phase of life was complete.

Life was a series of leaving and being left.

It had crossed her mind, though. She'd considered finding a ride to Goldfield, running up the steps she could walk in her sleep, and giving him one last hug. One for Ginny, too. And Leonard. And Cliff.

But time had been a thief to them all, and inserting herself on the cusp of leaving felt unfair. So, in her heart, Central Nevada existed only as a memory, no longer a home. She looked in the mirror, tousled her hair, and whispered the word that had become at once an enemy and steadfast companion, *"Goodbye."*

On her way out the door, the phone rang. She ignored the noise, ready to disappear into the summer heat and find the local diner she'd heard was a common meeting place for kids her age. Peggy came from her bedroom and answered the phone.

"No, she's just stepping out the door," Peggy said.

Kitty stopped just shy of her exit. There weren't many people who could be calling for her. Jeb had called from time to time over the near year he'd been in jail. His calls were always short and stilted. Turns out the dynamics of their father-daughter relationship withstood the test of time and distance. No matter if he was home or in the slammer, they still had no way to relate to one another. This disconnect was the only steady consistency upon which Kitty counted.

"I don't know, Jeb, and what's it matter to you?" Peggy spat.

So it *was* her dad. Kitty eavesdropped from around the corner of their small apartment. She couldn't hear Jeb's end of the conversation, but her aunt loved giving him a hard time. Hard enough that even Kitty felt sorry for him once in a while.

"Oh, yeah?" Peggy retorted now. "Father enough to leave her dried out in the pits and parentless. We're in Kansas, Jeb. Like it or not, that's where I decided to go."

Kitty cringed. It would be one thing if Peggy were defending her honor out of love, but no. Peggy loved tangling herself up in a good fight any chance she could.

Peggy huffed into the receiver. "Yeah, like you had nothing to do with it! Come on, Jeb. Take some ownership." The room went silent for a moment as her father clearly took a turn to speak. Peggy gasped. "Don't you dare! Well, I have never . . . You know what, you piece of junk, you'll be lucky to receive a postcard from us in the future. For all I'm concerned, you can go to—"

Kitty slipped through the door to the building's main hallway, which smelled of old popcorn and wet dog. The lights flickered overhead in the way they constantly did, and the pipes banged in the walls like they could burst at any moment. She hurried past the noises and flung the metal door open wide. Sweat prickled on her skin in an instant. The heat here was different, and her lungs felt the odd sensation of being wet and dry at the same time as she drew in a deep breath.

It was time to realize that goodbye meant goodbye.

It was time to start over.

13

Lia

1937
Galia, Oregon

I CAN HEAR them taunting me. When Tenn rolls over in his sleep, the letters speak their threats from beneath our mattress. *We know your secrets. And unless you find a better hiding spot, he's going to find us, and we'll tell him everything we know.*

I can't move them right now. I will have to wait until Tenn leaves in the morning for work. But I won't sleep a wink until then because every creak in the mattress splits my eyelids open. I don't know why Tenn would wake and think to himself to check between the mattresses. But what if he or I turn over, and somehow, he hears the rustle of the pages? The whispers of my secrets?

My eyes well at the thought, and I curl into the fetal position, clutching my stomach as it brews with my plight. My pulse beats steadily in my neck, pounding like the thoroughbreds we once saw race at the Santa Anita grounds.

That was the night he asked me to be his wife, getting down on one knee just after Azucar won the race with the stands roaring around us. Deep down, I'd known where our relationship had been heading, but I had lived in denial. As he awaited my response to his question, I'd fallen instantly ill. Surely, over the uproar around us, I'd misheard him? Though, him being down on one knee only confirmed what I had already known.

There were two distinct reasons for me to say no. For me to end the whole charade right then and there. But I could never have explained them to him, and above all else, he deserved an explanation. So, against the upsurgence of shame and guilt inside, I told him yes. I would be his bride.

What a sham, he'd say now if he knew. *You fraud. You devil.*

His unsaid and, as of yet, unthought words resound louder and louder in my head. I look to the curtained windows, pleading for morning's light to trickle through the sheer fabric. But it's only darkness. The soul-sucking kind that holds no mercy.

I need a plan. A place he won't ever think to look. Of course, one might suggest that I burn what letters I've written thus far and forgo writing any more, but I can't. Spilling my heart onto the page is too cathartic, too relieving to stop.

So, I will write. But I will search for a more covert spot to hide the evidence.

A secret about my secrets.

What's one more, anyway?

14

1981
Galia, Oregon

FOLLOWING MY MEMORY of the drive and hand-drawn directions from Donna at the hotel, I drove myself to Thimbleberry Cottage the next morning. The fog from my night of tossing and turning was thicker than the fog rolling in from the coast, but I pressed on, determined to get an answer to yesterday's discovery.

When I arrived, I checked in at the desk and found Maggy pacing the sitting room with her baby doll in tow. She moved from chair to chair with a sour expression painted on her face. I lifted a hand in a friendly wave as I approached.

"Good morning, Maggy."

She continued to pace, and I realized by the chewing of her bottom lip and the frantic worry in her eyes she wasn't simply pacing but searching.

"Are you looking for something?"

This time, she paused and regarded me. Her sour expression softened. Was that recognition flashing in her eyes? How must it feel to only remember flashes of your life?

"Hello, dear." Her voice wobbled with a sweet little lilt, a kindness that looped around her words as if she spoke in cursive.

"Hello, Maggy," I said and took a seat on the nearest chair. I patted the one next to me, inviting her to sit as well.

She obliged but distractedly scoured the room with her eyes.

"Is there something I can help you find?"

"There was a little girl in here." She pointed vaguely in the direction of the windows along the far wall.

"A little girl?"

"I'm afraid she's lost her mother," she said, biting her lip. Her eyes never ceased to move. She pulled her baby doll onto her lap, and I noticed the strength by which she gripped the child.

"The little girl is safe, I'm sure," I said.

She narrowed her eyes. "Are you her mother?"

"No."

A blade of mistrust entered Maggy's eyes.

"I'm Kitty. Do you remember meeting me yesterday?"

"Kitty?" My name came out like she had already placed me, though I doubted the sincerity of her actually remembering. "Kitty," she muttered again under her breath as her gaze returned to the window. "Now, where did that girl go?"

"Oh, you know what?" I clapped my hands with authority and put on a cheerful smile. "The little girl's mother just picked her up to bring her out for ice cream."

Her brows shot up at the mention of dessert.

I giggled. "Do you like ice cream, Maggy?"

A sneaky smile crept onto her thin lips. She leaned closer to me and whispered conspiratorially, "Yes, but it's a secret."

I suppressed my grin. "Your secret is safe with me." I pointed to her baby doll. "Does your baby like ice cream too?"

She nodded absently. Her lips moved with inaudible murmurs as she spoke to herself, and I thought I heard her repeat my name yet again.

"What's your baby's name?" I coaxed.

"Kitty," she mumbled unblinkingly.

She was hooked on my name. I smiled.

"Kitty?" I heard my name again, though this time louder and from somewhere behind us. I turned to see Joy striding over. She sat in the open chair beside her mother and leaned forward to speak to me. "Have you spoken with Abbi about the picture yet?"

I shook my head. "I only just arrived. I'm heading to find her in a minute; I just saw Maggy in here and figured I'd say hello."

"I wish I could stay and hear what Abbi has to say, but I was asked to pick up my granddaughter from preschool today."

Could this be the little girl Maggy was so concerned about?

"Oh, no problem. I'm sure this whole picture mystery has a simple explanation."

"Whatever the case, I'm dying to know what it is." Joy glanced at the gold watch on her wrist and clasped Maggy's hands in hers. "Mom, I have to leave, okay? I will be back again in a few hours."

"Okay, dear." Maggy locked eyes with her daughter. I wondered if she knew her in that moment.

"Don't go wandering off anywhere. Okay, missy?" Joy lifted her mother's weathered hands to her lips and kissed the backside. "Love you, Mom."

I wondered what a painful thing it must be to watch your parent deteriorate before your very eyes. But what a privilege and a beautiful gift to be able to care for, serve, and honor them in such a way. It was a feeling I would never know.

Briefly, a twinge of envy caught my heart by surprise. Joy had this opportunity, as painful as it was, to care for her own mother, and yet, I would be forever denied that with mine. And with my father too. I never even had the chance to say goodbye to either of them.

My heart ached for my children back home as I watched Joy and Maggy interact in the only capacity they could. It seemed that Joy was making the most of the time she had left, even if it meant forgoing reality and joining the world in which her mother now lived. If one day my body failed me in such a way, would my own children care for me like this?

"Kitty, let me know what you find out if you feel like sharing," Joy said to me.

I nodded. "Of course. Oh, I was going to ask you something. If, for some reason, I return here after today, would it be alright if I brought ice cream to share with your mom?"

Joy's face twisted, and I thought for certain I'd somehow said the wrong thing. "Ice cream? Mom hates ice cream."

I let out a hearty laugh. "Well, she told me today that she loves it." Though the fact *had* been divulged to me in confidence. I winced inside.

Joy rubbed her forehead and rolled her eyes. "She keeps surprising me in her older years. It's like learning to love a whole new person. I guess if ice cream is what she wants, then by all means, knock yourself out."

We said goodbye, and I walked down the hallway leading to Abbi's room. Her door was open, and she sat on the side of her bed, holding a handheld mirror while applying lipstick. I knocked softly to announce my presence.

She gasped in delight and set the mirror and lipstick aside to wave me in. She gestured toward the Venus flytrap chairs. "I didn't think I'd see you again, but here you are."

"Here I am," I said and tentatively sat down. Even with my careful precision, the chair rocked and sucked me into its cushions. "Abbi, these chairs . . ."

She covered her mouth, but it did nothing to hide her

mischievous smile. "If I get rid of them, I'll lose half of my fun."

"And if you keep them, you'll lose half of your visitors."

She pointed a finger at me. "You may have a point there." She smacked her bright red lips and said, "Remind me of your name?"

"Kitty. Kitty Fisher."

"Ah, right. Well, you can't have come back just to visit an old bat like me. What brings you here today?"

"It's a funny reason, actually." I wasn't sure how to broach the subject, but I knew I didn't want to waste any time. "Yesterday, just after you left and we were finishing cleaning up the mess, I found something I wanted to ask you about."

She raised her brows. "What was it, hon?"

I motioned toward her armoire. "Do you mind if I just show you?"

"By all means."

"If I can get out of this death trap, that is." I rocked forward twice and with enough momentum, popped to my feet. From the drawer in the armoire, I found the picture of myself and handed it to Abbi. I sat down beside her on the edge of her bed.

As soon as Abbi unfolded the small piece of newsprint and brought it to her eyes, she said, "Oh, good. You found it. Do you see now why I said you looked familiar?"

I swallowed hard. She seemed so unfazed. "Who is that, Abbi?"

But of course, I already knew the answer. I remembered being in a set of curlers with a baby on my hip and another child hanging onto my leg when I had first opened the package stamped from Goldfield and withdrawn a copy of the newspaper, only to find a note attached from Ginny: *Had to celebrate by proxy. Cheers to ten years and many more.* I had set baby Gloria down and given Alan a toy, then unfolded the paper at the dining table. I flipped to the page where I found a photo of Claude and I on our wedding day with the caption:

"Former Goldfield couple, Mr. and Mrs. Claude Fisher, are celebrating one decade of marital bliss. They currently reside in CO. Mr. and Mrs. Fisher are the son and daughter-in-law of Mr. and Mrs. L. Fisher of Goldfield."

The snippet had gotten straight to the point, but the sentiment behind the basic message was there. But now, this picture cut from a copy of the *Bonanza* was missing one thing: my husband. Claude had been clipped out of the photo, leaving only my smiling face by itself, a crease line running just beside my cheek.

"Who is that? Well, I don't think I actually know," Abbi said.

I closed my eyes for a moment. "Abbi, it's me."

She tapped the photo with her pointer finger. "You mean this right here is *you*, not just someone who looks like you?"

"Yes, that's me alright. That was my wedding day. Why and how would you have a picture of *me*?"

I kept my eyes on her, waiting for an answer or, at the very least, a falter in her demeanor, anything to give me an indication that she knew more than she let on. But Abbi remained steadfastly confused.

"I have many things that aren't mine."

"Can I see it again?" I asked.

She handed it over. My fingers traced the yellowed edges, soft from years of wear, and my mind wondered how far this scrap of paper had traveled. In how many pockets had it been tucked away? In how many sets of hands had it been held? Who had thought this faded memory of me valuable enough to fold up and save?

I cleared the lump from my throat. "This was from a newspaper, obviously. But it's not the complete photo. You see this edge here? That's where my husband's handsome face should be."

Abbi took the photo from me and felt the edge herself. "Interesting. Maybe the other half is somewhere in the drawer? What was this picture from?"

I told Abbi the story behind it. The information only puzzled her further.

"How long have you had this in your possession?"

She took a moment to think. "You're tootin' the wrong ringer. I can't remember for certain. Sometimes, I get a bit mixed up on things I have. I've been here for six years, after all."

"But you found it here at Thimbleberry?"

"Pah." She let out a breath and pursed her lips in thought. "Could have."

"But you don't know for sure?"

"Well, some of my collection has been found here, yes. But there could be a few things from before my time here. And you know, I've had old friends mail me photographs here and there throughout the years. I had a friend who passed not too long ago, and her daughter sent me a box of things from our younger days when we traipsed around the country together. Who knows if it came from her?"

I glanced at the picture cradled in Abbi's weathered palm and crossed my arms over my abdomen. How had this simple photo, a forgotten piece of my past, become a shard of glass in my peace? Was it not strange? The strength by which this small slip of paper gripped my thoughts unsettled me.

A thought fluttered through my head. *I was distracting myself with a silly coincidence to put off what brought me to Galia in the first place.* But this mystery certainly didn't feel silly, though maybe I was more desperate for respite than I realized.

"My eyeballs are floating," Abbi suddenly declared. She chortled as she stood and moved to her walker. "I'll be right back. Too much coffee just fills me to the brim if you catch my drift. You'd think I'd learn not to drink so many cups in a day, but at my age, I'd rather almost pee my pants than give up the beans."

I snorted. "They must make a mean cup of joe around here."

"Well, coffee's one of the only pleasures I have left to hold onto."

Her words made me sad. Had she not any hope? When Abbi returned minutes later, she looked at the clock on her wall and gasped.

"Everything okay?"

She twisted her painted lips. "Well, bingo is starting in ten minutes. I would skip, but the thing is, Frank's on a winning streak and has gotten a bit cocky about it lately. He bet me that I wouldn't beat him today. If I don't show, he'll think I chickened out, and I'll lose out on the chance for him to pay me fifty bucks."

"You bet on a game of bingo?" My lips twitched as I suppressed a laugh at the sweetness of the ordeal.

"You bet I did."

I wondered if the lipstick she was applying when I walked in was in preparation for the game. "Well, I certainly don't want to keep you from such a high-stakes match."

Abbi suddenly lit up. "Can you come back tomorrow? This afternoon, after my nap, I'll go through my things and make a phone call or two. This is important. I want to discover the source of your picture as much as you do."

I smiled weakly and nodded. I was no closer to having any answers. Doubt took root in my core that I would ever find them. The thought tunneled through my heart and reminded me again of the peace I could no longer feel, the unease that had wormed its way inside.

While I deflated, Abbi beamed, and I wondered if something hid behind her enthusiasm. "Tomorrow," she said, taking a step toward the door. "I'll see you then."

15

1948
Knoxville, Tennessee

THE SIMPLICITY OF life was gone, replaced now with keeping up, with the drive to fit in and line her lips in the right fashion or don the clothes of a girl that said, *"I'm free; I'm fun. The wars are behind; the future's ahead. It doesn't matter if I don't have roots. Look at me! I live an adventure!"* Because as soon as Kitty grew accustomed to one city and the ways and flows of its streets and people, Peggy got antsy and uprooted them again.

Kitty thought it might've had a thing or two to do with the revolving door of men in Peggy's life and her subsequent search to cleanse herself by dragging them to church. But church was never enough to remedy Peggy's sullied reputation, so they'd pack up and head for the next city. Whatever the case, leaving became routine, to the extent that too much time in one place began making Kitty antsy too.

Maybe she was born for leaving after all.

Maybe the apple didn't fall too far.

The brevity of her moves were protection, a shield behind which to hide. She knew she could run at any given day; Peggy's marching orders were often given without warning. So, she let herself be tangled up in whatever atmosphere she found herself in, and these days, it was a luscious land of greenery and waterways, a distraction from the pull of a desert far away. But the feeling of flightiness was also reinforcement that she didn't quite belong and never would.

The only sense of belonging she'd ever felt was with the Fishers. They'd made her feel like she had worth, like she wasn't dirt on the bottom of a shoe, even though they knew the truth. She'd never made up a story about her past, never felt the need to change details to make herself more palatable as she often did now with new friends. She'd never even had the chance to construct a lie with the Fishers, but still, they'd accepted and loved and *treasured* her just the way she was, background and all.

She tried not to think of them. Remembering made things worse. But as her body changed, and her heart shifted, and attention from boys became a thing of the norm, she couldn't help but think especially of Claude. Who had captured his attention back home? Anyone? Who would he settle down with one day? Whoever it was would be gentle and kind, fun and disciplined. Her parents would mesh with his own, and they would have happy memories of joint Christmases and family vacations.

It wouldn't be Kitty, of that much she was sure. Not that she wanted to think of courtship and marriage anyhow. But the simple fact that she could never be a prospect for him gutted her. Nevada was a location of the past, first of all. And secondly, her father had taken too much from the Fisher family. Claude deserved a girl who didn't remind him of losing his brother, a girl who didn't learn beauty tricks from her supposedly-aprostitute aunt, a girl who knew how to stay. Now freshly seventeen, all Kitty was learning was how to run and be satisfied with the crumbs that life tossed out.

Of all the places Peggy had dragged her to so far, Tennessee was her favorite. Today, the afternoon sun warmed Kitty's skin as she swayed and danced alongside her friends in the crowd in downtown Knoxville. Live music sent something through her body, a feeling she didn't quite recognize. It was the feeling of being alive. As her body lifted to the rhythm, she felt her heart unspool. As her feet shifted beneath her, her worries untethered themselves. On the street, hidden in the safety of the music, her spirits swelled, and she felt a little more free. But the music ended, as it always did, curtailing her freedom and dispersing the crowd.

On this particular day, when the Midday Merry-Go-Round ended, Kitty and three of her friends headed for the lake to cool off after an hour and a half of sweat-inducing dancing under the sun's joyful rays. They made it to the water and quickly saw that many others had a similar idea as well. There were the usual fishermen dotting the docks and the kids jumping in to beat the heat. But there was something else today, too.

The girls sat on the shore and plunged their tired feet into the refreshing waters. Kitty squinted at the decent-sized gathering just down from their spot. A man stood in the lake, the water up to his waist, and waved at someone to join him. A woman from the shore waded in, carving a rippled path until she reached him.

"What're they doing?" Kitty asked.

"And why's everyone else lined up and watchin' like that?" Jan said.

"Look." Bernie pointed to the man in the water, who now held an arm of support across the woman's back. "It's a baptism."

The woman in the lake relaxed into the man's arms, and he

tipped her backward until she dunked beneath the surface. When he lifted her back to her feet, her arms triumphantly reached toward the clear blue sky, and then she wrapped them around the man's neck as the crowd on the shore erupted into an enthusiastic cheer. Before the woman made it two steps toward land, another two people ran into the water toward the man, who held out an inviting arm.

"They sure are giddy about a bath in this gross water, aren't they?" Jan laughed, and it came out as a scoff. Their other friend, Kate, laughed alongside.

But Kitty noticed Bernie shaking her head beside her and turned to see the furrow in Bernie's brows, a mist clouding her eyes.

"I think it's beautiful," Bernie whispered.

Kitty looked back in time to watch the next two strangers be submerged underwater, one after the other, each of them emerging jubilant as praises sang from the shoreline once again.

"What're . . . what're they doing, exactly?" Kitty asked Bernie. She could feel a stirring behind her own eyes, but she hadn't an idea why.

"I seen a baptism or two at church. You know, you give your heart to Jesus, and He makes you a new person. Washes away all the sin and stains. Baptism is symbolic of that."

The only experience with church or religion that Kitty had had was Ginny encouraging her as a younger girl and the few times Aunt Peggy had dragged her to different congregations in search of something. The topic made her prickle.

"You really think that's true?" Jan rolled her eyes and lifted a foot from the water. "So, my feet must be pretty clean and new and free from sin then, huh?"

"You're missin' the point, Jan." A tear fell down Bernie's cheek, but there wasn't a frown to accompany it. Strangely enough, Bernie was smiling.

"Have you ever been baptized?" Kitty asked quietly.

"Me?" Bernie shook her head as the man in the lake began to speak.

"In Christ, you can walk free! In Christ, you are not in bondage to your sin! To your past! Christ says you are redeemed! You are His! Your identity is no longer found in the things of this world but in Him and Him alone!" The man projected his message with gusto, his hands cupped around his mouth to amplify his words. "Matthew 11:28 says, 'Come unto me, all *ye* that labour and are heavy laden, and I will give you rest.' If that is you today, weary and burdened, come! Lay it down! Trust in the Lord! Follow Him! Be baptized in Jesus' name!"

Jan muttered something that Kitty didn't catch because her focus was directed toward the man. She longed to believe that these things he said were true. Was it that easy for your burdens to be taken away? Would plunging herself under the water suddenly dissolve the endless pit in her stomach? She knew it wouldn't, but why, then, were more people flocking to the water? Why, then, was Bernie now rising to her feet?

"Wait. You're not going down there, are you?"

Bernie looked down at Jan and flashed a genuine smile. "I been told 'bout Jesus my whole life. Heard the stories 'bout how He set me free. I don't think I ever understood it till now. So, yeah. I'm goin'." Bernie took off, skipping down the shoreline until she reached the crowd. Her hands raised into the air to cheer for the young man who'd just come out of the water.

The water tugged at Kitty and blurred before her eyes. She plucked her feet from its coolness and drew her knees to her chest. None of it made sense to her, so why couldn't she dismiss it the same way Jan could? Why did she look at the beaming joy on the faces along the shore and feel that it was pure? Bernie waded into the water now, and even from Kitty's vantage point, the smile that spread across her friend's entire face was visible.

All these people had gladly entered the water without a care as to who was watching or who was judging them like Jan or Kate. All these people believed the lake man's words, the words that were supposedly in Scripture, the ones that promised deliverance. Death to life. Darkness to light. For a moment, Kitty imagined herself rising and joining Bernie's side, letting herself be cleansed of everything that plagued her. She felt her heart give a cheer of its own, a plea for freedom, for something that lasted longer than an afternoon concert, something that was said to stretch into eternity. She imagined what that freedom from darkness might do for herself, for her father, for her aunt. Maybe even somewhere out there . . . for her mom.

But fear gnawed inside as she imagined wading up to the preacher, who might look at her and say, "I'm sorry, but I wasn't speaking to you. This kind of freedom isn't for a girl like yourself." Her stomach soured with rejection at the make-believe in her mind. Of course, she couldn't do such a bold thing. Of course, someone of her stature wouldn't qualify for such a lofty promise. The spark fizzled out inside of her, and she remained on the ground.

Kitty watched as Bernie exchanged words with the man. Bernie plugged her nose and leaned into his sure arms, trusting and confident as he tipped her backward. When he brought her upright, Bernie doubled over, her mouth open. Kitty leaned forward, straining for a better view, a band of worry stitching her heart tight. Had Bernie inhaled water? Had the man hurt her somehow? Had she made the wrong choice?

But pain wasn't etched into her friend's face. Sure, Bernie wept in the breast-high water, but the tears were a thing of beauty and surrender, accompanied now with a smile so wide that tears sprung loose in Kitty's eyes as well.

She'd never witnessed someone so free.

16

Lia

1937
Galia, Oregon

I SIT ON the edge of the bed in defeat. Everywhere that seems a decent spot to hide away one's darkest secrets seems much too obvious. Tucking them into a nook or cranny is only welcoming someone to find them. I don't want them somewhere a houseguest might stumble across. So that leads me back here, to our bedroom, the room a husband would hope his wife wouldn't be leaving secrets at all.

The kitchen is one thing—slipping in extra sugar here and there or keeping a recipe secret for posterity's sake. The garden is another—the secret to how I get the roses to bloom in such a way (it's all about the pruning). But the bedroom? Preposterous! Yet here I am. Desperate.

The baby plays on the rug, completely unaware of who her mother is. It's incredible that she loves me in such a way. Would that love change if she knew the truth about me? And the truth about her? She stacks wooden blocks on top of one another and giggles as they fall down. My secret, I know, is safe with her for now.

I gaze across the room, fixating on the wedding photo of Tenn and me hanging on the wall. *I'm so sorry*, I think with half a mind to rip it down and smash it on the floor. To scoop up my little girl and run from this house and these lies because I'm a coward who cannot face the truth and own up to what I've done.

I need to stay. I cannot run. Though the temptation to destroy our photo remains, and it's not Tenn's fault, in the least.

Destroyer.

Destroyer.

Destroyer.

The words bounce in my mind. I cannot make them stop.

17

1981
Galia, Oregon

I SLUMPED BEHIND the steering wheel. Claude needed me back at the hotel, but a heaviness pinned me to my seat. I rested my forehead against the wheel and wondered how I'd muster enough energy to drive home. My limbs felt as heavy as the great boughs that hung from the surrounding green giants. I wanted to sleep alongside the forest, to dissolve into its safe branches and the quiet solace they promised.

"Okay, Lord," I murmured. "Is there a reason I'm here? Is there something you're doing with all this pain?"

The Lord provided rest, I knew, but my plea trailed out the open window and dissipated with the heaviness of my unbelief and inability to understand. My fingers curled around the wheel, and I bit back the taste of my youth. For a moment, I was fourteen, stomping amongst the sagebrush and kicking up dust, retreating to an old Model T that housed me safely when the world got too loud.

I started the engine, backed out of Thimbleberry's parking lot, and took to the road. The breeze blew through the window and carried out my resolve. As the road dipped and curved, I felt a part of myself unravel along with it. I punched off the low buzz of "The Winner Takes It All" coming through the radio and gripped the wheel tighter.

Miles went by in silence until I realized the town wasn't opening before me, and ocean waves weren't crashing into view. I pressed the brakes and slowed until I came to a turnoff on the road. I parked and grabbed the paper with directions from the passenger seat. My eyes flicked over the meticulously drawn map, and I saw the problem. I'd been on this road far too long. My turn was miles behind me, and I'd completely missed it, winding myself further into the forest rather than closer to the coast.

The paper fluttered to the floorboard as I got out of the car and slammed the door. The sound cut through the still forest like a knife. I winced. In a way, I didn't mind being lost, for it mirrored how I felt inside. I had never been to Galia, yet the entire place crawled with reminders of all that I'd lost and all that I'd never had in the first place. This new phase of life felt foreign as I entered middle age, parentless and floundering. My feet carried me away from the car with the aimless steps of a drifter. In the quiet, I heard the small voice of a younger version of myself ask, *Who even am I?*

You're mine, a voice disguised as my beating heart said.

The breath left my lungs. My chin dipped, and I couldn't explain the shame that suddenly burned within me. How could I doubt Him? He'd never given me a reason to, and yet I allowed my emotions to fester and that small voice to argue back, *"Are you sure you want me?"*

My eyes burned, but I spotted a trailhead just off the turnoff. I moved toward the opening and stepped onto the path. The forest pulled me in. Maybe a fifty-year-old woman could run away. At least for a little while. Long enough for her to come to her senses.

Moss dripped from a tree, and I ducked beneath its lazy, drunken fingers. Magic covered every inch of the place. Ethereal flickers of light dappled the leaves, and pine needles crunched underfoot. I inhaled the musty earth, its scent a mixture of death and new life, of decay and rebirth, the quintessential epitome of life.

I continued on. My body felt relieved to move. Pine cones and animal droppings littered the path, and I stepped around them as they came. A rustling overhead diverted my gaze. Through the endless trees that used the sky as a canvas, a raven took flight. I felt a part of my heart gloss over, like the pouring of lacquer on an old piece of wood. For a moment, the world didn't feel quite so wrong.

It was the Lord who shone the light that pierced through. It was His light, His forest, His story . . . I was merely living in it.

"It's all Yours, isn't it?" I whispered.

Including you. I felt His truth course through me this time.

My feet suddenly turned as if obedience had been whispered to them in a private word, and my heart softened. In spite of the gentle nip of the shaded wood, a warmth spread through my core and reached the tips of my fingers and the tips of my toes.

I wanted answers. My whole life, I'd wanted answers. But just as I'd been reminded in Abbi's room this afternoon, some answers would never come. Some things would never change. Mysteries would remain. Questions too. As much as I wanted to understand the parts of myself that still suffered the sadness of being unwanted by my mother, maybe it was never meant for me to know.

She may not have wanted me, but God always did.

"I'm going to keep trusting You. Even when none of this makes

sense." I sniffed and wiped my nose as I made my way back to the trailhead. In spite of everything, a bleat of hope escaped my heart. *"But if you could make it make sense, that'd be awfully great."*

Once I finally found my way back to the hotel, I hurried to the second floor and slid the key into the lock on our door, ready after the day to fall into my husband's arms, to feel the love of Christ shining through them, but when I opened the door, the room was empty, and the bed was made.

"Honey?" I called. "Claude?" But no reply came. He wasn't in the room.

A handwritten note on hotel stationery was propped up on the desk near the window. *"Feeling better and heading to the beach. Come find me. Love you. – Fly"*

I took a minute to freshen up and swapped my heavier sweater for a light cardigan, as the sun was now burning through the fog. It would only be a matter of time before cloud covering came back again, though, forcing the sun into yet another game of peekaboo.

I left the hotel on foot minutes later. Every step closer to the ocean became saltier, and the breeze pushed my hair from my face, the sandy waves I hadn't seen for years coming to life with the coastal humidity. As I stepped from the boardwalk onto the gently-sloping sand, I spotted the backside of my husband. He stood with both hands in the front pockets of his khaki trousers and the ocean breeze tousling his golden and graying hair. His plain white t-shirt hugged his strong frame. Taking off my penny loafers, I walked barefoot toward him.

The day nagged at my mind, the imminent sendoff of Dad's ashes ever-present as the waves broke and lapped at the shoreline in a fizzy, foaming burst. I stepped over a glob of seaweed, and when I reached Claude, I wrapped my arms around his back and wanted to melt.

He reached around for me and scooped me to the front for a

proper embrace.

"It's nice to see you upright and on your feet." I reached for his cheek. No more fever.

"I have no choice. I've been out of commission for only two days, and you've already begun scouting nursing homes for a replacement."

I leveled him with a glare. "Hardly."

"Are you sure about that?" He gave my midsection a squeeze. "I'm not quite what I once was."

"You might want to join those men on the pier with your fantastic fishing skills. You might be fishing for compliments as opposed to seafood, but still." I patted his chest and reveled in the way his eyes washed over me. "I could never find another you. You're irreplaceable. The only one ever made for me."

The smell of his cedarwood soap from home overpowered the brine in the air as he pulled me closer.

"I love you, Kitty."

I tilted my head to study his face. "Do you think we'll ever get to the point of our health and age separating us from one another? Like that woman Maggy and her husband?"

He raked his fingers through my windblown hair. "I've stuck by you since the days we were babies in diapers, and I fully intend to do the same in old age."

A laugh rattled forth. "You mean you'll still love me into incontinence?"

"Yup."

"Even if I don't recognize you anymore?"

"Absolutely."

"Even if I turn ornery?"

"You mean you aren't already?"

I glared at him.

"Careful," he murmured. "You're proving my point."

It felt good to laugh. If only all of life were as easy as this.

"Did you unearth any answers today?"

"No." I angled my body toward the slapping white caps. I had been given a good reminder, though. *I know You care, Lord. I know I'm Yours. But I feel that security being nipped at, and I'm ashamed to admit it.*

"Are you prepared to receive no answers at all?"

I wanted to be, but was I really?

"I'm not sure why this whole thing matters so much to me," I said softly.

After a moment, Claude squeezed me in his arms. "You're thinking of your mother, aren't you?"

"You say that like you already know the answer." I bit my lip and squinted as far as I could see, zoning in on the horizon. Maybe admitting the truth would give me freedom. "But yes. You're right."

I took a moment to gather my thoughts, and Claude patiently waited. Finally, I said, "I guess the photo felt like a breadcrumb. I just . . . I know I'm a grown woman, and I've lived my whole life without her. Thank God I had your mother to braid my hair, kiss my scraped knees, and keep me fed. But I still can't help wondering where she ended up. And if she ever regretted leaving."

The wind picked up and carried mist onto our faces. I blinked against the salt.

"I've prayed for her for years, and with my dad now gone and being around everyone at the retirement home, it's got me wondering if she's gone too. I feel kind of lame admitting it, but she still matters to me. Even now."

"God knows your mom, Kitty. He will see things through however they're meant to be. He's heard your every prayer, and if she's sent them up, He's heard your mother's too." He rubbed my arm. "Do you . . . wish you would have tried to find her? Are you . . . wanting to?"

"Sometimes," I admitted. "But the road goes both ways. She could have come and found me all these years and didn't. She knew more about how to find me than I did her." A lump formed in my throat. "With all that's happened in the past few months—Dad dying, your parents' house fire—it's dredged up a lot of emotions. That's all."

He squeezed my arm, and in that simple gesture, I knew he understood. I dug my toes into the cool sand and leaned against him.

"Tomorrow, I plan to visit Thimbleberry Cottage again. Is that alright? Abbi said she'd look through her things and maybe make a phone call to someone on my behalf."

"That's fine. Can I join you?"

"Absolutely." I perked up and pecked him on the lips. "It's a date."

"Speaking of dates . . . I already knew this week would be tough for you, though neither of us planned for the chain of events that have happened so far. But I want you to know how much I've been looking forward to alone time with you. Dating you. Being Kitty and Fly again. I wanted to turn this would-be sad week into a favorite memory, to celebrate your birthday and date the heck out of you."

"But instead, you've been food poisoned, and I've ditched you to hang out with strange old women."

"I just want this week to be different for you." He kissed where the ocean spray had landed on my cheek. "Will you let me date you for real?"

I arched my brow. "And what does *for real* entail?"

His eyes danced, and everything around us fell away. "Kitty Fisher, I am asking you out on a *real* date right now. If we hurry, we can make low tide. I have an idea."

18

1949
Tonopah, Nevada

THE CEILING FAN whirred, and the room smelled stale, like the former inhabitants hadn't quite left, but the light coming through the second story windows laced a ribbon of silky condolence around Kitty's heart.

The view opened to endless dirt, puffs of sagebrush sprinkled across the ground, and dying grasses reaching toward the sky like hands pleading for a cup of water. Everything here was parched, much like her own soul, which longed for a rush of cool waters, refreshing and nourishing. But this desert only reminded her of what once was and what never would be.

This desert had soaked up her tears, too stingy to ever return the favor and leaving her more bone-dry than she'd ever been. It didn't matter what Ginny Fisher had once told her here in this very town. *"God hasn't forsaken this desert,"* she'd said. *"There's nowhere His presence can't be found."* But instead of feeling Him, it was the steady shriveling of her own heart that Kitty felt.

Peggy hadn't been able to stay away. As much as she loathed the barren land and the reminders it brought of her husband's untimely death—he'd been killed in a training accident at the Tonopah Army Air Field during the war—Peggy also couldn't stand leaving him behind. The home he'd bought her, the life he'd promised, the grave he now claimed.

And so, after years of running and trying to stave off reality, Peggy dragged them back to the heat that coursed again through Kitty's veins. But of course, the home her husband had purchased, and where they'd lived before, had been sold. So, Peggy secured a job at The Mizpah Hotel, and instead of a home, they rented a single room to share for the time being until their housing situation could change.

Kitty made her way to the main floor of the hotel, sidestepping the casino. She quite enjoyed the Mizpah's lounge, where the bellhop often could be found, always ready with a joke, and the bartender gave her Shirley Temples on the house. She slid onto a stool, and William slid the soda over as soon as she sat down.

"So, you've been back here for, what, a week now?" William said.

Kitty shrugged. "Something like that."

"And I still haven't seen you running off with friends. Why's that?"

Because I don't have any . . . Kitty kept the thought to herself. "I just haven't gotten reacquainted. School hasn't started up yet and all."

He gave her a knowing look. "Seems to me if I was a kid on summer break, I'd want to be having fun with my friends. You should pay someone a visit and let people know Kitty Ralph is back in town."

She knew he was only trying to help, but did she want

everyone to know about her return? Did she want them to see the continued failure of her life? She wished for them to forget, to picture her living out some elaborate dream rather than see her reality. She'd returned to the place she could be seen clearly for what she was: trash blowing to and fro in the wind.

"Actually . . ." William leaned down and gave a quick nod toward something behind her. "It seems like someone might be paying *you* a visit."

Kitty turned.

A boy her age stood there, offering a polite wave and the smile of a heartbreaker. She lifted her hand in return, and he took her acknowledgement of his presence as an invitation to join her at the bar. He plopped down on the stool beside her and smoothed a hand over dark hair that fell perfectly into a comb-over. His eyes were dark and brooding, the kind that made a girl want to patch up any brokenness behind them. Kitty could sense his familiarity, but her heightened nerves made her mind fuzzy.

"Hey," he said, his voice low and his lips forming into a natural pout. "Are you . . . Kitty?"

She tried to place him. "Old classmate, right?"

"Jack."

That's right. She remembered him now.

"I thought you moved?" he asked.

"I did," she said, stirring the straw around in her drink. "My aunt and I just moved back."

"Oh." He smiled without showing his teeth. "I'm really glad you're back. Are you here to stay?"

Who knew?

"For now," she replied and glanced over her shoulder in case any other former classmates were waiting in the wings. "What are you doing here, by the way?"

Jack gestured over his shoulder. "I'm having lunch with my family. But I noticed you sitting over here alone, and well, I thought I'd come say hi."

"You recognized me?"

Sheepishly, he shook his head. "Not at first."

She wasn't sure if that relieved her or made her feel worse.

"Well, thanks for saying hi." She chanced a glance at William, who stood off to the side, drying glasses with a towel. He vaguely lifted a brow, and the motion pressed her to keep talking. "I haven't really seen anyone since coming back. Getting settled and all, you know."

He drummed his fingers on the bar top. "Well, a group of us are meeting up later to hang out. Do you want to join?"

Kitty froze, and her eyes darted back to William. A little smile quirked at the corner of his mouth. If she didn't accept this invitation, she'd never live it down. Immersing herself back into the town was a necessity, she knew, unless she wanted to live like a bitter old hermit, sipping Shirley Temples at a bar and brooding about the past. She shivered at the thought of turning into anything remotely close to Peggy.

"Sure. I'd enjoy that. It'll be nice to see familiar faces again."

He gave her a playful little nudge. "Well, how about I pick you up tonight then?"

Her stomach soured. She hadn't agreed to a date, had she? The last thing she wanted was a boyfriend of any sort, especially here. Of all places, here. So close to . . .

She swallowed hard. A distant memory threatened to resurface, but she pushed it into the recesses of her mind. She had to start over; she had to move on.

"Sure."

"Great. Where do you live?"

She opened her mouth but paused. What would anyone think if they knew she didn't have a real home? A permanent place to lay her head? "Just pick me up here."

"Okay. Six o'clock work?"

"That's perfect."

—

Not much seemed to have changed in Tonopah. Kitty began running around with familiar faces, the classmates she'd had for a brief time becoming her friends again. Jack always seemed to be hanging around, ready to offer a ride, ready to open a door. He'd asked her out on a proper date on more than one occasion, but Kitty always declined.

"Why?" he asked one evening as he walked her back to the hotel, where, by now, everyone had figured out she lived. They'd just come from a movie at the Butler Theatre with friends.

"I'm not dating at the moment."

"Well, what's it going to take for you to start?" Jack asked.

The sun had already gone down, and when they reached the Mizpah, Jack stalled outside. He leaned one shoulder against the brick exterior and watched her under the light.

"It's complicated." *And the last thing I want to discuss*, Kitty thought to herself.

"Is there someone else you like?" His dark brows rose with the question. A shadow fell across his face as he took a step closer.

Kitty felt her pulse in her throat. Her eyes darted away from him briefly. There wasn't anyone. Not anymore. Why, then, couldn't she stand the thought of giving her heart away? No matter how many times she promised it wasn't bound to anyone else, she always felt like a liar.

"No," she heard herself say.

"Are you scared of something?"

I'm scared of everything. She could never say as much out loud. When she didn't respond, he said, "It's okay to be scared. To be honest, I'm the one who's scared."

"You?" The idea seemed ridiculous. Jack was *too cool* to fear anything. "Scared of what?"

"Of you."

Her mouth went dry.

"I . . . I like you, Kitty. I don't normally fall like this for girls. And that scares me."

Suddenly, she felt quite scared indeed. Scared of the discomfort she felt, the nagging betrayal that wouldn't silence itself inside her mind, the idea of a boy delighting in her. Scared of everything to come in her life, the uncertainty that walked beside her every day, the fear that her best days were behind her.

"Come on," he said with a lilt in his voice. "Let's get you inside."

Tidbits of rumors had tickled Kitty's ear, little scraps of conversation here and there between her friends about Jack's proclivity to date around. She wasn't interested in a playboy, but was this playboy really interested in her? It flattered her to think that of all the girls Jack Knackey had dated, she was the one who made him scared.

19

Lia

1938
Galia, Oregon

YOU WOULD LOVE *the way her hair smells when she wakes from a
nap, the way she giggles so hard she can barely breathe whenever I
snort like the pigs that my grandpa used to raise. You would've loved
those pigs, I'm sure. Friendliest pigs I've ever met. All love, no
rottenness. I don't know what it was about those pigs that Grandpa
bred . . . but he somehow transferred the glow of his personality right
into each one.*

*Except for little Abaddon, whose name says it all. I'm not sure
what went wrong in that pig, but you didn't want to be caught near
it! I can assure you of that.*

*I often wonder at the meaning of names. Abaddon was named for
his destructive, mean behavior, so the behavior preceded the name. But
my daughter lives up to her name. And you . . . do you live up to yours?
Pure and clear? You are without fault. Who could blame you?*

"Great excellence" is the meaning of my own, and I fail to report good news in the way of how I've lived. But you know that already, don't you? At least by now you must. And if you don't, then you are much purer in heart than I ever thought.

I write to you from a place of shame and honesty. I have been running scared for a long time. I always thought as a child that I could spread my wings, fly if I wanted, let my bare feet glide over the tall prairie grasses, let the wind tangle my hair into knots and sweep me from my feet, scooping me in its warm cradle and carrying me for miles to deposit me into the breaking waves of the ocean I'd only ever dreamed about. I wanted to live a thousand different lives, to travel beyond the aching walls of my wind-battered home, to create on the blank canvas of the future a scene that mimicked the longing of my heart.

I got a taste of that from my school time in Syracuse, but when the money ran dry and forced me home, I was back to where I'd started: longing for someplace else.

You must wonder what happened to me. Maybe you've created extravagant stories with the wild imagination I assume you must have. Perhaps you've written me off entirely. I wouldn't blame you. It's what I deserve. It's why I've never attempted to come back.

And now, there's another reason.

I can't do it again. Twice. Leave, I mean. I cannot leave Tenn, leave our daughter, or leave the new life growing inside of me. It wouldn't be fair of me, but again, how is it fair to you?

Perhaps you've heard the saying, "You've made your bed; now lie in it." No matter what I do, I continue to hurt people. By staying, I hurt you. By leaving, I hurt them. And no matter the case, I am hurt regardless, though it is only by my own doing.

And I know it will only be by God's grace that He makes this all okay. Tenn stumbled into a revival meeting and now talks to me about God. We've even started to attend a sweet church in town. "His grace! His grace is enough!" they all say. But how could it ever be enough for me?

I was not handed a torch from my mother that shone with the brightness of tenderness nor of grace. She did not illuminate me with the warmth that I longed to feel, and according to her, she did not receive that same from her own mother. (Though in her defense, Grandmother was only ever kind to me.) But my mother handed me a torch that was smoldering at best, a light nearly extinguished that she expected me to use to illuminate the future paths on which I'd walk.

And any plans I had in rekindling the fire were squashed as I set you up to inherit nothing from me. Not a light of any kind at all. I'm sorry.

I'm learning as I look back that we cannot control the circumstances into which we are born, the families who were given the chance to love us and failed. But we can work toward setting ourselves and future generations free from repeating the same mistakes. Changing doesn't right past wrongs, but it does prevent future ones.

And should it align with the splendid blessing of forgiveness . . . well, that would be far more than I deserve. But it's what I want, what I hope for. I don't know how, but one day . . . maybe.

I ensure the ink is dry before folding the letter, not that there aren't already smudges on the page. I tuck it into the pocket of my apron and reach for my spade. I never know when my heart will seize with thoughts of the past, so it's easier now to carry a piece of stationery and a broad nib pen wherever I go. Be that to the garden, the market, or, for crying out loud, the powder room at Tenn's office.

What I can say is, I'm finding some sort of peace, deserving of it or not. Is that selfish of me? Because I wonder if, instead, I should doom myself to suffer. But my suffering bleeds into the rest of the family, and isn't that the very thing I'm trying to avoid once again?

My peace could be an illusion; I have enough sense to admit that. Because with my logic, I can't configure a manner in which all of this would end up okay. And yet, against my logic, I feel a nag, nag, nag to let it go.

I really should find my gardening gloves. The last time I saw them, my joyful little girl was filling them with dirt and prancing around the meadow, sprinkling the ground with her makeshift confetti. Who was I to interrupt such a parade?

Besides, the soil is cool to my hands, and I don't mind the grime. The grime signifies hard work. The proof of worth. And she really gets a kick out of going to the brook in the woods and letting the icy waters wash our hands. And in a way, I do too. The cleansing reminds me of what Tenn says about Jesus and how He can wash away our sins. Regardless of whether it's true, I'd like to lay in that stream for a while and imagine all of my stains washing away.

20

1981
Galia, Oregon

"NO, NO. YOU'RE not allowed to help. Let me make the sandwiches."

I opened my mouth to protest, but Claude pointed a finger at me.

"And no arguing."

"Okay, but—"

"You only like a thin layer of mustard, I know."

"And—"

"Extra pickles, yeah, yeah."

I crossed my legs and sat back in the wicker chair. My foot jiggled up and down with a mind of its own. Claude had fashioned the desk into a makeshift sandwich counter. Fixings were strewn across, and crumbs claimed the space like mighty warriors conquering a new land.

He glanced up from the jar of mayonnaise and said, "I've got this, babe. You're free to do whatever you want."

"What if what I want is to make the sandwiches?"

"That"—he pointed the spreading knife at me—"is off the table."

"That's funny," I said and gestured to the mess. "Because to me, it looks like it is on the table. All over, in fact."

"Pretend we haven't been married for thirty-some years and that I'm preparing a whole surprise picnic for you, will ya?"

"Oh, are you going to chivalrously pick me up too?"

"Oh, I'll do more than just that." He winked at me, and I rolled my eyes, though inwardly I bubbled with glee.

Once the sandwiches were made and packed, we secured our bike rentals from the hotel. Claude set the sandwiches in the wicker basket on the front of his bike, and I put the cans of soda and a picnic cloth in mine.

We took our bikes up the coast, away from craggy cliffs and looming trees, and rode beside the ocean on the hard packed sand of low tide. The wind stole our voices and tangled my hair, but few words were needed as we pedaled like the young kids we used to be, heading off to a new adventure.

As unpredictable and painful as life could be, the things that remained constant made up for those that didn't. Years ago, in my darkest moments of grief, I met Jesus. I'd met Him before, through the love of the Fisher family, but I didn't know Him by name until Claude introduced me. The fact was, Jesus had always been there. When I didn't know how to cope with losing my mother, father, or home; when I didn't know how to cope with the fear of caring for the new life growing within me . . . Jesus has been my rock, an even more steadfast one than Claude. In Him, I had peace with the past and hope for the future.

My mind briefly darted to the ashes that waited securely in our hotel room, and my heart swelled in spite of the sorrow inside. Maybe I could do this after all. In Him, I could do anything.

We dodged driftwood and deepened our laugh lines, and my mind continued to draw tally marks in my heart for all that I had to be grateful for. My Savior, my husband, my children, my family, blue skies, bike rides. The taste of glee. The cliffside that had loomed ahead drew nearer with our pedaling, and with the tide pulled far into the sea, a cave became more evident with each rotation of my bike's tires.

"We're almost there," Claude shouted with a satisfied smirk on his face.

I wanted to be this way forever.

Rocky earth guarded the cave's entrance. We left our bikes and picnic in the sand, wanting to first explore the site before the tide played any tricks and returned early. Unencumbered by clouds, the rare fullness of the sun beat on our backs as we picked our way across the rocks, and I couldn't help but thank God for His orchestration of the weather.

I'm here. I'm with you. I always am. My heart felt the words as strongly as the salt on my lips.

Anemones flaunted vivid colors in tide pools outside the sea cave's gaping mouth. A lone crab scuttled into the dark shadows of the hollow walls. I reached the entrance just ahead of Claude and entered first. Algae-wrapped regurgitations from the sea littered the inside, and only tufts of course sand stood amidst the endless crust of rocks. Water dripped from overhead and landed on my scalp, sending a chill down my spine.

On the cave's wall, running parallel to the ocean, light spilled through an opening just large enough for a single person to slip through. I headed for it. The doorway opened to reveal giant boulders jutting from the water, leading away from the doorway like a pier.

"Honey, look." My whisper echoed, and as I took another step, I slipped on a slick algae-crowned rock. Claude's arm instantly slid around my waist from behind as though to say, *I'm here. I'm with you. I always am.*

His love for me was like that of Jesus.

My worth had been under question from the moment I'd cried for my mother's breast, and she failed to appear. Additionally, it was attacked by a father who found comfort in a bottle rather than in his offspring.

But God.

God had placed Claude's hand around my heart with a vice grip and the life mission to rectify my deep-rooted misunderstandings.

By no deed of my own, I was loved before my father fell to alcohol, before my mother left, before my parts were even knit together in her womb. Loved enough by my Creator for a Savior to cover my yet-to-be-committed sins. For nails to drive through flesh. For death to believe it had the upper hand. For it to be conquered. Christ had thought me worthy enough to save, and through the love of my husband and lifelong friend, His love and grace had been made known.

I leaned into Claude's warmth, and he rested his chin on my shoulder. I sank into him, freed from the nagging strain of life. Together, we peered through the rugged opening at the expanse of the ocean ahead.

"Look at this place," he whispered. "It's . . ."

"Perfect," I finished as I thought to myself, *Here. This is where I'll let Dad go.*

21

1949
Tonopah, Nevada

IT WAS THE morning of Kitty's first day of senior year at school. The day came faster than she anticipated. As she woke up from a sleepover at her friend Bethany's house, nerves elbowed her excitement aside. The girls got ready together. Kitty took the curlers from her hair, dusted her face with makeup, and swiped a pale shade of pink on her lips. Bethany slicked down her bob and colored her lips a vivacious red.

"So, anything I need to know before my first day?" Kitty hoped for a crumb, any remnant of information about her former classmates in Goldfield whom she'd learned had integrated with Tonopah over the last few years.

Bethany dabbed at her lipstick. "No, not really."

"Oh, okay." Kitty smoothed her skirt, disappointed. She hadn't expected the news that Goldfield's high school had merged with Tonopah. She'd hoped, with fear tagging along, that maybe one day she'd run into the Fisher's at the store, but never had she thought her daily life would again involve Claude.

Maybe Claude had a girlfriend now, some girl in school she didn't know about. Maybe he'd somehow graduated early or dropped out like Cliff had always wanted to do. Maybe he wouldn't remember her much at all.

Her stomach churned. "Why do I feel like I want to puke?"

Bethany looked at Kitty and said, "Don't be nervous. You're going to be fine. I bet the boys are going to be all over you. Not that it matters," Bethany prattled, "with you and Jack and all."

"Beth, Jack and I are not—"

"I know, I know. You're 'not' an item." She lifted one eyebrow. "He seems pretty smitten if you ask me, though."

"Well, he can be smitten all he wants. It still doesn't mean anything."

Jack's interest in her was flattering, but somewhere deep inside, a warning bell rang out, though Kitty did her best to drown it out. It was only the past, she told herself, trying to prevent her future. The two couldn't coexist at the same time.

When they arrived at the high school, Kitty forced herself to smile, to act collected as she operated under the control of her nerves. In truth, she felt stiffened with sadness, but how could she burden anyone with such a thing? It was the first day of school. It was supposed to be a jovial day, not a pity party. She swallowed her pride and forced herself to move, to bend, to laugh at the jokes her friends told. She kept her eyes trained on things directly in front of her and her mind on the next necessary action. Walk up the stairs. Enter the classroom. Sit in a seat. Scanning the room for familiar faces would prove detrimental to her ability to function at all, so she sat beside Bethany in the front row of the already full classroom.

Maybe she'd changed enough that no one from home would recognize her? She'd grown, matured, filled out. Maybe they'd forgotten that Kitty Ralph existed at all.

The school day began with Mr. Reynold's instructing the students to give a summer spiel, one by one, starting with Jack. He moved to the front of the classroom, directly in front of Kitty.

It was hard for Kitty to meet his eyes, knowing somewhere behind her, Claude was in the room. The last thing she wanted was to hurt him more than she already had. The thought pricked her heart. *How selfish of her to even think that he still thinks and cares about her at all!*

"I'm Jack. You all know that already. Um, I guess the most exciting thing I did this summer besides fishing was trying to make a certain girl go out with me."

The words, coupled with his pouty smile, were meant to send butterflies fluttering through her stomach, but instead, they felt like a sucker punch to the gut. Bethany playfully nudged her, but Kitty didn't budge. Jack sat down, and the line moved around the room. Kitty recognized familiar faces and smiled from the front row as old friends took to the front of the room to talk about their activities over the break.

But then, Kitty's heart nearly stopped, a dead hollow organ suspended in her chest, when Claude moved to the front of the room. She couldn't look up, couldn't bring herself to meet his gaze. But his voice—oh, his voice!—simultaneously calmed her nerves and made her shake. It was him, but deeper, surer, older. She couldn't focus on his words—something about his dad?—because his voice unlocked a door to the past, a lifetime of memories.

Running through the desert.

Exploring abandoned cabins.

Biking on the dunes.

Bible stories on the porch.

Late night radio shows.

Kick the can.

Playing catch.

It was a whoosh of nostalgia, the deep sense of longing suddenly bringing an ache she'd long suppressed. She'd loved him. She'd loved his family. His mother, Ginny. His father, Leonard. His brothers, Vern and Cliff.

She wished for him to know the depths of which she loved them all, the incalculable gratitude she had for each of their lives. She wanted to set eyes on him, to see—she hoped—how well he was now. To have faith that the years had been good to him, to them, in spite of everything that had happened.

But he sat down before she could muster the nerve to look up.

When it was her turn, Kitty drew a brave breath and stood, offering the best, most confident wave she could. "I'm Kitty Ralph. Actually, I'm originally from Goldfield, but I attended here for part of my eighth-grade year before I moved away. But my aunt and I came back this July."

She swept her eyes around the room, waiting for the moment they would fall on Fly. *Did he still go by Fly sometimes?* Her gaze drifted, and then—

She lost the air in her lungs as his eyes locked with hers. He was different, no longer the young kid he was when she'd left. He sat taller now, his legs sprawling under the desk, one ankle kicked over the other. His shoulders were broad, his muscles evident even under his plain white t-shirt. He was teetering on the precipice of manhood, the sight before her convincing her of nothing less. This boy was new and different, but as her eyes bore into his, she saw he was also the same.

The summer sun had lightened his hair, just as it always did, rendering him into a version of his late brother Vern with the golden highlights and sun-kissed glow. His eyes were still warm, reassuring like the daily sun, rich, colored with the earthy tones of a woodland forest, and kind, inviting her in like he knew the inner workings of her heart and loved her in spite of its disfigurement, like he would still catch her anytime she fell.

It was too much, too easy to fall over the edge and tumble back into his life. She couldn't do that to him; she couldn't subject him to her. Her eyes flicked away, but she wished deep down that he knew all she wanted to do was gaze at him forever.

22

Lia

1938
Galia, Oregon

OUR FAMILY IS growing. It's a splendid feeling. Soon, I know that more laughter and cries and coos and ahhs will fill our home. They will dampen the echoing of the silence.

These letters are overtaking my bedroom, though no one would ever know. I've written so many that I'm having to use multiple frames. Tenn just thinks that I'm on a decorating spree, early nesting. I think he enjoys the new photographs displayed and the art I've picked up at flea markets.

Little does he know what lays behind them.

This season has been busy, and for that I am grateful. We've revamped one of the guest rooms to be a nursery for the new baby. And our firstborn is beginning to speak well. Having someone to converse with has made all the difference in the world. Even if she doesn't use the right words half the time.

Sometimes I think of the words I missed out on, the ones you said, the little ditties you made up, the funny quips and songs. I wish I could hear your voice. Is it high and raspy like hers?

I will never know.

I'm sorry I will never know.

I asked Tenn's office assistant the other day for a telegram form. She insisted I tell her what I'd like to send and to whom and where so she could file it for me as she normally does. But her pressing made me nervous, and I told her it was for a later date. I have no intention of allowing this telegram out of my sight. I'll be the one to send it myself, even if I have to sneak by walking down to the telegraph office, if and when I ever do.

I haven't found the words to say yet. Or the heart by which to say them. Sending it feels as though I'm betraying Tenn more than I ever have already. I'm not good at this, balancing two worlds at once. The past and the present. But no matter which way I think of it, you're still my present. Because you exist, you live, albeit outside of me and far away.

I'm not sure how long I've spent searching the Scriptures over the last few months, and I'm even more unsure of how much I understand or retain, but my grandmother would have been proud. I have found comfort in acknowledging my state of disrepair, and yet, there is a thread running through the Book that promises hope, that promises a rest from it all. Not to say that our mistakes are okay, passable, or even permissible, but they can be forgiven, and the God who created me and you and her and this new baby is the same God who promises better things to come.

I've never disputed the fact that God is God at all. It's always made sense to my soul that we came from somewhere, that our lives and this earth are intentional and designed. But I never knew the point, and that is what I'm trying and starting to learn.

Maybe the point is surrender. Maybe the point is love. Maybe the point is an illustration of how greatly good can outweigh bad, of how light can overcome darkness.

I'm still trying to figure it out. Still searching. I will let you know what I find out. Please don't give up on me just yet.

23

1981
Galia, Oregon

MORNING MIST LULLED the forest to sleep. A brown paper bag crinkled in my arms as we stepped out of the car under gray skies. The chimney puffed with a smoker's breath, and Thimbleberry Cottage was quiet.

In terms of tranquility, the estate was unparalleled. However, I couldn't help but wonder about the practicality of having a retirement home in such an isolated location. What if a resident escaped like Maggy and ended up in the woods or fell into a stream? A river? But this facility didn't normally accept flight risk residents. That was Joy's concern, after all.

I adjusted the bag that held the box of ice cream, and Claude followed me through the arched doorway into the softly lit foyer. One of the caregivers came from around the corner.

"Morning," she greeted as though by instinct. Upon looking at me, she said, "Oh, I remember you from the other day, right?

You helped Mrs. Monroe. What brings you back?"

I nodded. "Actually, we're here for two reasons. I spoke with Maggy's daughter, Joy, and she said it would be alright if I brought some ice cream to share with Maggy today. Abbi also invited me back for a visit."

The woman pursed her lips. "Well, Maggy's in her room, but I'm not so sure today's the best day for an ice cream social. You're welcome to go say hello, but . . . she's in one of her moods today."

"Moods?"

The woman smacked her lips and pointed down the hall. "First door on the left if you'd like to see for yourself." She gestured to the bag in my hands. "Would you like me to put that in the freezer for you?"

"Oh, sure. Thank you." I handed it to her, and she left for the kitchen. I turned to Claude.

"Do you want me to come with you?" he asked.

I didn't know. The last thing I wanted was to further upset her. "Maybe I'll meet you in the sitting room once I check on her?"

He agreed and snuck in a kiss before following my direction down the opposite hall while I headed for Maggy's room.

Her door was open, though the lights were off. I stood in the doorway. Maggy's room paled in comparison to the rest of the facility's homey, storybook feel. Her walls were bare, most of the shelves unadorned. Maggy stood with her back to me, fussing with her quilt, which spread over her bed in lumpy hills.

I watched her for a moment, then said, "Hi, Maggy. What have you got under your covers?"

She fussed with the corner of her bedding some more before answering. "Everybody always wants to know." Her tone was crisp and pointed.

"Oh, do they?" I kept my voice chipper in great opposition to the darkness lacing hers.

"But it's a secret," she whispered with a hiss. She patted the blanket with resolve and turned to cross the room for seemingly no reason. "Now, where did I put that?"

"Put what? Can I help you find something?"

"That baby!" she snapped and turned to face me with an expression clouded in anger. "Did you take her?"

My jaw dropped at the accusation, though I couldn't help but feel compassion for her confusion. I shook my head.

"No, certainly not. I think . . ." I shuffled through excuses in my mind. In her present mood, I doubted Maggy would accept any of them. But still, I needed to try. "Uh, Joy is taking care of her today. They're having a playdate."

Maggy's eyes narrowed. "Joy?"

There was no recognition.

"Joy. Your daughter?"

A beat passed. Nothing.

Her eyes went wide, and she pointed a shaky finger at me. There was fire in her eyes, and I felt like a child, as though I'd done something wrong and were being scolded. Maggy squinted, dropped her hand back to her side, and turned away with a head shake.

"Forget it," she mumbled. Her hands resumed their busyness, and she pawed over the top drawer of her dresser in search of something.

"Forget what?" I asked, wondering myself if she had already forgotten the very thing she had told me to forget.

My question passed over her ears, unheard or ignored, and I wondered if I was wrong for pressing the matter at all. She really *was* off today. Maybe my visiting was a mistake; maybe inserting myself into the lives of these strangers at Thimbleberry was wrong for me to do. But watching Maggy broke my heart, and I felt compelled to try something to turn her mood around.

But what?

I looked at her lumpy bed. What had she hidden beneath that quilt? Inching closer, at the expense of being caught, I lifted the blanket and peeked beneath. From what I could see, she'd stowed away a few small picture frames, a wadded-up napkin, and a dentures case labeled JERRY.

Oh, sweet Maggy!

With her still busy at her dresser, I scooped up the belongings as quietly as I could and stepped out of the room without her seeming to notice. At the office, I stacked the assortment of treasures on the desk before the facility's administrator.

She raised her brows and rummaged through the objects. "Let me guess, Mrs. Monroe is back at it again? Well, at least she didn't manage to shatter these frames. They look like the ones that belong in Carlisle's room. I'll return them. And Jerry's dentures too." She shook her head, whether in amusement or frustration I couldn't tell.

"Would you mind if I use the phone to make a quick call?" I asked.

"Knock yourself out. Just no long distance."

When she left to return the stolen items, I took Joy's number from my purse and dialed. On the fourth ring, she answered. Worry saturated her voice.

"Hello?"

"Joy!" I said with as much cheer as I could muster. "It's Kitty Fisher."

"Oh? Kitty? Hello."

"Is this an okay time to call? You sound a bit . . . upset?"

"Yes. I mean, no. It's . . . I'm sorry." She blew into the receiver, and I was sorry I'd called. "It's been quite the day already, and my blood pressure spikes when the phone rings. I keep worrying that my mother has run off again."

"Oh." Her worry that every time the phone rang, bad news could follow pained my heart. "Well, I can assure you that your mother is accounted for. I'm actually over at Thimbleberry right now."

"Really? What are you doing there?"

"I came back to speak with Abbi, and I brought that ice cream I mentioned."

"Oh, that's right. So, is everything alright?"

I waffled, realizing now that I was the bearer of bad news. But wouldn't she like to know? "Well, I wanted to mention to you that Maggy seems a bit off today."

"Off? In what way?"

"Angry. Guarded. Stealing, uh, random picture frames and dentures."

The pain in Joy's sigh could be felt through the phone. "Please tell me she didn't destroy anything."

"No. Everything is fine."

"I don't know what it is, but since she lost her memory, she fervently steals any frames she can find. Sometimes dismantling them, other times smashing the glass. It's the oddest thing."

"She seems concerned today. Searching her room for something."

"She gets that way. Coupled with the anger that comes, too, it's . . . it's the worst way to see her. It's why my dad adamantly avoids her. He just can't bear it, and it gets worse when he's around."

A few muffled sounds came through the earpiece, and I heard her cover the phone on her end to talk to someone else. "Sorry," she said a moment later. "I will get there as soon as I can. I'm in the middle of a whole ordeal over here. My dad's deciding to . . . Oh, never mind. You don't need to know all of our family's dirty laundry. Anyway, I will be there for the afternoon as soon as I can get away from here. Does she have her baby, Kitty?"

I didn't remember seeing it in her room now that I thought of it. "I'll make sure that's not the problem," I said.

"Thank you. And thanks for calling. The staff doesn't always inform me on days when she's like this, even though I've asked them to. She's my mom, you know? I want to know these things."

When we hung up, I checked again on Maggy. She was curled up in her bed, asleep in the fetal position. So childlike, so vulnerable. I hoped a good nap was all she needed. I grabbed the throw blanket folded at the end of her bed and covered her gently, then crept from the room to find Claude.

He was seated at one of the two extended dining tables across from a man in a tan button-down shirt and dark green suspenders. Perched on the man's wide-set nose was a thick pair of glasses, and to his left sat someone who looked nearly identical, minus the color of shirt and the absence of glasses.

"Hello, gentlemen," I greeted as I approached. Claude pulled out the seat beside him for me to sit.

"This is my wife, Kitty," he said to his new friends.

The man beside Claude raised his brows. "As in the famous Kitty?"

I paused. I guessed word had gotten around. "Guilty as charged."

"Frank." He held out his hand for me to shake.

"As in the famous Frank with the lucky bingo streak?"

He barked out a deep laugh. "You got me." He nudged the man next to him with his elbow. "This here's my twin brother, Arnold. He's on a bingo streak of his own—the losing kind."

Arnold's cheeks reddened, and he laughed a gummy smile. Like his brother, he politely offered his hand for me to shake.

"We heard a rumor about ice cream," Frank said with a sneaky grin.

"I might know a thing or two about that. It's not too early?"

"For ice cream? Never."

I laughed. "In that case, I'll be right back." I left and found a staff member who happily agreed to serve the dessert momentarily. I made sure she knew that anyone was welcome.

Back at the table, I took a seat across from Claude, Frank, and Arnold.

"So, you're brothers?" I said to Frank.

"They're twins," Claude chimed in. He seemed so at ease. "Just like Rand and Henry."

"You've twins in the family?" Frank asked.

"Our nephews," I said as a woman with long silver hair paused at the head of the table. With a terse mouth, she lifted her chin and continued along, sitting instead at the other table alone.

Frank carried on as though he didn't even notice the woman's presence. "Well, I hope your nephews are close. Twinship is a special bond."

"They are," Claude said. "Those boys have been through a lot."

"I think God knew they'd need each other to lean on," I added.

Frank narrowed his eyes. "How do you mean?"

"Well, losing their father in Vietnam was hard enough." It still pained me to broach the subject, especially in front of Claude. "And then one of them went on to serve in the very war that claimed their father's life. Drug addiction ensued. Their poor mother . . ." I stopped. Why was I divulging private details like this to a stranger?

My eyes flicked to Claude. A pensive smile rested on his lips.

"Wow," Frank breathed, his brow puckering. To his left, Arnold's lips twisted as though he had something to say.

"The family's been through a lot," Claude said. "It's only been by the strength of the Lord that any of us have made it this far."

"How true is that for all of us," Frank agreed. "Arnie and I both served alongside each other in the Second World War.

Army infantry. Stationed in Norway. Not sure how we got so lucky—and I use that term loosely—to be stationed with one another overseas and not be split up."

"And to both come home," Claude offered.

Frank nodded, and his eyes spoke of unspeakable pain. "Not without our own demons, but we made it home, nonetheless. Arnie lost his ability to speak when shrapnel got lodged in his throat and severed his vocal cords. The doctors said . . ." His voice trailed off for a moment, and a staff member appeared from the kitchen, balancing several bowls of ice cream and steaming cups of coffee on a tray.

"Will Abbi be joining?" I asked the woman.

"No." She set a bowl in front of me. "She said she's too busy preparing something for you and asked me to pass along the message that she'll be ready for your visit when you're finished with dessert."

I smiled. What could she be preparing?

When the staff member left, Frank returned to his thoughts. "They said it was the utmost miracle from God that it didn't sever Arnie's carotid and that he didn't bleed out then and there."

I covered my mouth, and my eyes darted to Arnie. He took a bite of his ice cream and gave me a wink like he couldn't have cared less.

"He can make guttural sounds but hasn't spoken a true word since . . ." Frank blew out a breath. "Well, since 1943."

"That's an incredible story." Claude picked up his spoon and used it to point between the brothers before taking his own bite. "How long have you both been here?"

"At Thimbleberry? He's been here for three years now. When my wife passed two years ago, I figured I might as well move in here too. Spend whatever time I have left with my brother."

I couldn't help but think of Cliff and Vern, should either of them have lived to ripe old ages. I could imagine the pair being just like Arnie and Frank. Never far from one another. Much like these twins, they were. But their fates had been long sealed. The memory of them rattled in my ribcage like a loose film canister on the floorboard of a moving car.

Claude scooped another spoonful of ice cream and gave no indication of his thoughts. Was he remembering them now too? Whatever the case, the sight before me made me smile because for a split second, I saw Cliff and Vern sitting there on either side of my husband, shooting the breeze like nothing had ever changed, like Claude hadn't lived so much of his life without them.

"So, you rescued Maggy on her outing the other day, did you?" Frank changed the subject.

I burned my tongue on a sip of my coffee and only managed a nod.

Frank laughed and leaned back in his chair. "We've all heard about the famous Kitty. Of all the things to slip her mind, that's one name she won't soon forget."

"My name?"

"Well, yes. Always muttering under her breath, Kitty this and Kitty that."

"She does seem to have latched onto it."

"We were all sure worried when we heard she was missing," Frank said. "I had a feeling she'd be alright, but worst-case scenarios kept creeping into mind. They let me help scour the grounds of the property, though it sounds like she went much farther."

"Much farther indeed. She was taking a nice little shopping jaunt on the seaside."

The silver-haired woman cleared her throat, and the sound made me jump. She'd been so quiet and unassuming that I'd forgotten she was seated at the table just behind.

"I was hoping this would be the straw that broke the camel's back, but alas, nothing seems to have been done," she said, her nose in the air. I detected indignation in her voice.

"What do you mean?" I asked. I caught the roll of Arnie's eyes as I twisted in my chair to face her.

The woman cleared her throat again as though what she was about to say held high importance. "Maggy's a fine woman, but she has no business being at this estate."

"And why's that?" Claude asked.

The woman leaned in. "It's obvious, isn't it? This is a *retirement home*," she hissed. "Not a skilled nursing facility for patients who can't remember their own names."

My mouth fell open. The woman straightened her shoulders.

"You know, Martha," Frank said, his voice steady and relaxed. "I seem to remember a night not too long ago when too much wine on the patio had the same effect on you."

My stomach clenched to suppress my laughter, and I caught Claude's dancing eyes.

Martha pushed her chair from the table. "Throw your daggers all you want, Frank, but that doesn't change the fact that Maggy doesn't belong here." With that, she flipped around and strode from the room, her silver hair swinging behind her.

"It's an intimate setting here. A place designed to make one feel like they're at home, rather than some sprawling nursing home where people quite literally come and go on the constant," Frank said. "But some residents seem to mistake this place for an exclusive resort, as you can see."

"Everyone else I've met here has been so polite and pleasant."

"Yeah, well, Martha is here to balance out the tone."

I snorted. "As Abbi would say, 'Every party has a pooper.'"

"Every home as a Martha."

"Speaking of Abbi, I am going to excuse myself and pay her a visit," I said, nerves cinching my stomach tight. Would Abbi have any answers for me today? I stood and collected my dish and mug. "It was a pleasure meeting you both," I said to Frank and Arnie. They each politely tipped their heads. To Claude, I said, "Care to join me?"

24

ABBI WAS POISED and perched on the edge of her bed, awaiting my arrival. A folding table had been set up in front of her, the bed and set of chairs creating an L-shape around it. Strewn across the table were many objects I recognized from her drawer collection.

"Hi, Abbi!"

She lit up at the sight of Claude and me in her doorway. She motioned to the chairs. "Come in! Sit."

"Careful," I said to Claude. "It's a trap."

Abbi giggled and wagged her pointer finger at me. "Don't scare my guests away before you've even introduced them."

I held onto Claude's arm and said, "This is my husband, Claude."

Abbi gingerly extended her hand to him, and if I wasn't mistaken, a true burst of red appeared under the layer of blush she'd applied to her cheeks. Claude and I sat in the Venus flytrap chairs, and this time, I did so with a shred more dignity.

I clapped my hands. "So, where are we with everything?"

"I'd like to see the photograph in question if I could." Claude rested his elbows on the table.

Abbi passed it to him, and the already unfolded cutout seemed so small in his hands. A wistful smile played on his lips as he traced the edges. "This is a good one. I can see why someone would want this."

Abbi leaned forward now, a spark in her eye. "But why would anyone ever think to cut *you* out of a photograph? Unless they kept it for themselves, which is what I would have done," she said under her breath but not quietly enough for us to ignore.

"And discard me?" My mouth fell agape. "Abbigail Banks, must I remind you that Claude is a married man?" I pointedly lifted one brow.

"I'm a rusty, dusty old broad. You've got nothing to worry about," she said through a wheezy giggle as Claude drummed the table with his fingers, an amused grin spreading from ear to ear.

I snorted. "That's all part of your charm."

She waved the comment off with a laugh and looked at the spread before her. "Well, I did make a phone call, but turns out everyone I ran around with has kicked the bucket. So that was a real dead end"—she cupped a hand around her mouth and lowered her voice an octave—"if you catch my drift."

This elicited a soft chuckle from Claude before he said, "Sorry to hear that." The chair creaked as he leaned forward.

She pursed her lips. "One of my friends sent me a box of random things years back. I was hoping maybe this little photo was one of them."

"So, does that mean this is the end of the road? Case closed? Mystery . . . unsolved?"

"Pah!" A soft sigh escaped from Abbi's lips. "Don't jump ship just yet. I thought maybe we could piece together a story from what I have that didn't originate from me. I went through the drawer and sorted everything, and this is what I have." She gestured to the assortment on the table just as a knock came at the partly open door.

Frank announced his presence with a grand, "Hello!"

"Go away, you," Abbi teased.

He ignored her and stepped one foot inside. "At least I have witnesses now to the way you treat me."

"I'm a sweetheart, and you won't convince me or them otherwise," she stated indignantly.

"And I would never attempt to try."

Abbi's fixed jaw melted into a grin. "What do you need, Frank?" If I wasn't mistaken, she said his name with an air of dreaminess.

"I'm looking for a chess partner and was hoping I'd find one in Claude."

Before Claude could answer, Abbi said, "Can't find your own friends? Or must you encroach upon mine?"

"I believe I met Claude first," Frank said coolly and put his hands in his trouser pockets.

Claude glanced at me, and I shrugged. This meeting with Abbi didn't exactly seem promising, so it wasn't like he'd miss out on much if he left.

"Alright," Claude agreed and stood more gracefully from Abbi's chairs than I ever could.

"He just wants something else to brag about besides bingo," Abbi muttered.

Frank's belly jiggled as he laughed and walked out the door with Claude.

"That man's a troublemaker." The grin on her face told me she didn't mind.

"He seems like a hoot."

"Oh, he is. I never said being a troublemaker wasn't fun."

"He reminds me of someone else I know."

Abbi's eyes narrowed into slits. "You best not be talking about me."

"Never." I shook my head, though she and I both knew who I'd meant.

Turning her attention back to the table, Abbi said, "Most of this junk isn't doing me any good. I mean, what am I going to do with one pearl earring and one dangle gold hoop? Can you imagine me being caught wearing two different earrings?"

I laughed. "Talk about the scandal of the century!"

"You're telling me!" She held the earrings up to her ears and opened her mouth in the shape of an *O* as though the idea was preposterous, but with the hairdo she wasn't aware she was sporting (crazy pieces sticking up in random red tufts), the scene made me laugh even harder.

She slipped into a wheezy giggle fit, the infectious kind that leaves your abdomen aching. I wiped the corners of my eyes and hoped the bit of mascara I'd put on wasn't now running down my cheeks. Abbi brought the earrings down from her ears with a sigh and suddenly stared in a melancholic way at her table of lonely keepsakes.

"Sometimes . . ." Her words fell short.

"Sometimes what?" I cocked my head, intrigued by what she might say.

"I feel like one of them." She nodded toward the items before her. "A halfway version of what I once was. Like pieces of me are missing, and there's no hope of recovering them. I'm a little . . . useless, pointless, I guess you might say. What good is an unmatched earring without its pair? What good is this tiny key if I don't have the diary that it unlocked? What good is anything or anyone that's only half as good as they once were?"

My heart broke for her. And commiserated, too. I'd only just turned fifty and already had worrying thoughts about my place in life. Time was edging us all toward old age, toward eternity.

"Oh, Abbi. You still have so much to offer. You're no less important than you were in any other state of life."

"That's a kind thing to say." She pushed the earrings into a small mound of other loose jewelry.

"Do you feel that way about any of your friends here at Thimbleberry? That simply because they aren't in their prime, they are no longer golden?"

"The only thing golden about us is our golden years. But no. I guess I don't feel that way about anybody else. Just . . . myself." She looked down, avoiding my eyes. "The truth is that some days I feel like I have pep in my step, and other days like I'm only stepping closer to the grave." Her voice grew small. "And that scares me."

I couldn't help myself from asking, "What exactly are you afraid of?"

She licked her lips then pursed them. "Whatever comes next, I guess."

Whatever comes next. The words steeped into my pores while seeming to hang on Abbi's tongue. There was something haunting in them, and I couldn't imagine not having solid hope for what was to come after this life. I wanted to wipe the fear from Abbi's mind, for I remembered a time when I, too, feared what lay ahead. Never knowing where I'd be, whom I'd be around, how I'd make it through. But now I knew and could rest in the assurance. If only Abbi could as well.

"You've lost many people close to you, it sounds like," I said softly, hoping to glean a better understanding of her heart.

"I'm one of the last left standing. That I know of, anyway. If my sister's still around, I wouldn't know it."

"Oh. Did the two of you not have a good relationship?"

She leaned back slightly and crossed her ankles. A beat passed as her eyes saw something on the far wall of her room that I knew wasn't really there. Whatever she saw, it was in memory only.

Finally, she answered, "I never made time for the people who would have gone to hell and back for me. I only made time for the ones who didn't care if I went there myself."

"Oh." I took a soft breath. "I'm sorry, Abbi."

"I made my bed," she murmured with a wistful sigh. "I thought my life was so important. So much more important than my own family. I thought they were fuddy duddies, to tell you the truth. And I spent my life doing all the things I thought would fill me up, as though the limelight might warm my skin and the extravagant parties would fill the void. But the glitz has only turned to rust, as it turns out."

Her grief and remorse filled the room, not with the heavy, dense fog of a lone decision but with the collective weight of eighty-some years worth of confetti. The memories seemed to fall around her, a deafening and inexistent flutter. Abbi closed her eyes, and I watched the way her mouth fought to stave off tears.

"Abbi—"

She held up a hand, and I held my tongue. "I lived in such a way that the eulogist at my funeral should have a grand list of reasons my life was so great. But if greatness as I understand it now were the criteria, the page would be filled with empty lines."

"I'd like to politely disagree. Already you've blessed me in the few days I've known you."

She clasped her hands in her lap and offered a kind smile. "That's nice of you to say."

"Look at this." I gestured to the table. "You've been so kind and helpful to organize all of this to help a stranger."

"And yet I've totally derailed our visit with sob stories of a life almost passed." She shook the sadness from her face and sat up straight. "Let's get started before I kick the can too."

Her hands landed on a group of photographs. She pushed them closer to me. "I suppose we ought to start here, since this whole thing started with a photo in the first place. These are ones that either don't belong to me, or I don't recognize anymore."

I picked up the small stack and sifted through them. A few portraits of strangers. A group of friends posing at the Statue of Liberty. A sleeping and swaddled infant. A few colored, albeit blurry, ones that involved livestock. Nothing that gave me any answers.

I turned each of them over, hoping for a clue on the backside. The photo of the women had the documentation, *"Girls outing: L. to R. Amelia, Patsy, Nancy G., Nancy M."*

"You don't know these women?" I rattled off their names.

Abbi took the photo and squinted at the faces. "Could have. But even if I once did, I don't anymore."

"Okay." I set it aside and picked up the portraits. "And these?"

"Nope."

On the back of the black-and-white photograph of the infant, someone had scrawled the faint words, *"not goodbye."*

"And this one?"

"You know, I always thought that was the saddest. Clearly, that little babe was adored."

"It's not one of your children by chance?"

"Oh, no. I never bore children. I found that in the crease of the sofa out there, but no one has claimed to recognize it."

"Not Arnie or Frank?"

"No."

"Maggy?"

"No. I even asked her daughter."

"How about everyone else here? There was a woman named Martha at the table earlier."

"Martha is newer here. I found this far before she arrived. I took it to June and Jerry and Bernard and Patsy and Lilie and Carlisle."

"And the staff?"

"I don't know what they'd be doing bringing such a dated photograph to work with them, but I did try, yes. The staff turns over from time to time, so there might have been someone I missed asking. But maybe it belonged to the previous owner of the sofa if the facility owners purchased it secondhand. Whatever the case, no one seems to recognize this poor, forgotten baby."

"Wait a second. Didn't I just say Patsy a minute ago? Could she be the Patsy in this photo?" I picked up the picture of the group of women again.

Abbi frowned. "Well, that would make sense, wouldn't it? I'm sure I've asked her, but maybe I'm loonier than I thought. I'll take it to her later and see."

Nothing was written on the back of the last photos, so we moved on. But with every item, my hope dwindled. A dropped grocery list. A phone number scribbled on a scrap of envelope. A dirty bus ticket. A diary key. Loose earrings. A necklace charm. No clear-cut answers. No crumbs or clues.

"That's the end of the items I couldn't place. The rest on the table are things I know I've received from friends."

Together, we combed through the assortment, but nothing jumped out as though to say, *"It's me! I'm the item that can solve this mystery!"* At the end of our search, Abbi handed me the newsprint photo that had started the whole thing.

"I'm sorry to send you away disappointed," she said softly, sounding as dejected as I felt. "Why don't you keep this?"

I took it and slipped it into my pocket.

"There's gotta be some way of tracking this down, though." She tapped her forehead in thought.

"It's alright. Maybe it belonged to your friend who passed after all. Or maybe it's just some weird happenstance." I couldn't imagine what that happenstance would be, and I couldn't believe I'd convinced myself that it somehow mattered. "Maybe someone came across my photo, and it reminded them of someone they knew. An uncanny resemblance or something of the sort. Maybe they saved it to show someone else but then lost track of it."

"Perhaps. I could do some more digging if you find the time to come back tomorrow."

The way she said it gave me the sense that she only wanted to keep me returning, suspending my hope like a string dangled in front of a kitten.

"Yeah. Maybe."

<h1 style="text-align:center">25</h1>

1949
Tonopah, Nevada

SHE HUGGED HER sweater around her, angry at the words that danced in the air. The wind seemed to snatch them and keep them near, strangling her. He still cared. He still loved her. He was still protecting her, trying to warn her, to save her.

But by now, didn't Claude know she couldn't be saved? There would be no Prince Charming, no savior, no hero. Those were reserved for the deserving. For people who weren't her. It didn't matter if what he'd just divulged to her were true, if Jack really had bragged to a friend about only pursuing her for impure reasons, if Jack was only curious about what it would be like to bed a hooker's niece.

Unable to block them out, the whispers in the surrounding wind grew louder. *You are nothing. You are nothing. You are nothing.*

Claude waited for her to say something back, and in that

space, the words tightened themselves around her throat. Was his revelation supposed to frighten her? Provoke her? Send her into his arms? The wind lifted dirt and tickled her bare ankles, each grain like a slice, a reminder, a tiny carving of who she was. Who she always would be.

The niece of a hooker.

The daughter of a murderer.

The offspring of a deserter.

The ground crunched beneath his boot as he took a step nearer. "I'm sorry," he whispered. "I just thought you ought to know. Are you okay?"

"I'm more embarrassed than anything," she murmured. She tilted her head back and let her curls fall away. The sun washed over her face. Talking to the sky, she said, "But maybe he's not wrong. I fought so long thinking I belonged to another family—yours. Believing I was more than my own lineage, somehow above it. But there comes a point when you can't keep hiding from what keeps seeking you out."

"Kitty." His voice was full of alarm. "What are you saying? Please don't tell me you're thinking of giving yourself up to a guy like Jack."

"If it's any of your business, I plan to wait for marriage."

"Then I hope you won't waste your time on Jack because he's certainly not the type to wait. Kitty, I don't want to see you hurt. I don't want you settling for someone who treats you like you're not worth a hill of beans. Why not find someone who treats you the way you deserve?"

"Maybe he is."

"Is what?"

"Treating me the way I deserve."

Distance. Avoidance. That's what she'd focused on since the start of the school year. Creating as much space between herself and Claude as possible. She could only keep him safe if she kept him at arm's length. Too close and danger would encroach, the danger being the way he made her vulnerable, pining heart hitch in her chest.

And now, he was close enough to fall against. She knew he'd catch her and hold her in the way she could only dream about. But the strength of his arms should be reserved for someone else, she believed. It wasn't a space she fit into anymore.

But he continued to try, arguing with her views, saying all the truths that only felt like lies as they entered Kitty's ears. How could he think she deserved something more than Jack? More than how she'd been treated, neglected, and discarded all her life? How could he think he knew her now after so many years apart?

They'd fought many times before as kids, back when the most important things at stake were winning a game or claiming the last piece of watermelon. But now, he pried into a private place that was only her own. He'd suffered the past few years, too, but no one knew what it was like to carry the burdens she had. He didn't know of the weight that kept her pinned like a slave.

Years of suppressed anger boiled inside of her, and they shouted with equal fury until brimming tears finally spilled, and the fight was knocked out of her with the punch of his words. They dripped with truth, but the truth was drowned out by the breaking of her heart as she ran as far away from him as she could.

26

Lia

1938
Galia, Oregon

I DON'T HAVE much, but what I do have, I treasure. The past is with little evidence here in the present. Aside from the letters I write that feel like ticking time bombs, I have a few photographs that remain hidden too. There are two, to be exact: one of her, one of them. Thus far, they've been stowed in a cigar box in the closet. But I take them out now and move them to reside with my hidden words.

Rain tap dances against the windowpane and drums on the roof. It's a comfort most days, and today's no different. Though for my daughter's sake, I'm praying for the sun. She wants to run across the meadow to dip her toes into the brook. But right now, her chubby hands are pressed to the glass as she watches a rain droplet race on the outside of the window.

It's breathtaking how quickly she's grown and changed; she's on a one-way train to independence, and there's nothing I can do to stop it. The minute changes are enough to make a mother itch for control. It's all going by so quickly. But what control do we have outside of ourselves? I've experienced the damage caused by generations striving for control, dictating movements, thoughts, and beliefs. When the world feels too unpredictable, it's almost human nature to overstep the bounds of your own autonomy and dip into the space of another's.

My mother often slandered my grandmother for doing this to her, though ironically, my mother turned around and did it to me. Never were my efforts good enough. Never were my opinions right. If I wasn't in perfect alignment with how she felt or whatever she thought, I was punished. All simply for being myself.

I don't want to follow in those footsteps with my own children.

I look at the photographs in my hands, at the faces over which I have no control or influence at all anymore. I relinquished any right to their lives, and yet I long to know they're okay. A warmth spreads through my stomach and makes me ill. I will never know their state of being and will never see the domino effect I've had on their lives. How my ubiquitous absence has affected their course.

I'm sure it's for the better.

Is it for the better? The thought consumes my mind. I look at my daughter and place my hands on my growing abdomen. Would it be for their betterment if I left too? My stomach roils. *To even have such a thought makes you unfit for motherhood!* How can I do this? That fear of being inadequate, of being alone with dark, immutable thoughts, was what led me to run in the first place. I have traveled so far and yet haven't progressed at all.

Something inside tells me to hang on, but today suddenly tastes of defeat. How prideful that I ever considered myself a good mother. Have I been foolish to tuck hope inside my chest? To imagine one day a reunion? To think that God would orchestrate such a thing on my wicked behalf? And most of all, to fancy myself a good mother to this little girl?

My breath catches in my throat. My fingers twitch. The photographs become like lead in my lap. I don't want to look at these faces anymore. Don't want to carry the weight of their reminder. It's too painful today, dredging up the past. I want to forget. I want to watch raindrop races with her and not think about all that's continually slipping through my fingers.

I scour the room for scissors and find a pair inside the desk near the window. I lean against the structure for support. My hands shake as I hold the photographs, the last remaining traces of a former life lived. Just as I lift the scissor's blade, a puff of warm breath tickles my neck.

"Mama?"

I freeze and feel her tiny hand on my shoulder, only to realize she's climbed onto the desk chair behind me. I set down the scissors and turn. She leaps into my arms without thinking, and I catch her. Just as I always do.

Just, I realize, as I always will.

My heart softens, and she relaxes in my arms.

"Is it?" she asks, and without looking, I know she's spotted the photos on the desk behind me. Sure enough, as I turn, she wriggles in my arms and points, asking once again, who is it?

"Someone I once knew," is all I can manage. The answer satisfies her, though as soon as I set her down, she reaches for the photographs and studies them. I hold my breath and wait. Her curiosity is satiated as she sets them down and runs back to the windowpane.

Not today, I decide. I can't let go today. The scissors are tucked back into their drawer. The photographs scooped back into my hands. These will stay for now. I glance at my daughter and, seeing she's distracted, take a picture frame from the wall and unfasten the backside. I slip the photographs inside, seal them in, and return the frame to its position.

27

WHEN I CAME from Abbi's room, I found Claude and Frank locked in an intense chess match in the sitting room. Both of them sat in identical poses. One forearm resting on the table, the opposite elbow propped and hand covering their mouth. I wasn't planning on interrupting their focus, but Claude caught sight of me in his peripheral and gave me a quick nod. He vaguely gestured with his head toward the patio door, and in the space of that small moment, Frank made his move.

That sneak.

Claude's attention snapped back to the game, and my gaze traveled to the patio doors that stood open just before the dining room's entrance. A tear-filled Joy sat outside, bent over her stomach in a chair.

My heart sank as I headed toward her. Was Maggy okay?

The patio had a gentle sloping ramp that led to a recessed

cemented area enclosed with granite boulders. Cafe-style patio furniture decorated the space. Nestled down amidst the rock with the surrounding pines brushing the gloomy sky above, the area felt like a safe haven, like a good place for a cry, where the hanging fog felt like a hug and the humidity reminded us that waterworks weren't always a bad thing.

Joy lifted her head as I shut the door. She wiped her nose.

"Do you care for company?" I asked, pausing my approach.

"You can find better company than me at the moment." She sniffled. "But come. Take a seat."

I moved a bistro chair closer and sat. Without thinking, I reached for her hand. "Is everything okay?"

"It will be." But her voice lacked hope.

"How's your mother? Is she still sleeping?"

"I ducked in there a minute ago, and she was still snoozing away."

"She must really need the rest."

"Her and me both." Joy rubbed her temples.

"You mentioned something on the phone. It sounded like trouble within the family? I don't mean to pry, I just . . . I'm here if you need an ear or a shoulder."

She exhaled deeply and took a moment before answering. "My dad is selling our childhood home out of nowhere." Her eyes fixated on her lap, and I knew there was more to the story.

"Oh. I'm sorry. What brought him to that decision?"

She looked at me now, her face blank. "He doesn't want to be alone in such a big home, or so he says. Someone approached him and offered a pretty penny for the property out of the blue. You know, things have been"—her eyes closed and flickered beneath their lids as though the words for which she searched would suddenly appear written on the underside—"*tough* since my mother's dementia."

The forest's heavy, mild breath took our words from the air, and we sat in silence. What advice did I have to offer, considering the vastly different paths we'd walked in life? I took a slow breath. In the stillness, I almost convinced myself that the ocean's distant rumble could be heard, calling to me a reminder of its presence, of the job I'd enlisted it to complete. I swallowed hard and packed away my own problems to listen to the present ones that Joy had entrusted by sharing with me.

"I can only imagine," I managed to say. "I'm so sorry this is all happening."

The corners of Joy's lips drooped lower. "I feel like I don't know either of my parents anymore, and how sad is that? Dad has become so cold, so distant. Like he's cutting off all reminders of their life together, including my mother entirely. I think it's his way of coping with everything, but still."

"It doesn't excuse how hard it still is for you as their daughter to watch your mom progress in her disease, to see your father turn from her, to learn that your connection to your upbringing is being sold."

My mind flitted to the charred remains of our homes in Goldfield. I supposed I could relate to Joy after all. I didn't relish this feeling of being homesick for a home that no longer stood. It had always been a comfort to know that our Goldfield houses were forever beacons of light. But not anymore.

"I know I'm grown, but that house has always been home to me. Does that make sense?"

"More than you know," I said softly.

A sliver of sun slipped through the gloom, its appearance sudden and piercing. A thought occurred to me. That light breaking through was the same light that had filled our now-ruined homes in Goldfield. The beam danced away, hidden behind a cloud once again but not gone. Just like, I realized, the light from our childhood homes. For they had never been illuminated with an extinguishable source but by the One whose beams reached me even now.

"My siblings and I always thought our home would be kept in the family," Joy said, pulling my attention back to her. "But everyone is already settled into their own spaces, and my dad always has been swayed by the right price tag. The thing is, though, he has a bad back and can't handle the move alone. Apparently, Dad accepted the offer weeks ago, and there's a deadline for him to be out. So, the process is a hasty, expedited mess."

"How long do you have?"

"Two days."

"Two days?" My brows shot to the sky. "That's it?"

"I told you it was hasty. I can't believe he didn't tell us all about this sooner. Dad said he'll keep whatever is packed over the next two days. Otherwise, it's being donated. I just . . . I want the time to sort through their belongings, you know? The family heirlooms, the memories. I want to have time to memorize the space I'll never see again."

Mist coated her eyes. I wanted to help her, to mend the places where fire had singed her heart too.

"Can't your siblings help?

A sharp exhale escaped her. "Jason doesn't talk to my dad anymore. They had a falling out last year which time hasn't yet healed. And my sister Connie desperately wants to drive down from Tacoma, but she's slammed with work and has a boss that deserves a good neck-wringing."

"So, it all falls on you?"

She confirmed with a nod.

"I'm sorry." I could see the distress etched into Joy's every feature. "Where is your father going?"

"Dad has enough money to retire at a five-star hotel for the indefinite future if he wanted to. I told him to come stay with us, but he hasn't committed. I know he won't. He's keeping everyone at a distance these days. I think he'll eventually find a small house and settle in. Maybe in a seaside cabin somewhere like he always dreamed. It's like he wants to separate himself from the past, and it makes me feel like I'm some sort of orphan," she said, and her face fell flat. "Sorry. I didn't mean . . . I know I'm not . . ." She sighed. "I wasn't thinking of your . . ."

I held up my hand. "It's okay. I think I understand how you feel better than anyone."

Her eyes brimmed with tears again, and I stood from my chair to wrap my arms around her. For being someone I'd only known for a few days, she didn't feel like a stranger at all. Joy carried an easy sense of kinship that reminded me of the familial warmth I'd felt from the whole Fisher family my entire life, like the warmth of the sisterhood and friendship I felt with Maisy. It was like stepping into a ray of sunlight that spilled through the window on a cold winter day.

Joy's burden was heavy; I could feel the weight of the world on her shoulders as she hugged me in return. My heart pleaded silently for her burden to be lifted, that she might be untethered from this stress.

She pulled away and wiped her eyes. "I really should go check on Mom again and start figuring out this mess. By the way, what happened with Abbi?"

"Oh." At the tone of my voice, her face fell. "It was unfruitful. No answers."

"Really?" Joy said with obvious disappointment. "I'm sorry, Kitty."

"It's okay. I'm not sure what I really expected anyway."

And this was the truth. Had I hoped to uncover something hidden about myself? Didn't we all long for answers that we would never get this side of Heaven? My stomach soured, and I didn't want to discuss this disappointment that I was ashamed had taken root and given me false ground in which to misplace my hope.

Changing the subject back to her before we parted ways, I asked, "Is there anything I can do to help?"

A short laugh escaped her, though it bordered on hysteria. "Short of packing up a lifetime's worth of belongings in two days, no."

28

1949
Tonopah, Nevada

THE FILLED GYMNASIUM erupted into a collective cheer of victory as the game winning shot sank into the basketball hoop. These were the moments that made her forget. The bursts of frivolity sustained her, carried her to a fleeting place of respite like the country music on the streets of Knoxville, and she sought them out as often as she could. Parties. Parades. Sports. Extracurriculars. Anything that made her feel, if but for a moment, like she belonged to something bigger than herself.

Kitty celebrated alongside her fellow cheerleaders on the baseline and watched the team gather into a line to shake hands with Gabb's defeated team. At the end of the line, Richie slapped Jack's hand, only confirming their bond even more. Jack caught Kitty's stare and winked. She raised one of her oversized tissue-paper pom-poms and smiled. When he turned away, she scanned the bleachers for the umpteenth time that night. Most of the school seemed to be present. Everyone except for one person.

Claude.

The chasm between them was for the best. As much pain as the divide wreaked, unnecessary closeness hurt more. Reconciliation was out of the question, no matter how badly Kitty burned for it. But the truth seemed to be that deep down, Claude operated on a separate wavelength from their peers. He stood a little straighter and ran his mouth a little less. And it made him all the more unreachable.

If she was honest, Kitty was embarrassed by their fight. The embarrassment was added to the other things she hid behind emotional masks. If only she could fill that empty space inside of her . . . But nothing ever quenched her spirit. Endlessly, she went to bed with a pit in her stomach, a hollowness resounding deep inside.

Bethany snuck an arm around her, smacking her pom-pom into Kitty's face. Kitty batted it away, and Bethany said, "I think I'm starting to like Richie."

Kitty rolled her eyes. "It's because of that game winning shot, isn't it?"

Bethany grinned. "No. It was how *cute* he looked after making said shot."

Kitty laughed, and the pep band began to play another song, drowning out whatever Bethany said next. In front of her, parents moved from the bleachers to the gym floor to congratulate their sons. How would it feel, she wondered, to have a parent present for milestones and big moments? To hear them say, "Good job. I'm so glad I'm yours."

She didn't understand why Claude wasn't on the team, for he was an athletic guy, but if he was, she knew his parents would be in the crowd too. She pictured Ginny screaming her lungs out, getting all worked up as she did with competitive events. The memory made her smile and pricked her heart with guilt.

After all the Fishers had done for her in her life, she could've at least paid them a visit and thanked them. But with the mess she'd made with Claude, how could she now?

As the crowd began to thin, the team shuffled toward the locker room, but suddenly, Jack turned around and jogged across the court to where Kitty still gathered with her squad. His dark hair was caked with sweat, and a bead even rested above the natural pout of his lips.

"Kitty," he breathed.

"Yes?"

"I want to take you out tonight. Can I do that?"

Kitty felt the eyes of her friends on her, and if she was to guess, the show was exactly what Jack had been looking for. But shouldn't she be pleased he wanted to publicly make it obvious he liked her? He'd done so time and time again. And as her friends pointed out, they'd never seen him try so hard to win a girl's hand. Her stomach fluttered in spite of herself. She had turned him down so many times, and yet, here he was, trying yet again. And besides, the idea of being taken out sent a thrill through her. Anything to forget. Anything to distract herself.

She shrugged her shoulders. "Okay, Jack. Sure. Why not?"

"Best night of my life." Jack grinned. "I'll be out right after I shower and change." He leaned forward then and planted a kiss on her cheek. The spot burned as he walked away and disappeared through the locker room doors.

29

Lia

1938
Galia, Oregon

TENN AND I *did something we haven't for years: danced! He pushed aside the chairs in the sitting room and put on a record from the other room. My protruding belly made the affair a bit comical at first, but we figured it out. For hours, the two of us danced well into the night. I felt his strength, his tenderness for me. I wished to fall asleep in his arms and let the back corners of my mind (where I stuff all my worries) melt away.*

He whispered into my ear, "My, how I love you." My eyes welled with tears, and I can't entirely blame my heightened emotions as I carry our child. Ever since that revival meeting he went to, he's a different man. Not that he wasn't good to me before, but now, the man walks like he has clouds under his feet and not a worry in the world, save for the yet-to-be-redeemed.

It all intimidates me to a degree, but also, it's bred a stitch of hope into my heart. The other day, he came from a meeting at the church, all wound up in the best way. "Don't these people know? Honey, these people . . . they, they've gotta hear this! Don't they know how easy it is to be free? Free indeed?"

I asked him what exactly he'd meant, and of course, he wasted not a second to respond. "Doesn't matter what you've done or where you've been, Christ came for the broken. If only everyone knew the great weight He lifts, the penalty He's paid on our behalf!"

He'd have ripped his beautiful locks out if I hadn't stopped him. The topic makes him that passionate, and quite frankly, leaves me wondering if, in fact, I am as forgiven as he says, as the passages I've been reading in his Bible say.

Could Christ's sacrifice be enough to cover my own sins? The ones I'm too ashamed to even speak out loud. Is His love great enough for me?

I sit here now, the rain drizzling outside yet again, and wonder if Christ's freedom feels something like dancing with Tenn. Like a thrill and yet like rest. Like comfort and like peace. Could I dance with Him? With Jesus, I mean? Is He really holding out His hand like a proper partner, waiting for me to accept His invitation and take to the floor?

30

CLAUDE KILLED THE engine and turned to me. His eyes were soft and thoughtful. "I think you should help her."

"Help Joy? With the house?"

"Yes."

"Why do you say that?"

We parked at a lookout spot that led to the water's edge. He opened his door. "Come on, let's walk."

Hand in hand, we followed the path that dissolved into rocky, seaweed-strewn sand. I had thought the fog was burning off, but now it felt thicker and weighed down my white-sneakered feet as we stepped over driftwood and kelp. The area was wild and rough, a nod to the forest that climbed the rugged cliffside behind it.

"She has no one else to help with the house, right?" Claude asked without expecting an answer. "By the way you talk, it sounds as though you feel a deep calling to help her, and if that's the case, any prompting from the Lord should be listened to."

I looked up at him. His mossy hazel eyes searched my face, and under his tender gaze, I couldn't deny the validity of his assumption. "I just know if it were me, I'd be grateful for the help."

The reasons for my desire to help Joy were hazy but undeniable. What good was I if not a useful tool for the Lord? But another thought nagged my mind and nipped at my heels. Was I only distracting myself yet again from the reason that drove me to the coast in the first place? Was I still prolonging the inevitable with Dad's ashes, just as I feared I'd been doing with Abbi's photograph? Witnessing the mother-daughter bond between Maggy and Joy while also reeling from my parentless state had driven me to latch onto the ridiculous mystery. I'd allowed my heart to revert and hope for a shred of my heritage, for a crumb of my long-gone mother.

For so long, the enemy had fought for access to the thorn in my side, longing to twist the brier, to bring me to my knees. But what the enemy failed so often to remember is that in weakness, the Lord is made strong. But that never stopped him from trying. And I felt now the inklings of a war waging around me. A war for my peace, a war for my usefulness.

I'd lived with a quiet fear of being a burden, of not wanting to take up too much space, of not having any worth. And but for the grace of God, those thoughts might have bested me all my life and sent me down a path that mimicked those of my parents. But the mother-shaped thorn in my side and the part of me that longed for her validation and love had been touched by those who loved me well and pointed me to the Redeemer of my soul.

It was through Claude, who had never failed to lift me up even in my weakest state; through Ginny and Len, who had always been more like parents to me than my own; through

Maisy, the sister I never knew I needed; and even through my own father, who transformed into a new creation before my very eyes, that I knew Christ's unending love for me and the power He had to transform lives and hearts. The power of redemption, even in those who seem like the furthest of the lost and least deserving, was the power of the Gospel.

I knew this. I'd seen this. I'd lived this. But why, then, did a tear fall onto the beach as I let go of the coveted hope squirreled away for my mother? Shame swirled in my belly as though everything leading up to this moment hadn't been enough, shame that I still felt a mother-shaped hole in my chest.

No one ever told me much about her, and there came a time when I stopped asking. I grew too busy being a mother myself to remember her in such a heavy capacity, other than the passing thought here or there. The pitter-patter of wild toddler footsteps through the house, the acrylics spilled across the floor, the dishes that begged for constant attention took up room in my head more than the empty ghost that had haunted me for so long.

I knew I didn't need her. My life thus far was proof that Christ carried me without the need of her presence other than to be the vessel by which I was brought forth into this physical world. But as I'd sniffed my babies' sweaty naptime heads or nursed them in the quiet house, I'd often found myself wondering: *Did she regret missing out on this with me? Did she regret missing out on all of the descendants that she'll never meet?*

I've never not pondered her reason for leaving. Never not wished I could simply see her, ask her, have her care for me and me for her. Like Joy and her mother. A prick of jealousy bled into my heart. The beautiful reciprocation of mother and daughter. Parent and child.

"Do you really think I should help her?" I asked Claude now.

"I think you want to help her."

I did. I wanted to fight against the snare I sensed the enemy laying. I wanted to bless this family. I wanted to give from a place of open arms, not an envy-filled withholding. The thought of caving into my thorn, of abandoning Joy in spite of the short time I'd known her, felt wrong. The conviction gripped my heart.

"I do want to help. And I'm sorry. I know our time—"

"You don't have to come up with an excuse or talk yourself out of it. Don't apologize for being who you are." Claude held my gaze. "You are the most giving, loving person I know. You're just like my mother in wanting to help another in need."

I opened my mouth to respond but paused. Being compared to Ginny Fisher was the ultimate compliment, a testament to her lifelong influence in my life. But the comment also left me wondering if I was like my own biological mother in any way. Had I inherited my love for fruity sweets from her? Or my nervous habits? Perhaps my love for swing dancing? Was she at all reflected in the ways I cared for my family, or was she only manifested in the anxious feelings that plagued my gut from time to time? If I didn't have the steadfast love of Christ to give me a sound mind, would I succumb to even more negative outlets?

"What a gift that God is choosing to use you to bless this family." Claude's words brought me back to the present.

"You really think that's what's happening?"

"They say He works in mysterious ways. I think that those who are willing, He equips and makes able. And for whatever reason, your path has crossed with Joy's, and He's placed her on your heart for a reason."

If this was His desire for my time here, I wanted nothing different.

"So, what do I do? She only has two days to do what she needs at the house, and we only have a few days left here. Between your food poisoning and my visits to Thimbleberry, we've hardly gotten time together."

He waved me off. "We've had our entire lives together, honey, plus forever to go."

"You're such a romantic."

"You're one yourself, too, you know."

"Am I?" I had never fancied myself as such.

"Look at you. The way you see others, the way you can appreciate all they have to offer, and the conviction you have to help others? That's pretty darn romantic to me."

His tender smile stretched, and my heart swelled with the belief that my usefulness and my life mattered. "Okay, I guess I should call and offer my help."

"*Our* help."

"Our? You'd really join?"

"You might need some muscle to move heavy objects, don't you think?" Claude flexed his bicep and wiggled his brows. Some things, thankfully, never changed. "I may be hot on your heels to fifty, but toots, these guns still shoot like cannons."

I laughed. "You sure those aren't just pop guns?"

He suddenly stopped walking, dropped my hand, and stretched his own high into the air. "I've about had it up to here with you, Kitty Fisher."

"Only to there?" I feigned surprise. "Surely you're more fed up with me than that."

Claude's lips twitched into an almost smile, and as he fought to play along, not a shred of sadness blocked my view. For the time, however fleeting, I felt free, unburdened.

He worked his jaw. "Your sassiness leaves me no choice. A spanking should set you straight."

"You wouldn't dare."

But the look in his eyes told me he would. Slowly, I took one small step backward. I thought of what Abbi said the first day I met her: "*Grow up, but don't grow old.*"

"Move another muscle and I—"

I took another step. Our eyes remained locked.

"I'm warning you, Mrs. Fisher. Don't you even think about trying to—"

I darted. I knew I only had a few exhilarating seconds before Claude would catch me, but I ran like a dog from a dogcatcher, and when he scooped me from my feet, I squealed like a young girl in love.

The swirl of both gray sky and ocean made my mind dizzy as he spun me around. I couldn't separate up from down, but when the world stopped turning and he began to run, I realized his plan.

"You wouldn't dare!" I yelled as I watched the gap between us and the swells grow smaller.

"I can't hear you over the wind!"

"It's only a breeze, you old man! Clean out your ears!" I screeched and clung to him, wrapping my arms farther around his neck. "If you don't put me down right now, *you'll* be the one getting a spanking!"

Claude stopped moving immediately and looked me in the eyes, one eyebrow arched high. "Is that a promise?" He winked, and I wriggled from his arms, playfully swatting his behind as I ran away from the water's edge.

I sat in the rough sand, out of breath, my lungs heavy as the fog. When Claude reached me, he held out a hand and helped me back to my feet.

"You keep me young, Fly."

He snorted. "You call fifty young?"

It took all I had not to laugh. "What am I going to do with you?"

"I believe you're stuck with me."

"That's true. I lost the receipt for you ages ago."

The wind picked up without warning and blew sand across

the beach in a flurry. Claude tugged me up the beach, and through squinted eyes, we pushed back against the wind and the sand that shrouded our vision. It was reminiscent of the gusts that would stir up the desert dirt back home and create rashes on exposed skin.

When we reached the car, we struggled to open the doors. Sand littered the nooks and crannies of our Dart when we finally dropped into the seats. My car door nearly clipped my hand as the wind slammed it shut. Rain began to din against the hood, and I flipped the visor down and checked the mirror, laughing out loud as I saw the disarray of my hair and the sand that freckled my already freckled cheeks. It crusted my brows and the tips of my lashes too.

I brushed and blinked away the grains, then turned to Claude, only to be met with his lips pressing against mine. My hands came to his face on instinct, and sand that clung to his stubbly beard fell into my cradling palms. The gales whipped around our car, and the waves raged and crashed with the fury of a thousand men. But here inside, we abided in peace.

31

1950
Tonopah, Nevada

SOMEONE DOUSED THE fire behind her, its hiss the mark of a night ended, a phase of life complete. Most of their fellow just-graduated classmates had already departed the desolate desert party, leaving only a few remaining to the bitter end. Kitty stumbled as she stooped and collected what she could of their contraband beer, dumping the bottles and cans into the makeshift trash—the bed of someone's truck. Bethany tossed in two cans of her own.

"Come with me, Kit. Just apply." Bethany's words slurred slightly together, and it wasn't clear to Kitty if it was from tiredness due to their late night or the amount of alcohol she'd ingested.

The alcohol churned in Kitty's own stomach. She'd watched her father let the drink control his life, had firsthand felt the reverberating effects, and yet here she was, letting it proclaim ownership over her too.

But what had she learned over the past handful of years? Certainly not that she was different from her parents. In fact, the very things that made her despise them had worked their way into her, as well. Like an absorbed splinter, the uncertainty of her future dissolved. There was only one path forward, and it meant walking backward.

"We can dorm together," Bethany's plea came out as a prolonged whine. In a short time, Bethany would be heading for the University of Nevada, Reno. Everyone seemed to have plans and goals. Everyone except for Kitty.

Bethany looped her arm into Kitty's and dragged her toward the car. But out of nowhere, Jack intervened and slipped an arm around her waist, pulling her away from Bethany and into him. Her head spun, but she didn't have the energy to resist.

"I'll bring you home," he murmured into her ear. "I want to talk to you about something."

Her thoughts were jumbled, but she assumed it would be about a long-distance relationship, maybe. He was heading to Fresno for college. Maybe he was trying to recruit her just as Bethany was.

Kitty didn't care who brought her home so long as she could sleep. And soon. Whether it was at Bethany's house or the rental home she now lived in with Peggy. After hugging goodbye, Bethany ducked into a car with three other friends, and Kitty slid into the front seat of Jack's passed down Packard.

Kitty's mind buzzed. She slumped down in her seat. Jack said something about college, but his words didn't quite reach. All she wanted was to sleep, to rid herself of her stagnant mind, the one that couldn't be silenced even now as it swam with the alcohol she'd had no business drinking. It was the same routine; once the distraction wore off, the pain returned. What would it take to silence it for good?

Jack put a hand on Kitty's thigh, and she hardly realized it was there until his car suddenly came to a stop. Kitty sat up and peered out the window, unable to see through the blackness of the night.

"Are we here already?" She looked at Jack, and his face bobbed before her. His grip on her thigh tightened.

"Kitty." His voice was thick, and the wafting scent of liquor plunged Kitty into the past, the memory of her father's breath sour in her mind. "Come here."

"Where?" she asked, confused, her voice laced with sleep and innocence.

In a blur, Jack moved her to the backseat. She could hardly tell up from down, but there was no mistaking the way he smashed his lips against hers and moved her clothes aside. She tried to say his name, to tell him to stop. But her voice . . . where was her voice? He pressed his body against hers, and she pushed against his chest. A scream lodged in the back of her throat. Her instincts told her to fight, but her heart said, *"What's the use?"* Jack couldn't be overpowered, and furthermore, she'd known all her life that she wasn't worth fighting for. Maybe Claude had tried to convince her otherwise, but the entire world seemed to scream the opposite.

A tear slid down her cheek as she let herself slip,

s l i p,

s l i p

away.

32

Lia

1940
Galia, Oregon

JOY LEADS THE way to our sanctuary, the sweet clearing nestled in our patch of woods beyond the meadow. My heart sings there, as does hers. She runs, sure on her feet, trampling over the earth like she can't fail.

With Him, you can't . . .

Baby Constance stirs against my bosom, and I pat her small back as I try to keep pace with her sister's exuberant spirit. She ducks between the trees. I'm close behind, only entering our secret hideaway a step behind her.

It is cool today, and the clouds are heavy. But we're dressed for the occasion, and not much can deter Joy from rushing for the brook or leaping from logs. The sureness by which she moves astounds me, and in her animation, I find rest.

She gasps suddenly and points. Upstream, a doe dips her

muzzle into the water. Her round eyes manage to catch mine in the dimness of the forest, and she freezes. So do I. I don't want to blink and miss a moment of this creature's beauty. My eyes burn as I hold back the sudden burst of tears I feel.

"That God?" my daughter shrieks.

The doe gazes lazily for a beat longer and then is gone. I crane my neck for another peak, but the forest has swallowed her up. Joy tugs the hem of my dress.

"Is it?"

I cradle the baby's head as I bend down. "Is that God? Is that what you asked?"

She nods. The question has been repeated over the last week more times than I can count. *Is that caterpillar God? Is the postman at the door God? Are those thunderclouds in the sky God?* I've said no each time. *They're His creation.*

I look back upstream. Was that God? No, not Himself, but was it *Him?* Because just last night I'd sat with Tenn, listening to him read the Forty-Second Psalm as I rocked the baby to sleep. I look back upstream, and a knowing settles in my heart. It's a feeling undeniable, as though I finally feel peace lacing itself around me, as though His hands are resting upon my shoulders.

The more I seek Him, the more I've come to realize that He does care.

And so do I. I want Him. More and more.

"Yes," I say to my daughter. "I think it was."

33

1981
Galia, Oregon

JOY CRIED WITH gratitude when I called to offer our help. I couldn't bear the thought of her father leaving their family's legacy. What I would have given to visit the Fisher family home for a final time to rescue all the history that I could . . . Not that material items mattered. But they did remind us of time gone past, jiggling our memories, keeping our minds from forgetting from where we came.

Joy gave us the address, and Donna from the hotel drew us one of her elaborate maps. In the morning, we set out. Trees densely lined the roads, and the air drifting through our open windows was heavy with the sweetness of creation. The Monroe family home was further inland than even Thimbleberry, in the southernmost reaches of Galia, almost running into Neskowin Beach.

We pulled down the lane and parked behind Joy's car. The

massive southern-style home, which had a long porch jutting out from the front door, was surrounded by an expanse of open green lawn. A pathway led from the driveway to the porch, where yellow interior light spilled onto the wood through the windows.

I rang the bell, and a deep *clang* resounded inside. *Now,* that *would wake a sleeping baby.* The thought sent an ache through my heart, and I longed to hold my grandbaby. Just a few more days, and we'd be home.

I shook the thought from my head and looked to Claude for encouragement, which he offered in the form of a smile. My purpose and the task directly in front of me needed to be my focus. My efforts would be stunted by my sadness if I became too homesick.

The door opened. "You've come just in time," Joy said, inviting us in. "Coffee's ready."

We followed her through the foyer, where a grandfather clock ticked, and a wide staircase swirled upward, disappearing into the second story. We walked under an arched transition and past a sitting area that boasted the coziness of a crackling fireplace. In the kitchen, just to the right, coffee mugs waited for us on the marble island counter. Joy grabbed the carafe and filled each mug.

"I'm going to miss that sound," she said, nodding toward the fire as she retrieved cream from the fridge. "When we were growing up, my dad always got up early with my mom. He made the fire while she made breakfast. Us kids would come down one by one from our rooms, and one of the first things I'd hear was the crackling of the fire followed by Mom's low humming as she kneaded dough for biscuits and then the flipping of newspaper pages as Dad sat reading at the table. Those little things . . . I hope they stick, even when I'm old and gray and can't remember anything else."

I swallowed the sudden lump in my throat and poured a splash of cream into my coffee. "It's the feeling of home you're going to miss. That steadfast, familiar comfort."

"I feel like I'm losing the one constant I've had throughout my life. This home has been the guardian of our family." Her brow furrowed. "I suppose you both know that better than I do, though."

"I've been thinking about that same thing the past few days myself." Claude set his mug on the counter, and it made a small *chink!* I could tell by the sheen of his eyes that he had something important to say.

"How do you . . . come to terms?"

I waited as much in anticipation for Claude's wisdom as Joy did, I think. He pursed his lips, letting a moment slip past, but finally, he spoke. "By realizing that it won't last, whether you sell this home or not. It's in this house's nature to wither and fade, be sold or burn down. It wasn't ever meant to live on forever. Leaving those memories behind in a physical sense is . . . hard, but it was never the physical things that mattered, was it? Our memories and connections with our loved ones are the only things we can take with us."

Claude's words sent a sad chill through me.

Joy's chin trembled as she looked into her mug. "And what if we lose our memories?" she whispered.

"Right." He took a moment to collect his thoughts before answering. "I believe that though our bodies may fail in this broken world, God does not. No matter if it appears like all traces of someone are lost, the soul inside isn't. They're still known by the One who made them, the One who will, in the right time, restore and resurrect."

Nodding, Joy seemed unable to speak.

"It helps if we can hold onto gratitude that God let us be housed in walls full of love and fond memories at all," I said.

"Even when the walls we find ourselves in have changed, He's still with us. So, are we ever really not home?"

The revelation surprised even me, and a sob lodged in my throat. But I didn't feel like crying; I didn't know if I could stop once I'd started. I purposely took a big swig of coffee, burning my tongue to keep the tears at bay.

But Joy let her own tears fall, though she wiped them away with haste and a resolute nod. "You're right," she said. "Thank you."

"How can we best help you today?" Claude asked.

She groaned and rubbed her temples. "I'm afraid of how much work there really is to be done. We should get started. Would you like a quick tour of the grounds first? I can show you my favorite spot. It was my mother's favorite too."

While I silently wondered if Joy was procrastinating, I happily accepted the invitation.

Through the back door, we stepped down wooden steps and passed an overgrown garden and untamed flowerbeds. The morning air was still, and with the sun's emerging presence, the day had the air of new beginnings. We traipsed across the luscious meadow that sprawled behind the home, aiming for the forested tree line ahead.

"I know it's a bit of a walk," Joy said. "But I promise it's worth it."

When we reached the forest's edge, Joy motioned for us to follow as she weaved between the aged cedar and spruce trees and stepped over decaying logs until we came to a small clearing where the world stood still. It was like the trees had all stepped aside in the manner of gentlemen, opening a dance floor sized space of earth for its esteemed guests. And at this magical moment, we were the honorees. Claude's breath audibly hitched, and he touched a palm to the small of my back as we stepped farther into this wooded sanctuary.

The chatter of water reached my ears. I turned. A brook snaked toward the west and drew my steps nearer. Water so clear it made me thirst rushed steadfastly over protruding rocks that donned mossy wigs. It took great restraint not to kick off my scuffed-up sneakers and plunge my toes into the earth's tears.

"My mother discovered this spot when we were young." Her voice weighed heavily with nostalgia as she sat on a nearby stump like it was her designated spot at the breakfast table, a place she'd sat a thousand times. "She used to take us out here to play and have picnics all the time."

This sweet, mythical-like forest had been at the fingertips of the Monroe children all their growing up years. Claude and I had endless supplies of dust and sagebrush at our childhood disposal, but somehow, in spite of the beauty that dripped with moisture around me, I felt a distinct form of gratitude that the not-so-barren desert had been what formed us.

"This is beautiful, Joy. I can see why you'll miss this," I said.

She didn't respond, too focused on what I could only assume was a crashing of the past, present, and future before her. Claude caught my eye from where he stood near the brook and held out his arm. I stepped toward him, and he welcomed me against his side, pulling my shoulder into the crook of his arm, a puzzle piece clicking into place.

"It all flows together," he said, and somehow, I knew what he meant.

After returning to the house, we decided to begin with the most important rooms first, beginning downstairs in the study. We fell into a rhythm, and our work became a soundtrack. The light clapping of books stacked one atop another. The crinkle of newspaper wrapped around a figurine. The scraping of cardboard as another box was assembled. But perhaps the sweetest and saddest sounds of all were the gentle and frequent sighs of a memory unlocked for Joy. Our flow only changed when Claude opened a cabinet and discovered an alphabetized collection of records in pristine condition.

"Was your father intending to leave these behind?" he asked, dumbfounded as he extracted an album at random.

Joy set a file folder full of dated paperwork into a box. "I think he's trying to leave everything behind, if you ask me."

Claude and I silently locked eyes for a moment.

"I don't know your dad," Claude said. "But I'd venture to guess that as emotionally absent as he may seem, this journey with your mother has entirely rocked his world. Not that his actions are justified, but sometimes it helps to consider the different ways people cope."

His words made me think of a teenaged, heartbroken Cliff.

"He acts like he doesn't care. And yet here I am"—she dropped another file folder into the box—"clinging to everything I can. But it feels like I'm the only one holding on, and that's something I don't understand."

"And you may never," I said. A rush of sadness entered my mind like the tide. I had waited for what felt like forever for my dad to change and had foolishly clung throughout childhood to the notion that my mother might suddenly remember I existed and return for me. "We can't control the actions of others, but we certainly can pray for them to change."

At least one of my lifelong prayers had been answered.

Joy fussed with the cardboard flaps of the box and sighed. "My mother prayed, sometimes out loud. Half the time, I don't think she realized she was doing it. I used to pray all the time, too. But these days, I hate to say, I've been relying on my own strength." She paused long enough for the corners of her mouth to droop. "Maybe that's why I feel so broken."

"Our own strength is never enough," I said.

A minute ticked by. Claude turned the album in his hand and, in a decidedly swift motion, slid the record from its sheath and set it on the Victrola. There was a crackle and a pop before the instrumental jazz piece began. The music drowned out the fragility that resided in the air.

With the study mostly packed away, Claude hauled the boxes to the foyer as I followed Joy up the stairs. We carried rolls of packing tape and stacks of newspapers in our hands and flattened boxes awkwardly under our arms. I peered down from the landing and caught a glimpse of Claude neatly stacking boxes below. He must have sensed my eyes. He looked up just then and smiled in a way that brought heat to my chest.

34

Summer 1950
Tonopah, Nevada

"I'M GETTING OUT a little early," he said.

Her heartbeat quickened. The clarity of her dad's voice was like nothing she'd ever heard from him before, and she knew it couldn't be due to their phone connection.

"Oh. When exactly?"

"I think they're talking about July."

Kitty breathed uneasily. Four and a half years of physical separation were coming to a close. His release had been one of the furthest things on her mind. "Well, that's . . . good."

Fear weaseled its way in. Everything seemed to be coming to an end all at once and collectively begged the question that made her knees shake. *What comes next?*

"Yeah." He went quiet on the other end of the line.

"So . . ." There was too much silence and nothing to fill it with.

"So, I got some work I can do in Reno. I'll be heading there after I get out."

"Reno. I have some friends going to college there."

"Kit."

She waited, sure that he would continue, perhaps congratulating her for graduating or ask about *her* upcoming plans. But his words went unspoken, and Kitty heard them. A muffled sound on his end came through the phone. "Oh, I actually . . . I have to go. Bye."

When the line went dead, it took all her strength not to collapse as she placed the phone in its cradle. The summer heat sweltered inside the small home, and she wanted it to suffocate her. Claude had been right about Jack and his plans to use her all along. Her innocence being stolen in the black of night confirmed what she'd always known. As did the following morning when she'd walked to Jack's house and attempted to confront him but instead was manipulated and humiliated by Jack in front of Richie. Only the idea of her had ever been special to Jack. She'd been a fun chase, a game of cat and mouse, and he discarded her as soon as he got what he'd wanted. And now, she meant nothing to him.

But her meaning wasn't limited to Jack.

She meant nothing to her father. He hadn't asked to see her, even after all this time. Nothing to Claude. She'd made her bed there and allowed her insecurities to separate a lifetime of friendship. Of what could have been. And soon, she'd mean nothing to her friends who all had plans bigger than their hometown.

Her only companion now was a darkness that sickened her stomach.

35

1981
Galia, Oregon

THE HALLWAY UPSTAIRS was an ode to the Monroe family. Portraits and hand stitched quilts hung on the walls, creating a cozy atmosphere that shouted of the family's forgotten love and togetherness. The record still spun downstairs and reached our ears even as we stepped into the master suite. We set our armfuls of supplies on the bed. I pointed to a ladder of quilts that leaned against the far wall.

"Was your mother a quilter?"

"Yes. She was . . . a little bit of everything. Always keeping her hands busy." Joy assembled a box and slid it my way. "I'll start going through the dresser drawers if you want to start taking down picture frames."

I grabbed a few sheets of newspaper and got to work. Joy hummed alongside the jazz music as I reached for the nearest hanging photograph. A layer of dust coated the top and fogged the glass like dirty snow. How long had it been since these were properly dusted?

"If there's a rag handy, I'll dust these before packing them away."

She pointed to the adjoining bathroom. "I'm sure there's one in there."

A few washcloths were folded in the cabinet. I wet one in the sink, wrung it out, and returned to my duty, carefully wiping the glass front of the frame to reveal a family portrait. Something about it twisted a knot in my stomach. I tossed the rag aside and wrapped the frame in newspaper, set it in the box, and went on to the next.

Claude rejoined us, and Joy put him to work on shelves of knickknacks. I continued my task, filling the box with wrapped frames until the music suddenly cut downstairs. Joy hummed one misplaced note into the quiet air. A moment later, the staircase creaked under the weight of heavy footsteps.

"My dad." Joy's lips formed a grim line. She stepped from the room, barely making it a few steps before we heard her father's bite.

"Whose car is that in the drive? Did Peter get a new one? Sure is a downgrade if you ask—"

"Dad!" Joy hissed.

I looked wide-eyed at Claude. His hand was frozen in the air, a porcelain poodle in his grip.

"Since Jason and Connie can't be here, my friends have generously lent their time to help protect our memories before you go throwing them away."

"Come on, Joy Belle. That's not fair."

"Don't even get me started on fair, Dad." Her frustration roiled through the walls. "Did you see all those boxes downstairs?"

A beat passed.

"Yes."

"Don't they make you sad? You can change your mind, and we can start unpacking. Just say the word."

Silence.

Joy huffed, but it sounded like her fury fizzled out. "Look, I don't want to fight about this. Frankly, I don't have the energy. Would you like to meet my friends who are helping sort through all of *your* belongings?"

Claude and I both turned away from the door, as though occupied by our tasks and not at all listening to the spat on the other side. They entered moments later.

"Kitty, Claude, this is my father, Tenn."

Her father took up the space in the doorway with his broad shoulders and even broader pride. He looked like a man who had no time to waste. Claude moved across the room to shake his hand, and I followed suit. Tenn's scrutinizing eyes lingered on mine for a moment, and I felt like a specimen under a microscope. The space between his brows creased with a mark of confusion then released.

"Are you from around here?" he asked.

I shook my head. His eyes narrowed. My stomach lurched with an uncertainty I couldn't place, and I tried to smile. "What a lovely estate you have here," I said.

"It's been good to us, hasn't it, Joy Belle?" He sank his hands into his pockets and leaned against the doorframe. "It's just time for a change, something a bit more manageable. The home has outpaced me."

You seem to have outpaced your family, your wife . . . I shook the thoughts away. I didn't need to judge.

Tenn rubbed his head, and I was surprised at the amount of hair he still had on his head for his age. Claude's father had been bald for years, and I'd noticed the beginnings of thinning on Claude's own head as well.

"I, uh, understand that you played a tremendous hand in Maggy's rescue the other day." He didn't quite meet my eyes when he said it. Probably because he was ashamed that I'd spent more time with his wife in the matter of a few days than he had in months. "Thank you for helping her."

"No need to thank—"

"I insist." He withdrew a checkbook from the back pocket of his slacks.

"No, no. You don't—"

"I insist. It's my way of thanking you."

My eyes darted to Claude. He took a step forward.

"That's very kind of you, Tenn," Claude said. "But we wouldn't feel right about accepting money from you."

"Truly," I reiterated. "I was happy to help and see her back safe and sound. It's a deed anyone would have done, considering the circumstances."

"Well, then, for the work you're doing here at least." He pulled a pen from the inner crease of the book.

"Dad, please."

Tenn's eyes darted back and forth from Joy to me a few times before he finally tucked his checkbook away, though it wasn't without a sigh. "Okay, then."

I nodded resolutely. "Maggy seems like a wonderful woman. How many years have you been married?"

I sensed the topic of his wife made him uncomfortable, frustrated even. He looked to Joy for the answer.

"What has it been? Forty-five? Forty-six years?" His eyes widened for a flicker of a moment, as though he was shocked at the number.

"That's a considerable amount of time. I hope you're able to enjoy the years you have left."

A cloud descended upon his face. "Easier said than done when you're the only one who realizes you're still married."

"But you are," Claude piped in. "Still married, that is."

The remark could have been taken as a jab, but Claude's voice was warm and encouraging. Tenn clicked his tongue like he was about to say something. Whatever it was, he let it go.

"Well, I suppose I'll leave you to it," he said. "I have an appointment to get to."

"Another open house?" Joy asked with a bite.

He answered with a curt nod, and Joy's eyes flared.

"Have a nice time, Dad. I hope you find what you're looking for." She turned from him and resumed her work at the dresser.

Tenn watched her. In the crinkle of his forehead, I could see grief mapped out on his face. It wasn't the same route as Joy's, but the location of loss was there nonetheless. "I'll be back before long," he said. When Joy kept her back to him, he looked at Claude and me. "Nice to meet you both. Thank you for being such good friends to Joy." His eyes again lingered for an uncomfortable second on my face, and then he left.

Silence and tension worked in tandem to squelch the air from the room. When his footfalls could be heard descending the stairs, Joy knelt on the floor.

"Are you okay?"

"I don't know why I'm acting like this. I'm pushing him away, too, and that's not exactly helping." She let out an exhausted sigh. "Maybe we're more alike than I thought. I just wish I had something real to hold onto. All of this"—she gestured to the contents of the box nearest her—"is wonderful to have, but I wish I had my family again."

The words stung.

I lowered another frame from its nail on the wall and prayed. *Give her hope, Lord. Give her a reason to keep going.* Despite being less dusty than the others, I grabbed the rag and wiped the frame. Though, when I turned it over in my hands, something rattled behind the glass. Odd. A faulty loose screw, perhaps? I grabbed a piece of newspaper and wrapped it around the frame, but the rattling persisted.

This time, I set the newspaper aside and gave the frame a proper shake. Something was definitely shifting around behind the glass. Something much larger than a screw.

"I think there's something inside here," I muttered more to myself than anyone else. I tipped it over and heard a *slide* and then a *chink!*

On the backside, I unfastened the backing board and pulled it loose. Hidden between the backing and the displayed photograph on the front side was a locket necklace and a folded piece of paper. I lifted the locket and dangled the chain from my index finger.

"Joy?" I called. "I found something."

She looked up from across the room with squinted eyes. "What on earth?" She came closer and snatched the locket from my hand. "I . . . I recognize this. My mom used to wear this when I was younger, but I haven't seen it in years. Where did you find it?"

"In that picture frame."

"The picture frame. What would it be doing in there?"

I held up the folded paper I'd also found inside. "Maybe this will explain?"

Joy tucked the necklace into her pocket and took the paper. After a minute, she frowned. "This doesn't make much sense."

She passed the paper back to me to read for myself. One glance, and I knew Joy had been correct on her analysis. The cursive penmanship was nearly illegible, the letters squished and scribbled. If a magnifying glass was handy, perhaps we could make out a few of the less-scrunched, less-scribbled words. The only thing legible was the year 1980.

"This is recent." I pointed to the date.

"Yes, but what exactly is it? Was this the only thing in the frame?"

I rechecked and nodded, though my eyes drifted to the box I'd been filling. "Unless . . ."

". . . there's more?"

36

Summer 1950
Tonopah, Nevada

SHE HADN'T MEANT to fall in love again. Hadn't meant to see him at all. Certainly hadn't meant to unwittingly trap him into this impossible situation.

The mission had been simple: see Ginny and get advice about the growing reality of her situation. How could she have known that Ginny was hundreds of miles away, tending to Cliff and Maisy's new babies? She had planned on talking to the only woman she could trust, not being whisked to the movie theater on a date. But the moment Claude had laced his hands with hers, she experienced the feeling she hadn't for years. The feeling of home.

And now, a week after their unplanned first date, they were caught up in the cab of the Sheridan-Blue Ford that Claude so proudly drove in those days. Fresh ice cream cones in hand, the excess melting over the sides and onto their knuckles. A hefty drip fell from Kitty's hand onto the beige interior seat before she had time to stop it. She winced.

But Claude merely brushed it with a finger and smeared the remainder on the tip of Kitty's nose. She wrinkled her freckled nose and let her mouth drop open in a fake show of disgust.

"It's cute," he said. "You're like a white-nosed Rudolph."

"A white-nosed Rudolph, you say?" In a moment of pure spunkiness, Kitty smashed the swirly tip of her ice cream plumb into Claude's nose. "That's more like it."

He licked his lips and blinked a few times, the ice cream coating his lashes like chunky white mascara. Kitty couldn't help the giggles that burst forth. Claude locked eyes with her.

"You," he said, taking one finger to swipe through the mess on his face. "Are." Another swipe. "So." Another. "Beautiful when you laugh like that."

She covered her mouth with one hand, mostly now to conceal her blushing rather than to keep her laughter inside. He meant it, she knew. He meant it without ulterior motives. Meant it with all his heart.

In addition to Claude's face, their hands were a mess now, with melted ice cream coating them like lotion. They smeared as little ice cream on the door handles as they could and hopped out to sit on the curb.

"You missed a spot." Kitty scooted closer and leaned in, close enough to catch a whiff of his Ivory soap. She picked out a splatter of ice cream from his golden-brown hair. "There."

"You're not going to address this whole situation on my face?"

Kitty burst out laughing again. There was a fear that festered deep inside of her, but she ignored its sprouting as she looked at the white mess still smeared all over Claude's face. It dripped from his nose down around his mouth like a fu manchu, and she couldn't quit giggling if she'd tried. Infectiously, it spread to

Claude too.

"Oh, you're right. What are we going to do about that?" Kitty finally managed to say.

"We? I don't believe I'm the one who made this mess." Claude lifted his ice cream crested brows, his kind hazel eyes drawing her in.

She could close her eyes and draw his every feature. The way his hair naturally swooped to the left. The strong line of his jaw. The crinkle of skin at the corners of his eyes. He meant the world to her, so much so that his presence made her dizzy. She was lost in the hazy mist of falling in love, in its disorienting glow.

"Let me help you." She leaned closer, and her cheeks burned as she felt his eyes heavy on her. She wiped away the bulk of the mess from his face with her fingers, and he used his t-shirt to scrub away the leftovers.

"I'll help you clean the truck before your dad sees it," she said.

"It's the least you could do." He nudged her jokingly, and without thinking, she laid her head on his shoulder.

"I'm so happy I have you, Fly."

37

1981
Galia, Oregon

WE TORE OPEN the box and lifted out every picture frame while Claude gathered the few that remained on the walls. The three of us got to work prying every backing board away and found that, sure enough, sets of letters had been stowed inside of most.

"This looks like a task that might warrant more coffee?" Claude asked, and I ventured to guess that the offer was his polite way of giving Joy privacy. "I'll brew some more."

"Yes, please." Joy sounded relieved, and Claude excused himself from the room.

"Do you want me to call anyone? Your siblings? Your dad?"

She held up a finger to stop me. "No. None of them would be able to come right away, regardless. And I think this would upset Dad enough to whisk them away and toss them in the trash."

"Okay. Well, do you want time alone? I can start in another room while you read these?"

"That's the last thing I want. Look at me. I'm shaking!" And she was. Her free hand trembled when she held it up as proof. "Though I don't know if it's from nerves or excitement. I mean, what did we just unearth? I almost feel like we've landed in the middle of a great mystery novel, don't you?"

It wasn't my family, but it was impossible to not find sport in the ordeal. Still, I hesitated. "Are you sure? I don't feel it's my place."

"Why not? If it weren't for you, these may have never been discovered. So, should we start sorting through them? Organize chronologically if they have dates? Hopefully the rest are more legible than the first." Excitement oozed from her. She finally seemed like her energetic, go-getter self again.

"Well, I think it's safe to say you've figured out what your mother has been searching for."

Joy paused mid-reach for a letter. Her hand moved to cover her gasping mouth. "Wait. You don't . . . You don't suppose these are all *hers*? I mean, that would explain so much. Like how she's been stealing picture frames and destroying them."

"That's what I was thinking."

"There must be a part of her brain that still clings to whatever these letters are or whatever they meant to her. But . . ." Color drained from her cheeks. I sensed her panic. "What if there's something terrible hidden within these pages?"

There was always that possibility.

"Say these are from your mother or someone in your family. Are you sure you want to do this? I mean, that's a good point. What if you discover something you don't want to know? Something you can't go back from?"

"I can't pretend I never found these." Her voice was small. "Of all people to discover their existence, I feel I'm the one to respect my mother the most. I'd rather these be in my hands than someone else's." She wrung her hands. "What would you do if it were your mom?"

The question almost made me laugh out loud. "I wouldn't have the simplest idea. Being someone who never knew her mother at all, I'd . . ." In my facetiousness, it occurred to me that I didn't know how to answer. If presented the chance, would I care to get to know my mom when she never cared to get to know me? Would I want to know anything about her life?

"I'm losing my mom, and this almost feels like a chance to get to know her all over again," Joy said quietly. "If these are hers."

I couldn't fault her for that. In fact, the existence of these letters could be an undeniable blessing. Who was I to know? Suddenly, music returned from downstairs, this time from a Johnny Cash record.

"I don't think there's any harm in reading the papers," I finally said. "Just be prepared. Something hidden to this length may hurt to uncover."

"Right." She steadied herself. "For some reason, I have a feeling everything will be okay."

We sifted through the letters. Some had dates, but the majority didn't. We organized them the best we could, but it seemed best to simply dive in. Joy selected a letter and gestured for me to do the same.

"Read and switch?" A nervous smile spread on her face, one that conveyed hope.

I nodded, praying that hope was not crushed and still feeling uncertain about prying into Maggy's privacy in such a way. But still, I picked up a letter and read.

Do you laugh like she does, squeezing shut your eyes? Does your laughter make a dimple pop? I wonder about you all the time and can't help but feel trapped in the complexity of it all. Because this living, breathing soul that squeals with delight before me, and this kicking child inside my womb, would not be here if it weren't for the very thing that had the power to cut you the most.

I never owned a domino set as a child. We simply didn't have the money or the time to lend to pointless items, as my mother often said. (According to her, we'd wasted it on education.) But I had a friend who did. And just like those dominoes, with the flicking of the first piece—clack, clack, clack—a chain of events set off with you, with me. Unstoppable.

I stood at the precipice, watching the dominoes of life topple over, and now, I wait for the final blow.

Do you think you'd ever consi

The words ended there. A thought left unfinished. Short and sweet, but enough to gather tears in my eyes as I lowered the page. What had Maggy done?

My thoughts drifted to my own daughter, Lorraine, and the untraditional way in which she was conceived. The memory belonged to another person entirely and no longer had the power to hurt me. But I knew if it wasn't for that horrific act, she wouldn't be here today. God was in the business of creating beauty from pain, and out of the sin of another, He birthed something—someone—precious and kind and full of pizzazz, redeeming something so truly ugly.

Had Maggy and whatever hardship she'd endured been redeemed?

"This is so sad," Joy whispered, her eyes still darting to and fro across the letter she held. "This is a whole other side of my mother I never knew. She never showed her pain. I would never have known that she experienced anything like this."

"You're sure these are hers? Could they belong to a grandparent?"

"No. This is her handwriting, I know it." Joy quickly thumbed through a few other letters. "I see my name in a few of these. They have to be hers. Besides, I never really knew my grandparents. At least on my mother's side."

"You didn't?"

"I think they must have passed before I was born. Or maybe my mom had cut ties with them. We never had a relationship with that side of the family."

"I never had one with my mother's side either. Barely with my father's, and even then, I'm not sure how much it counts." I thought of Peggy. Whatever had become of her? She'd left Tonopah again after Claude and I married, and she never tried to keep in touch. I couldn't even find a number for her when Dad passed away.

Claude entered the room carrying two cups of coffee. He handed them over and settled into a rocking chair in the corner of the room.

"Thank you for the music," Joy said. "And the coffee. It helps."

Claude laced his hands on his lap and rocked. "I take special requests. Just let me know what record I should put on next."

Joy smiled with gratitude and took a sip of her coffee. I reached for the letter she'd been reading and exchanged it with mine. We proceeded to read through the stack. Sip. Read. Sip. Read. After a few more letters, I couldn't ignore the unease growing in my gut.

"These are all over the place," Joy said and ruffled a few pages. "I can't understand whom she's writing to. For example, in this set, the first page seems to be written to one particular person while the second seems written to someone else entirely, though midway through, she talks to herself, then to God, then back to the person to whom she was writing in the first place."

"In the one I'm reading, she writes about meeting your dad.

Specifically mentioned his name, Tenn."

Joy snatched the letter from me and scanned it. I took the final sip of my coffee as I waited for her thoughts.

"She's hiding something, but what? These all tell of her pain, but I can't figure out *why* she was suffering. The way her memory is now, we may never know the truth."

"Do you think she ever told your dad?"

Joy cast her eyes downward as she shrugged. "Judging by the tone of these letters, it seems she never had the intention to. But who knows . . . maybe whatever it was that drove her to write eventually drove her to admit the truth out loud? Maybe that's why he's been so distant over the past year or so?"

"Joy," I said. A knot twisted in my stomach. "I think your mother isn't hiding something, but rather . . . someone."

"I'm gathering something of the sort as well."

38

Summer 1950
Tonopah, Nevada

FROM THE MOMENT the vomit left her lips, a thousand truths were revealed.

The first truth: Just as she'd suspected and feared, her life had been forever changed. The seed of fear was, in fact, a seed after all. A physical one. A real human life. A baby hadn't been part of the plan, but neither was Jack taking advantage of her on graduation night.

The second: There was nothing she wouldn't do for the life sprouting inside of her. As another wave of vomit rushed past her lips, she knew she would endure a million more if it meant keeping that life, who'd had no say in his or her creation story, safe and protected.

The third: She had to come clean to Claude, the love of her life. She had to let him go. He hadn't signed up for a family when he started dating her, and she should have been upfront with him the day she went to find his mother and failed. Her stomach clenched again as she realized he was due to pick her up any minute now.

The bathroom door was open; she hadn't had time to shut it in her mad rush for the toilet. Peggy watched from the doorway, her arms folded across her chest.

"You're knocked up, aren't you?"

The tolerance Kitty and Peggy had built for one another was shattered in an instant. Kitty wanted to cry out, to ask her aunt for help, but the sneer on Peggy's face told her it was no use. She'd born no children of her own, though Peggy had felt the pangs of pregnancy before.

"We'll take care of that."

Kitty spit into the toilet and lifted her eyes to regard her aunt. "We'll take care of nothing."

Peggy snorted. "You're prepared for this? You know better than me? You're your mother in the making." Peggy passed the comment in disgust.

Kitty didn't know what the insult meant, and she didn't get the chance to ask as a dry heave clenched her stomach. The room spun, and she felt drained. Peggy flung a few more insults her way. Tears streamed down Kitty's cheeks, the saltiness creeping into her mouth and mixing with the acid.

Kitty wrapped her arms around her stomach as though to muffle Peggy's dirty words from her child's ears. Heat crawled up her neck and made her nostrils flare. It was a fury that Kitty had never felt before, one of protection and truth. No one would tell this child that he or she was a mistake, unworthy of life or love. No one would feed him or her with the same lies that had wormed their way into Kitty's own heart.

Too weak to argue, all Kitty said was, "Aren't you late for work, hypocrite?"

Peggy screamed a foul word or two and stormed out of the

house. Kitty crawled to the living room, too weak and dizzy to pull herself off the floor.

The final truth came as memories flitted through her mind: She was in for the hardest journey of her life yet, set in motion by actions of her own and the actions of others, but as she slid a hand over her abdomen and braced herself for what was to come, she knew that she would never again be alone. Even in her sorry state, as she blubbered and hated herself for what she was about to do to Claude, an unusual peace curled up within her, stretching out like it was there to stay.

39

"WAIT. WAS SHE . . . having an affair?" Joy clasped a hand over her mouth.

My stomach turned. This whole endeavor wasn't going to end well. I could feel it in my bones. *Maggy, what have you done?* My eyes darted to Claude, who still sat in the rocking chair. He caught my glance and winced. Even he could sense the gravity of the situation.

"What did you find?"

Joy read the letter out loud:

"'*We may never find each other again, and that is the seed I have sown. I have much to atone for, but an apology from afar will only go so far. For reasons I can't disclose, I have to tell you that I cannot return and come back to you. Not that you would have me anyway. I thought we were riding on the promise of something big, but I was only coasting on the promise of escape, and I fear I will never learn what it means to be settled. Why must I feel that there is always something from which to run, that my feet cannot be firmly planted anywhere. As soon as I begin to take root, I flee. Fear drives me. But I am trying to stop running. I am trying to make the most of the decisions I've made and go forward with what I can. I am sorry for the pieces left to rot and the questions you must surely have. Please take care of her.'"*

Joy waved the page in the air with frustration. "Take care of whom? What does this even mean? Had she been planning on leaving us?" Hysteria now outlined her voice.

I knew the pain of being left and had lived with the repercussions of it my entire life.

"You don't know that, Joy. Let's look at the facts, okay?" I did the best I could to keep my voice steady and confident. "Clearly, she was hiding something, but your mom didn't leave. She stayed. She . . . chose you."

My eyes stung, and for a moment, regret bound me. I wished I hadn't agreed to help her with this project. I was here on the coast to scatter the ashes of my lone parent who *had* stayed, and somehow, tears were gathering in a near-stranger's childhood home for the parent who'd left, who'd let me believe I was unfit to be loved.

Sometimes, I still wished I'd pursued finding her. Just to know. To have answers. To silence that nagging in the back of my mind. In spite of it all, I had found purpose and broken the curse that my mother had tried to hand down to me. As it turned out, I didn't need my mother, for I had God, who spared and cared and provided for me. But that had never stopped me from wanting her.

"There are photos tucked in here." Joy's voice wobbled, and she held up two photographs. She didn't have to say anything for me to know where her mind was drifting. She examined one. "I don't think this is my father and me. Perhaps it's Uncle David? Or . . . maybe it's . . ." She let the accusation fall as she handed it to me.

There was a familiarity in the photo, and I realized I had a similar one of my father holding Gloria when she was little. He consumed my thoughts now, and the man swimming before me in the photo began to look like him. I missed my dad. Wanted him back. Wished to redeem the time we'd had left sooner than we did. Eternity was ahead, and this brought me comfort, but still, I wanted him here.

Hold fast to the light had become our family's motto over the years. Death was something we were all familiar with. Hardships, too. We were no strangers to pain. And pain, I knew, was okay. It gave opportunity for beauty; it gave wings to faith. God had proven time and again that He would hold us up mid-flight and carry us through to the other side.

Hold fast to the light.

The tears fell whether I wanted them to or not. I handed the photo back to Joy and wiped my cheeks.

"Kit." Claude's voice was low, concerned. The rocking chair creaked as he leaned forward.

"Is this too much?" Joy set her hand on my arm.

"I'm fine. Just missing my dad." I felt Claude's eyes on me from across the room but didn't dare meet them. I knew I'd lose it if I did. After a deep breath, I asked to see the other photo Joy had found. She handed it over, and I paused.

"This is a duplicate," I said. "A copy of the one Abbi has in her room."

"What are you talking about? Abbi? From Thimbleberry?"

"Yes." I looked at the slumbering infant in the photo. "She showed me this exact picture in her room the other day. Said she found it and asked around to find its owner, but no one claimed it. She said she even asked you."

"Now that you mention it, months ago, I think she did. But I didn't recognize it. I don't know who that is."

"It isn't you?"

"I didn't have that much hair as an infant. This baby looks only a few months old, if that."

"Is this the same baby as in the other photo?"

We compared the two, but it was impossible to tell.

"I wish I could just ask my mom." Joy paced over the Persian runner rug and flicked the photo back and forth in her grip. "This whole week makes no sense. First, my mother went missing, only to be rescued by you, which is more than ironic considering how ever since her progressing dementia, she's been calling that baby doll of hers by the name Kitty, and we've never known a Kitty in our life. Then, my dad suddenly selling the house. And now, finding these letters, I just—"

"What did you just say?" I swallowed hard.

Joy's forehead creased at my sudden interruption. "Um, just saying how this week has been full of the unexpected."

"No. The thing about my name."

"Oh. I just think it's ironic that you, of all people, found my mother. When her dementia began to progress, she started looking for her 'baby.' We didn't know what she meant, of course, but she accused each of us of taking it. That's when the doctor suggested we get her a doll. She would ask for 'Kitty' all the time, like the rest of us had disintegrated into no importance, and this baby doll was actually real."

An alarm rang out from somewhere deep within me. My lungs constricted. "I thought that after learning my name, she'd somehow been remembering it all week. By some weird fluke." The words tasted dull as they left my mouth.

"No." Joy smiled with naivety and looked back at the assortment of secrets on the bed. "Well, now here's a clue."

I wasn't sure I wanted to look. Wasn't sure if I could. I was already halfway out the door without having moved a single inch.

"It's like she started filling this out then changed her mind. Look."

I obliged. Joy held a yellow telegraph form. She flipped it over, though the backside was only filled with the Western Union printing information. She turned it to the front. "Now, who on earth would my mother have known in Goldfield, Nevada?"

My eyes flitted to Claude's with the pull of a magnet. He'd already perked up in his chair.

"Goldfield?" he said with surprise.

I tore my eyes from my husband and back to the telegram. The message area was blank, like Maggy hadn't brought herself to say what she'd needed. But there, on the line labeled "place," she'd written *"Goldfield, NV,"* in the same handwriting I'd grown so accustomed to reading all day. The rest of the information wasn't filled in, other than the "name" section. She had addressed it to *"J. Ralph."*

"Can I . . ." My voice threatened to give me away. In light of my warning to Joy about jumping to conclusions, I was on the verge of leaping off the metaphorical cliff myself. I cleared my throat and straightened my shoulders. "Can I see that locket again?"

Joy pulled it from her pocket. Concern painted her face.

My fingers fumbled to open the clasp, but I finally popped it open. The locket had an extra layer inside, which folded out so the wearer could store multiple photos within. Three of the four slots were filled.

Joy peered over my shoulder and pointed. "That first picture is me. Then the second is Jason. And if you turn the middle piece like flipping a page. . ."

The hinge protested as I did.

". . . that's Connie."

Heat crawled from my legs, up my spine, and to my neck. The point of origin for the fire, I knew, was the pocket of my pants, the same pair I'd worn just yesterday when visiting Abbi at Thimbleberry. I slipped my hand into my pocket, and my fingers burned as I pinched the newsprint photograph of myself between my thumb and index finger.

It was already folded in the manner it had obviously been for years, concealing the face of the woman—me—inside. My jaw hardened. I didn't need to try to make it fit. Something in my soul told me it would. Still, I pressed it into the locket's empty and final slot, and it stayed as though it had always belonged.

Gently, I set the locket on the bed. "If you'll excuse me."

40

1950
Tonopah, Nevada

SHE CLOSED HER eyes, memorizing every second of the moment before she shattered it. Claude's lips against her forehead, his fingers raking through her messy hair, the heat radiating from his body. If only they could exist this way forever.

But it no longer was a relationship between just the two of them. She was sure of it.

He begged to stay and offered his help because that's who he was. But she couldn't expect him to help with a child he'd had no part in conceiving. She couldn't expect him to carry such a burden.

His lips pulled away from her skin as he rested his forehead against hers and looked her in the eye. "You really want me to go?"

No. But this wasn't about her.

"Yes," she said softly.

His heart had broken before and because of her, yet again. A part of hers crumbled, too, as he unwove his fingers and stepped away. As he slid into his truck, she ducked inside the sweltering house, unable to withstand watching him drive away. Her light footsteps punctured the silence inside and punctuated her solitude.

"God," she whispered into the air. "If you're there, please—" Her voice fell prey to the lump in her throat, dissolving all traces of stoicism she had left. Words could no longer drift from her lips to the One above, but she figured, if He was truly there, He'd hear every one of them in her weeping.

Life was a culmination of one's actions colliding with the actions of others. And as the following days crept by, the weight of decision pressed against Kitty's heart. Firsthand, she had felt the pain when emotions commandeered the wheel: It had happened because of her mother and whatever whim or pain that had driven her away; her father and the deep-buried emotions that liquor attempted to numb; Peggy and the sorrow that led her to run; Jack and the selfish lust that came at her expense. She'd felt emotion's power in her own self even when fear kept pieces of her heart locked away.

But how different would her life be if emotions took a back seat? If people operated with intentionality and a pure mind rather than under the control of their impulses and brokenness?

She slid a hand across her flat stomach. What if she was wrong about her pregnancy? What if nothing had happened that night with Jack after all? Her heart twinged, and the thought of an empty womb both wrecked and relieved her.

The phone rang for the second time within the hour, the tenth time within the week. Not that she was counting. Unlike all the other times when she let it ring into oblivion, Kitty rose from the couch and answered it. Claude's voice on the other end was a comfort.

"I've been trying to call all week," he said in a voice saturated with worry. "Is everything okay?"

So, all of the calls *were* from him.

"I'm okay, Claude. I just wanted to give you time, that's all." Time to realize that he was better off without her continuing to weigh him down.

"Okay." He sounded frustrated. "My dad is picking my mom up tonight. They'll be here in the morning."

Relief spread its wings inside of her. Ginny, the only woman she'd ever truly learned to trust, would soon be home. Ginny would guide her through this. Ginny would help. Kitty would soon have answers, and all doubt would be removed. Her stomach tightened as realization dawned upon her. As much as she wanted the truth, she almost feared the fallout from it more.

"How are you feeling?" he asked.

She drew a breath. Claude was already worried enough; she didn't want to add to it more. But if there was anyone she could trust with her thoughts, it was him. "Scared." The word slipped through her lips. "Just really scared."

"When I get done helping Dad at the garage today, would it be okay if I came and picked you up?" Claude asked.

Hope burned in her chest. It wanted to break loose and run to the safety that he had always promised. *Steady,* she told herself. She couldn't let it run wild. "To do what?"

"Take you on a date."

In spite of her efforts, that burning hope barreled out of the gate, and she smiled into the phone. Shouldn't she say no? Protect both of their hearts from falling further in love in light of all that was going on? She wanted to bridle her emotions, didn't she?

But this didn't feel like something rash, something driven from a place of darkness or greed. It felt much akin to the way the sun rose every morning and set every night. It felt steady and right, as though the two of them together had always been in the making.

"I'll be ready whenever you get here," she blurted out.

And for the first time in a while, against all odds, hope billowed in her heart.

The feeling only continued to grow that day, from the moment she opened the door to find him shaking with nerves on her front porch to sitting blindfolded in his truck en route to a promised surprise. Only when she whipped off her blindfold to find that he'd brought her to their childhood hideout, a junker Model T, did her hope waver with a twinge of fear.

What did returning here mean for him?

The busted windows helped with the heat and the putrid smell, but inside the deteriorating cab of the Ford, Claude laid his heart on the line. "I'm ready to face this with you, to walk by you every step of the way, to have a life together, to raise that baby together, should you truly be pregnant. And before you give me a thousand reasons why I shouldn't, why I deserve something different, let me give you one reason that tells you why you're wrong: I love you. There's not much more to say except for that. I love you. I'll say it again and again if I have to. I love you. I love you. Do you get it yet? I love you."

Her head spun. Her chest heaved. She argued and reasoned, but no matter her angle, he had an answer, clear and pure. He wanted to spend forever with her, baby and all. As a family.

"Is there any part of you that wants to be with me forever?" he asked, pulling her hand into his.

"Yes," she replied.

"And setting aside all your shame and worry and fear, is there any part of you that doesn't?"

The decrepit Model T, beaten down from years of neglect, had been privy to years of secrets in their youth, and now, it housed their most important talk of all. Kitty relaxed against

Claude and curled her fingers around his.

"No," she said.

It didn't matter if she had to smell the sunbaked rat pee of these seats for all of time, what she wanted was to forever sit beside her best friend. And moments later, when he pressed his lips to hers, she knew that even forever wouldn't suffice.

41

1981
Galia, Oregon

MY NAME FADED into the background as Claude called after me. But he didn't chase; he let me go. The evidence washed over me. It seeped into the marrow of my bones. Fury carried me through the house and out the back door. I panted through the meadow but didn't stop until I stumbled into the concealed safety of the forest sanctuary. My foot caught an exposed root, and I fell to the earth's mossy, cool floor with a grunt, wishing for a moment it would swallow me whole.

The forest reverberated around me. The buzz of wings. The rush of the stream. I picked myself up on all fours. A guttural sob escaped my chest. The sound needed no words; God already knew the aching lament of this human soul.

Had my mother known how many times I'd cried for her? Prayed for her? Worried for her? For all I'd known, she was dead. On sleepless nights for fifty years, scenarios had fluttered through my mind until I exhausted myself to the point of sleep. *She'd fallen ill . . . been abducted . . . run over by a train.* Of all the excuses I'd made, never once did I consider that the only thing preventing her from returning was a new family.

My tears found a home in the spongy ground, and the forest's breeze chilled my wet cheeks. Time became nonexistent as my pain released. When enough strength returned, I moved against a stump and curled my knees to my chest, noting the ache that wasn't there in my youth. I looked skyward and only saw strands of the clouded heavens from between the trees.

"You knew this would happen." My voice was raw. Of course, He knew that my coming here—*here!*—was in the works. He'd been the one to bring me, after all.

But why now and not sooner?

Anger brewed. At my mother. At God.

My fickle heart twinged.

Was I still that child? The one who tucked herself away, who ran for the shelter of an abandoned Model T? I dusted my hands on my already stained knees and drew a breath. At least I knew now from where my propensity to run had come.

But I was not that girl anymore.

I pulled myself to my feet. There was no need to wallow in shame, alone and discarded. For I had Christ, the One who promised to journey with me through every shadowy valley, through every gusty storm. Though I didn't know how to face it yet, I knew I could do it by His strength.

A twig snapped near the entrance of the forest. I scanned the tree line, my heart already primed for whom I would find. Claude appeared between two cedars. A sea of unspoken words flowed between us. He slowly stepped toward me.

"Have I lost my mind?" I finally said.

"You can't lose something you never had."

I didn't want to smile but couldn't deny the pull of my lips.

He reached me and wrapped me in his arms. His warmth calmed me.

"How long have you been there?" I murmured against him.

"Long enough." He tilted my chin upward and kissed my tear-crusted cheeks. "Honey, we don't know—"

"I do." The strokes of a pen had revealed more to me about my heritage in a single afternoon than I'd experienced my entire life. As sure as I was of Claude's love for me, I was certain that Maggy Monroe was my mother.

His chest trembled as he took a deep breath. This discovery shook him to the core as well.

"I don't know how I'm supposed to feel right now," I murmured. "What . . . what do I do?"

"No one expects a lifetime of hurt to be untangled in a single afternoon. But we'll figure this out."

The emotions swirled again, and I squeezed my eyes shut. When I reopened them, the forest seemed dimmer. "All this time, she was out here building a new life with a new family. When I first started to read her letters, before the pieces had clicked into place, I felt compassion for her. But now, I just feel angry."

Claude nodded and rested his chin on the top of my head. "Do you remember when your dad wrote to you after being released from prison?"

"Yes."

"You didn't know how and what to feel then, either. But you gave him a chance, and look at the beautiful relationship it led to. Think of the years redeemed and the happy times we all had. It's almost like you're being allowed that now with your mother."

I scoffed. "Yeah, great timing. She doesn't even remember who I am."

"By the sound of it, you're the only one she does remember."

My heart lodged in my throat. I felt as though I was on a collapsing suspension bridge, too far in to turn back now, not that I could anyhow. My only choice was to forge forward, to trust that I would make it to the other side. But what waited for me ahead?

"How can I have a relationship with her now? She's too far gone, Claude."

"You're starting to sound like Tenn."

I hated that he was right.

"There's still a soul in there, Kitty. Maybe dementia has claimed part of her, but she's still your mother. At the very least, *you* can make peace."

I broke free from his arms to study his face. Did he really think there was something to salvage between the two of us?

"Of all the places, how did we end up here? How did I wind up bumping into my *mother* outside of a bookshop?"

"There are no coincidences with God."

"It's the only way to explain it, isn't it?"

"How else? It's easy to forget how deeply He cares for us, but He hears our cries and listens to our prayers, even from long ago. He heard your mother's, and He heard yours. Maybe it's not on your perfect timeline, but He still brought the two of you back together again."

I shivered against the breeze. "This changes everything, doesn't it?"

"Does it, though?" he questioned, and it made me falter.

Did it?

"I have something for you." Claude pulled a slip of paper from his pocket and handed it to me. "By the time you left the room, I could already tell where your mind was heading. Joy was confused and rightfully worried when you didn't return. But she read the last few letters in the pile and thought you'd like to read them too."

The pages shook in my hand as I worked to unfold them, but in my trembling, the breeze took advantage, whisking them from my grasp. My fingertips reached and snatched one from the air immediately, but the other was traveling as a hostage toward the brook's encouraging call. I stumbled after it, Claude at my heels, and watched as the page fell toward the earth in a roller-coaster plummet. It landed on the bank, the bottom edge submerged.

I scooped it up and used Claude as a crutch to catch my breath before laying the page flat on a log. Only the signature at the bottom of the page had been kissed by the stream. The name *Magnolia* bled down the page.

"Magnolia?" I felt her in there somewhere.

"Read it," Claude said.

I looked up at him. "Have you read it already too?"

"No. I thought you should first."

My body trembled beyond my control, and I wondered if I'd be able to see the scrawl on the page at all. Claude stooped down, wiped my tears with the pad of his thumb, and said, "This doesn't change who you are. You, Kitty May Fisher, can do this."

My chin quivered, but I managed to nod. "Okay," I whispered and gathered my strength—His strength. My husband was right; none of this changed who I was. There was nothing outside of Him that determined my identity.

I drew a breath and began to read out loud:

"'Joy splashes across the babbling brook that winds through our batch of forest. It's shady here, though the sun peeks through splinters and windows of branches above, illuminating small pockets of light on the forest's floor. Joy has been jumping from one to the next.

She's steady on her feet now. No longer does she need me for sturdiness, no longer is she reaching for my hand for comfort. She strides forward confidently. Even as the waters nip at her ankles, she balances on the slippery rocks at the bottom of the brook with ease.

She's getting out now, though it won't be for long, I'm sure. I'm sitting on the bank with my paper and pen, writing. Baby Constance is strapped against my bosom, fast asleep. Something has been brewing in my heart lately, and finally, feels as though it's brimming to the top. And I only realize it in totality now as I watch my daughter giggle and race alongside the stream with a leaf that's floating away.

A week ago, in this sanctuary of sorts, Joy spotted a deer upstream through the trees. Her shrieking excitement scared it away rather quickly, but I knew it had been thirsting for the cool waters that Joy is back to splashing in now. My soul has been panting with the same desperation as the doe's, with the need for living waters that will quench my parched soul.

I smile as I feel my heart turn to You. Finally. I have been running, hiding, turning every which way aside from toward You, shriveling into a heart so stale and dying. But now, I feel You. Now, I long for You. I want more. Can I just bask in Your goodness? Can I surrender myself to Your presence?

It's a desperate and irrefutable need I have to know You, to feel You, and I wonder at the miraculous words that detail Your care for me, Your will that I should desire You, and Your steadfast desire for me. You care for me in such a way? In spite of my failings? You know who I am. You know my faults, the depths of my sins. And somehow, You still love me? You still forgive me? Oh, how I want to know You more. To get a never-ending fill of Your sweet love, of the waters that quench thirst.

I don't know how to reconcile all of this. I don't know how to make it right. But You do. Somehow, You will. And Lord, You must know I am willing. That I desire it so! And You know that I long to protect my family in the process, for to hurt them would devastate us all. It's the last thing I want. So, You must orchestrate this. You must bring the pieces together and show me how and grow me in patience as You do.

Thank you for Your tender, loving kindness, Your mercy. I pray and hope with all my being that all my children experience the same. That they know You in spite of me. That from the wounds I've caused, You have created something of beauty.

Continue to comfort my sad heart, to show me that joy can still be found, for though I am suffering, little Joy deserves my joy. And Constance too. I don't want to fail either of them or the ones to come. I want to be the best mother I can be, to prove that I can do this and that it is only because of You that I do.

I will never leave them or this family that Tenn and I are building. I won't. I will be committed and faithful, but show me, Oh God, how to recompense for the past, how to unravel this tangled web, and how to do it gently for all involved.

I trust You with all the details, and I feel You asking me to let this rest. Work Your will, Lord. If I must suffer for the answer to be brought to light, so be it. But protect my family—both of my families. Please let Jeb and Kitty know how very sorry I am. And how very good You are.

It is time I stop walking as Lia and be the Maggy that Tenn knows me as. For the sake of all involved.

But as You know me,

Magnolia'"

The pages shuddered in my hands, and my mind went numb, like it was protecting me or, rather, shutting down. Claude touched my back, a reminder that I was still alive.

"Lia," I whispered to him. "That was my mother's name. Well, a shortened version of it, apparently."

He took my shaking body in his arms. "Come on. Let's get you inside."

42

1950
Goldfield, Nevada

LIFE HAD A way of changing in the blink of an eye. For better or for worse, like the promises in marriage vows heard around the world. The hard times wouldn't last forever, nor would the good. Things would change, slowly or quickly, on scales large or small. And in a blur of events penned by the Divine Author of her life, what began as an impossible journey had developed into a tale only before read in fairytales.

A life thrived inside of her, under the layers of lace and silk that now concealed her belly. *Married.* She was getting married. That is, unless her heart burst before the evening ceremony had time to commence. So much had changed in a short amount of time. She'd left the darkness of Peggy's home for the room offered by Ginny and Leonard. Specifically, Claude's room—the very one she found herself in now. Once Ginny and Len had accepted the news that Kitty was pregnant and that Claude intended on marrying her and raising the child as his own, they welcomed her with open arms. Claude moved next door in the interim to Kitty's vacant childhood home and worked on fixing it up to be their first home. They would officially move into it together tonight. Their wedding night.

"I've never seen anyone more stunning," Margaret declared with a clap of her hands.

"You truly are," Ada said as she reached up and cupped Kitty's cheek in her palm. "And it has nothing to do with the dress, I assure you."

"This is more than I ever could have dreamed," Kitty said, her eyes landing on each of the women who'd worked to bring her dress to life: Ada, Margaret, Edna, Jane, Matilda, and Beulah. "Thank you for this."

"Oh, honey," Edna replied. "It's our pleasure."

"Claude's become like family to us, which makes you family now too." Margaret pulled her into a hug so tight Kitty feared it would pop a few seams.

The ladies of *Wilted and Quilted* buzzed around Kitty, taking one final look at her in the wedding dress they'd adoringly crafted over the span of a week without notice. The women weren't staying for the small, discreet wedding but had stopped by the Fisher home to see Kitty in her final bridal ensemble. They passed along their compliments and congratulations one more time before Ginny walked the women to the door.

Kitty, now alone, took a deep breath. She moved to the window where she and Claude had held many private late-night meetings as kids. Usually when her father was passed out or on a bender, she'd tiptoe out of her home and wake Claude. He'd kneel beside this very window and tell her stories, made up or true, and help the night pass and the pain to pass, too.

She peered out, unable to see her old and soon-to-be new home around the corner. Instead, she watched the sun glide toward the horizon an inch more. She stepped away and ran her hands over the beautiful dress that fell perfectly over her. It was the novelty of the soft fabric brushing against her legs that made Kitty smile as she twirled like she used to as a young girl in a sundress. She paused and caught her reflection in the mirror that Leonard had set up for her to use in the room. In the chaos of getting ready and having so many women scrunched into the small space, she hadn't had the proper chance to really look at herself.

She took her own breath away.

One hand moved to her soft, flowing curls and the other moved to the pearls around her neck, but what really caught her eyes was the peace she saw staring back at her. A knock at the door startled her. "Come in," she called.

It was Ginny returning.

"Everything is all set up out there. Pastor James just arrived."

Every cell in Kitty's body quivered with anticipation. *Was this really happening?*

When Ginny had come home from her months-long trip assisting Cliff and Maisy with their newborn twin boys, Kitty divulged everything, from the suspected and unexpected pregnancy to the intentions she and Claude had made clear to one another. It was all a shock to Ginny, of course. Kitty was well aware of the return crash landing she'd made into the Fisher family's lives. They all had every right to politely shut the door on her, and yet, as the tendrils of her heart reached for their support, they each graciously offered it tenfold, in lengths she never expected.

Ginny wiped her eyes and reached for Kitty's hand. "I've always thought of you as one of my own."

Kitty's eyes moistened. Her place in the world had never felt more concrete. "Well, now it will be official."

"I'm so glad you came back home, sweetheart."

Ginny was a marvel. The years had been gentle to her, though her gray eyes wore the sheen of exhaustion. Taking care of others was her life's role, no matter how taxing. But it was clear that Ginny's strength came from a source outside of her own self.

"Thank you," Kitty said. "For being better to me than I ever deserved." She felt the words balloon inside her, reaching a place higher than she intended. As easy as it had been to doubt God's presence in her life, she undeniably felt it now. "Is Claude ready?"

Ginny's lips quivered as she nodded. "Are you kidding? He was born ready for this."

Kitty laughed. "This is really happening, isn't it?"

"I think it always was." Ginny squeezed her hand. "Kitty?"

"Yeah?"

"Do you know who you are?"

The question caught her off guard. But for once, she was beginning to understand, to feel the truth in the words Claude had read to her from his Bible, to feel the truth in the actions that the Fisher family had demonstrated over the course of her life.

She was more than the daughter of two great sinners, more than the sins of her own life. She was more than a victim of unfortunate circumstances, more than even a mother and soon-to-be wife. She was the unconditionally loved daughter of the Most High.

"I think I do," she finally answered.

"Good. Come to me if you ever need to be reminded, sweetheart."

Another knock came. This time it was Leonard.

"What's the status out there?" Ginny asked.

"Close to being ready."

Kitty swallowed hard and imagined the humble scene assembling in the living room. For a quick moment, she wondered what it would be like to have someone from her family out there. Her mother, her father, her aunt . . . anyone at all who cared enough.

"Mind if I have a moment alone with the bride?" Leonard asked.

"Certainly." Ginny kissed him on the cheek on her way out.

"You look beautiful, Kitty," he said.

"Thank you." She briefly glanced at the mirror. "Thank you for everything."

"Thank *you*," he said.

"For what?"

"Being you." He pulled the chair from under the desk and sat down. Kitty followed suit, carefully perching herself on the side of the bed. "Not every dad gets the privilege of knowing his future daughter-in-law for all of her life."

"I could say the same," she said.

The comment made him smile. "You've always cared for my son. No one's ever quite"—his voice cracked—"managed to make him light up like you. And I know I can safely say the reverse is also true."

A tear found its way from her eye and down her cheek. Leonard handed her a handkerchief, and she carefully dabbed at her face. She had a thousand words she wished to say to him. *"You've been a dad to me . . . Claude is just like you with your unwavering strength and loving nature . . . You should be proud of the son you've raised . . . It's an honor to be walking down the aisle on your arm . . ."* But she knew that lurking tears were vying for their chance to escape, and opening her mouth again would only unlatch the gate.

Leonard stared down at his clasped hands for a moment, and Kitty saw a tear fall to his skin. It seemed as though he was in a similar conundrum as her, and so they sat in silence, speaking a thousand words without having to say them at all.

Finally, he stood and extended one of his weathering hands to her and lifted her to her feet. He wrapped her in a hug.

"Len?" she whispered.

He pulled back. "Yeah?"

Tears gathered in her eyes, and she struggled to keep them back. He looked into her gleaming eyes and patted her shoulders. "I know, sweetheart."

She nodded, thankful that he could hear her heart.

"Are you ready to do this?" He righted himself and held out his arm.

She looped her arm in his. Her stomach squeezed, and her hands shook, but still, she said, "Yes. I'm ready."

Leonard slowly opened the door, hoping the noise would alert the gathered audience that the ceremony was about to begin. He poked his head out first, then ducked back into the room, saying to Kitty, "You'll still marry Fly even if he's peed his pants, won't you?"

She laughed out loud, thankful for the joke. "You don't think Ginny would mind doing his laundry just once more, do you?"

He grinned. "We'll ask her later."

They moved through the doorway and into the hall. In the living room ahead stood Claude. He adjusted his feet and pulled back his strong shoulders. His dark suit gave him the air of a budding silver screen star, as did his golden-brown hair styled in a quiff. He locked eyes with her, and reality cemented itself into her being.

This was real life. For better or for worse. But no matter what, for always. It was a feeling sought after by many but not always found. The feeling of forever, of peace, of home. The feeling of God's hand joining theirs together. It was the feeling of family.

43

1981
Galia, Oregon

AN ETERNITY CHUGGED by as I waited for Joy to respond. She sat in her mother's rocking chair, her gaze fixed out the window. I held her blameless. How was anyone supposed to accept such news? But despite her lack of response, I knew my words reached her, so I continued.

"The common theme in your mother's words has been the remorse and conviction that stemmed from her making a bad decision. It's evident that she left more than one person behind."

Joy gave a faint nod without turning from the view outside. I handed her the telegram.

"Your mother addressed this to a 'J. Ralph' in Goldfield, Nevada, correct?"

Another nod.

"Joy." I could feel a tremble building in my voice. I swallowed it away. "My maiden name is Kitty Ralph. My father was Jeb Ralph. And we were from Goldfield, Nevada . . .”

I spoke words I could never have foreseen myself speaking. Of my parents arriving in Nevada on the promise of a second gold rush and the disappointment that ensued. Of my mother fleeing and becoming the source of my questions and pain throughout my life. I picked up the photograph of the man holding the baby.

“You don’t recognize this man, but the moment I looked at the photo, I felt his familiarity. And I think that’s because this man is my father.”

“And you’re the baby he’s holding?”

I stared at the photograph again, this time with more scrutiny than before. The face structure, the dark hair, the squint of his eyes . . . all the evidence of my father was there. The only thing that left room for uncertainty was the photo’s lack of quality.

“Claude?”

He’d been waiting outside the room, giving Joy and I space to come to terms with the discovery. But he came within a moment, and I handed him the photo.

“What do you think? Is that my dad?”

Claude studied it. Of all the people in this world, there was a time he hated my father the most. And who could blame him? My dad was the catalyst to everything falling apart. He had taken so much from all of us with his selfish, hurting heart. A heart cut open by the woman I’d spent the last few hours with by means of her letters. But yet, my father had found redemption, walking as a new creation, his purpose directed away from whiskey bottles and sin. And Claude forgave him. As time passed, we all unlearned our brokenness, relearning how to love one another with fresh, willing hearts. He and Claude had been able to come together and find solid ground, the foundation being Christ.

Finally, Claude returned the photo and said, “If I had to

definitively guess one way or another, I would say yes, that's Jeb."

Me and my dad at a time when my family was still together, and the future was still at our collective fingertips. Dad looked happy and optimistic, like he was on the verge of discovering a gold mine. But there would be no striking it rich, no happy new beginnings, but instead unproductive mines and a flight-risk wife.

Silence stretched. The rocking chair creaked, and I realized that Joy was looking at me.

"You look like her," she said. "I never quite saw it before, but now, it's all I can see."

She rose and searched through the family photographs that had been removed from the walls until she found one of her mother.

"She looks about your age in this one," Joy said and held it next to my face. Her eyes darted back and forth. "The shape of your eyes, the rosebud lips, the chin shape . . . It's no wonder she trusted you from the moment she met you. You look like a younger version of herself."

"Or maybe she sensed something all along," Claude wondered aloud.

Did she know me deep inside, even now?

Joy showed me the photograph. "Don't you agree you look alike?"

I hadn't given the photographs more than a passing glance as I'd wiped and packed them away earlier. But now, I looked with fresh eyes.

My mother's face stared back at me, youthful and full. Breast-length, soft curls fell over her shoulders. A smile warmed her face. The Maggy I knew from Thimbleberry had plenty of wrinkles, the carvings evident of a life lived, and white hair shorn to her ears. But in this picture, and even in the Maggy I knew, I could see it . . . I could see . . . me.

"And so, this locket . . ." Joy toyed with it in her hands. "She carried you inside at some point and had even thought to hide it away. But when? And why? I can recall her wearing this when I was a child. I remember opening it and looking at the small pictures inside. Never was there anything in that fourth space before."

"That picture wasn't taken until 1950 or printed in the newspaper until 1960."

"How would she have obtained a random photo from a 1960's newspaper back home?" Claude asked.

"Well, she got her hands on it somehow," Joy said. "And obviously hid the locket away once Kitty's photo was inserted."

Part of me recoiled at having been a hidden secret all my life, and yet, another part took to the sky like a kid whose drawing made it onto the fridge.

"But the question is, when was it removed? Mom must have taken it out for some reason before she left for Thimbleberry, maybe even the facility before that. Wait." Joy's face went white.

"What is it?"

"In her letters, she . . . said things about going to jail if her secret were uncovered. If she left you and your dad out of nowhere, does that mean divorce papers were never formally filed?"

"Not to my knowledge, but that doesn't mean anything."

"It means she would have been committing bigamy this entire time."

"And your parents' marriage would be void."

Her chest caved, and she let out an audible breath. "I'm going to have to tell my father."

"Tell me what?"

We all jumped at Tenn's sudden appearance, and I felt the urge to run. He glanced at the mess of papers and picture frames and frowned at the way we stood with pale faces and stooped shoulders. He straightened his own posture and crossed his arms over his chest. "Tell me what? What's going on?"

"Dad . . ." Joy's voice shook.

"What?" His voice was cold and defensive, like he was already preparing himself for the worst.

"We should move to the sitting room. We have a lot to discuss."

Over the next hour, we shared our discovery with Tenn, presenting the facts and the evidence like attorneys in a courtroom. When we finished, Tenn's eyes were red and rimmed with tears. He started to speak once but failed, the anguish too raw. He held up a finger as though to say, "*Give me a moment,*" and then left the room. He returned with an envelope.

"I'd always known that the past haunted her. She was running from something. I knew it from the first moment I laid eyes on her. She was guarded, dodgy, but I didn't pry. I had things in my past I wasn't too proud of either. But I figured she'd tell me one day if it were that pressing. We fell in love, got married, moved from California to here. She was good to me. To our whole family. The best wife and mother, doting and caring and present. I thought she was happy."

He smacked the envelope against his knee and continued.

"A year or two ago, I found this beneath our bed. It's a . . ." He shook his head in disbelief. "It's a letter from a private investigator giving her information about a woman named Kitty." He glanced at me. "It's dated twenty years or so ago. When I found it, I first thought it was some weird mistake, but I couldn't really ask Maggy about it because, by that point, she was too far gone."

He slid the letter from the envelope and showed us. Something small fluttered from within the trifold. He bent to pick it up from the floor.

"Is that a scrap of newspaper?" I asked, reaching.

He handed it over. I searched for the locket amongst the pile of evidence we'd just presented and, from it, withdrew my photo. I smoothed out the creases and placed it within the original article where it belonged. There Claude and I were, together again in old newsprint. I felt a sob build inside.

She'd never let go.

Joy read a portion of the letter from the investigator out loud. " *'Lia, by what my search has turned up, Kitty is happy and healthy and married with children of her own. Hope this gives you peace.'* Wait. Lia? When did Mom ever go by Lia?"

"She didn't." Tenn looked like a statue in his wingback chair, and I knew reality was crumbling around him.

"Lia only existed in the past, in the form of my mother. Maggy hadn't been born until she met Tenn," I said.

"Maggy. Magnolia. Lia." Joy slowly rubbed her temples and groaned.

"She called me by the wrong name a few times," Tenn said quietly. "When I found that letter, it made sense why. I thought her dementia had turned her into someone I didn't know anymore. Turns out, I never really knew her at all."

44

Fall, 1950
Goldfield, Nevada

THE EDGE OF the letter peeked out from under a haphazardly thrown sweater on the dresser top. It seemed to float through the newlywed's house and follow Kitty everywhere, constantly reminding her of what was to come. The wind beat against the house, and Kitty glanced at the clock hanging on the wall as she entered their bedroom. Not that Ginny and Leonard would make a fuss, but she and Claude were already ten minutes late for dinner at their house.

Kitty grabbed her sweater from the dresser, and the letter rode a ribbon of air as it drifted to the floor. She bent down and picked it up, her pregnant belly not yet large enough to hinder her. She'd read the letter enough times that she could recite it by memory if she were asked. But were the penned words steeped in truth? That, she did not yet know.

She donned her sweater and tucked the letter into her pocket in case she decided to show Claude's parents at dinner. Her father wasn't often the subject of conversation, but tonight, there was news that needed to be shared.

"I'm ready," she announced to Claude as she stepped into the living room.

"Great." His smile wavered as he looked at her. He closed the Bible that had been splayed open on his lap and stood. "You okay?"

Kitty thought of the letter tucked into her pocket and the conversation to come that she knew would stir up the past. "I hope so."

The warm wind reminiscent of a sad autumn long ago whipped Kitty's long, sandy hair in front of her face as they walked from their home to Claude's parents' next door. They let themselves in without a knock and were greeted with the smell of roast as soon as they stepped inside.

"I was starting to wonder if you two newlyweds were going to show or not," Ginny quipped as she set a plate on the table. "Come on, take your seat. I'm dishing up."

Leonard's chair screeched as he pulled it out. "Claude, I was thinking about another fishing trip next weekend if you're up for it?"

Claude sat and looked at his father, whose warm eyes so closely mirrored his own. Claude shook his head and cast a glance at Kitty as she took her seat beside him. "Sorry. We've got plans. How about the next?"

"Oh, doin' anything fun?" Ginny set the final plate on the table.

Kitty knew the time to discuss the matter at hand would come, but she didn't anticipate it coming so soon. She opened her mouth, but Claude beat her to it.

"I'm taking Kitty to Reno for a few days."

Was he trying to protect her as he always was? Or was he, too, scared of breaking the news to his family?

She scooted her chair in a smidge and looked down at the plate of roast, carrots, and potatoes in front of her. "Actually, we're going to visit my dad."

The lull in the air was nearly undetectable.

"Oh?" Leonard dipped his chin gravely, as though the small nod were permission granted. "Claude mentioned that he'd finished serving his sentence."

"Yeah," Kitty said uneasily. "He got out a bit early even. Not that . . . Not that he should have, because you know, with . . ."

"Kitty." Ginny reached across the table and rested a hand on Kitty's wrist. "It's okay."

"But we're going to see him, and . . . you know, I'm just still so sorry for everything."

"You don't have to justify your reasons for wanting to go. You're his daughter." Ginny patted Kitty's hand, then pulled hers away. "And you don't have to apologize for him or carry his burdens anymore. They were never yours to begin with."

Leonard nodded his head in agreement. "We love you, Kitty. You're our daughter. Really, you always have been. And in fact,"—he locked eyes with his wife—"we've forgiven Jeb."

"How do you all do it?" Kitty's voice was small.

"How do we forgive?" Ginny asked.

"Yes."

Leonard cleared his throat. "Kitty, if there's anything we've learned from Vern's death, it's how badly we all need God." He took a breath and laced his fingers together in front of his lips. "Speaking for myself, I didn't prioritize God like I should have most of my life. I had faith, sure, but losing Vern sank me back to my knees, a place I hadn't been for a long time, and I was reminded that without God, there's nothing. No hope. No redemption. No forgiveness."

"I feel the same way," Ginny said.

"So do I." Claude rested a warm palm on her thigh, and she looked at him. When her eyes reached his, she felt a stir in her stomach, something unrelated to hunger or a growing baby, like her heart was using her abdomen as a springboard for a gymnastics routine, and she suddenly felt the answer speak into her bones.

"The more I'm figuring this whole thing out," Claude glanced at his parents, then back to her, "the more I realize that this life isn't about me anymore." He squeezed her thigh. "It's about serving and showing Christ to others. And how can I do that if I'm holding onto anger?"

Leonard lifted his fork. "Our inability to forgive does nothing to share Him with those who need Him most."

Kitty felt these truths swirl within her, as part of her now as the microscopic cells that streamed within her veins. She wiped her eyes. "I want to forgive . . . I want to be fully . . . free. I want my dad to be, too."

Maybe, she thought, he could find freedom. The only way she'd ever known her father was as a man who stumbled in late and couldn't hold down a job, who laughed at anything that evoked emotion or appreciation for life. He'd been distant and unavailable, wallowing so deeply in his own hurting heart that he didn't care that he was hurting her. Yet, while his calls from prison had never amounted to any fruitful conversations, there was no longer a slur to his words or a stumble in his voice. In his recent letter expressing apologies, she'd detected no lurching of his penmanship, no sign of drunkenness on the page. He was sober now and proclaiming to be different.

Maybe freedom was in the cards for both of them after all.

Leonard wrapped an arm around her shoulder and said, "I know. We all want that too."

"I think if your dad can learn to be honest about things, he'll find that freedom," Ginny said.

"What do you mean? Honest about what?"

"We can't expect God to heal us if we're guarding our wounds," she said. "It's like with any injury, you don't want anyone else to touch it, right? You want to guard it and protect yourself from further pain. But if you don't remove the splinters and stitch the wound shut, you won't heal. If we don't expose our wounds to the only One who can bring true healing, they're going to fester all of our lives."

"Well, let's pray my dad can do exactly that, then."

"How about we pray right now and then get to eating before the food gets cold?" Ginny winked and held out her hands to say grace.

45

1981
Galia, Oregon

"GINNY. IT'S ME."

The voice of the only woman who ever mothered me instantly soothed my nerves. It wasn't a voice that made me want to cry. It was a voice that made me strong. A voice that reminded me of sacrifice and love and resilience. I pictured her puttering around Maisy's kitchen, stretching the cord of the phone, her morning coffee in hand, smiling like her home hadn't just burned to the ground.

"Are you alright, dear?" Her voice had grown thin over the years. "You sound sad."

Only a real mother could tell such a thing.

"That's because I am. I'm . . . a lot of things all at once, and I don't exactly know how to even begin sorting them out."

"What's going on? Are you both okay?"

I already knew I'd stumble over all the words but trusted that

Ginny would decipher the message, that she'd find the thread, however bare, that linked directly to my heart. So, I drew a deep breath, the minutes of our long-distance call practically ticking in my ear and began.

When I'd finished, I was completely spent, and Ginny was silent enough to the point that I questioned our phone connection.

"I'm here," she said. Then, finally, "Kitty, when you believed that Maggy, the sweet stranger with an incurable disease, had written the letters, what were your feelings when reading?"

I'd been strangled with sadness. "I wanted to understand her, to keep reading and find the source of her pain. I felt compassion. I felt grief."

"In her own words, did you ever doubt her sincerity? This pain you just described to me in the letters?"

"No."

"I can't tell you what to do, honey, but it's clear that you have remained a part of your mother throughout her entire life. I think we as people dig ourselves into holes that seem insurmountable. We're so deep in that we stay stuck, trapped, so blinded by the glare of our sin that got us there that we can't see the hand reaching down into the hole to pull us out.

"Yes, your mother put herself in that hole. And the reasons sound like they run deeper than a generation. For a long time, you were trapped in a hole of your own. But God reached in and lifted you out, right?"

I pressed the phone into my ear. I didn't want to miss a word. "Yes."

"And He did that for your mother too?"

My voice wobbled. "Her letters were filled with prayer and longing. She seemed to have found Him, yes."

Ginny took a moment to reply. "When we cry with a pure heart to God, He hears our prayers every time, and His answer always comes. Sometimes immediately, in the form of a yes or a no. But sometimes, it takes a long time as He strategically moves the pieces into play. It seems like your mother finally got her prayers answered, didn't she?"

"It makes me wonder, why now? After all this time, now that Dad is gone? Now that she can't recognize me? Why now?"

"That's not a question for this side of Heaven. But you can rest in knowing that His timing never fails. Are you going to see her again?"

"Do you think I should?"

"I think you already know the answer to that deep down."

Claude tapped me on the shoulder. "Donna was just at the door for you," he whispered. "She said you have a visitor downstairs."

"Who?"

"Joy."

Dread filled my core. "Okay. Ginny, I have to go. Thank you for your advice."

"I love you, baby," she said.

"I love you too."

I hung up the phone and moved robotically to the door, my mind as heavy as the fog. Claude followed me.

"Do you want me to come with you?"

"Whatever it is, I think this is something I have to do alone."

He opened the door for me, and I walked over the threshold. "It's all going to be okay," he said.

I turned to face him. Deep down, I could feel God stitching hope into my heart. I knew the light was coming. It always did.

"Tell your sister hello for me," he said as he slowly closed the door.

I rolled my eyes.

"Tell her she's a little late on the holiday cards."

"Stop it."

"Oh, and the wedding gifts," he said through the narrowing crack.

I smiled. "Will you just wish me luck already?"

"Who needs luck when you have God?"

I found Joy downstairs sitting in an armchair next to the bookcases, a magazine balanced on her crossed knee, her sunglasses perched atop her freshly styled hair. A breeze blew in through the open windows. I sank into the armchair beside her.

"Kitty." Her voice broke, and she tossed the magazine aside. "How are you?"

"All things considered, I'm doing okay. How are you?"

"Rattled. Confused. But somehow okay, too." Her lips pulled into a thin line. "I have something for you." She handed over a manila envelope. "The pictures of you and your dad, the letters Mom wrote explicitly for you. We . . . we figured you should have them."

I smoothed my hand over the envelope. "Thank you. How did it go with your dad after we left last night?"

Her eyes grew distant. "Not well." She dropped her face into her hands.

I placed a hand on her back. "This is probably the wildest news any of us could ever have imagined, but when darkness is brought into the light, we should rejoice. I mean, I always wanted a sister. Do your siblings know yet?"

Joy lifted her head and looked at me. "They're yours now too."

I hadn't considered Joy's brother and sister. That was a new idea to wrap my head around.

"But no," she said. "We haven't told them yet. We're having a family meeting this weekend. When do you leave?"

"Tomorrow."

Her forehead crinkled. "Would you consider coming by Thimbleberry one last time before you go?"

My breathing slowed. If I said no, it would mean never seeing my mother again. Joy waited, and I traced the edges of the manila envelope. Finally, I nodded and said yes.

247

46

1951
Goldfield, Nevada

KITTY STROKED THE swirl of Lorraine's dark brown hair. She ran a finger down her soft, unblemished cheek. Lorraine sucked in a breath, a sleepy smile curling at her tiny lips, and fell deeper into slumber aside Kitty's breast.

Kitty breathed in the intoxicating scent of motherhood. As she reveled in the weight of Lorraine in her arms, a log all bundled with muslin blankets and innocence, she pondered on the thought of leaving. Not on her own urge to leave but on her mother's.

"I will never leave you," Kitty sang quietly. "You'll never ever be alone."

A light flicked on in the hallway. Claude. He padded into the living room, finding Kitty in the rocking chair. She gave him a nod, her tired eyes just wanting to close. Claude bent down and kissed her on the cheek.

"What are you doing up, honey?"

He didn't respond but leaned over Kitty to watch their sleeping infant. The one he claimed as his own. "How's our girl?" he asked.

Our girl. No one else's but ours.

"She just fell back to sleep," Kitty murmured.

"Think she'll stir if you pass her to me?"

"We can try."

Claude held out his arms and cradled Lorraine in them. She barely moved as she settled into him. He stepped toward the couch and sat down. Barely adults, the two of them only nineteen, Kitty felt they'd lived a lifetime already. She moved from her rocking chair and joined him at his side, curling her legs beneath her.

"Your dad is in for a real treat when he meets her today, isn't he?"

Kitty rested against him. Today was the day Jeb would return to Goldfield for the first time since Vern's death. She hadn't expected him to ever set foot in town again. Yet his willingness to face the destruction he'd left in his wake showed how far he had come. How far the Lord had brought him.

"Anyone who meets her is," Kitty answered.

"Do you want to go rest? I've got her."

Kitty nestled into the side of his bicep. "How about I rest right here?"

"Even better."

She closed her eyes and felt the pull of sleep. She didn't know how this day, not yet even dawned, would work out. A million scenarios fluttered through her mind of her father stepping back into this home, meeting Lorraine, seeing Ginny and Leonard again.

Whatever happened, she knew that everything would be okay.

47

1981
Galia, Oregon

I WATCHED HER walk and heard the tiny mutterings under her breath as she clutched the plastic, baby doll version of me to her chest.

The first human I ever knew. The first who ever knew me. But she hadn't stayed long enough to get to know this version of me. It was paradoxical to see my own flesh and blood moving in front of me. For so long, I'd wondered about her. And come to find out, she had been wondering about me as well. But it was too late—time and disease had not been our friend. What had we left? In her mind now, she had reconciled with me. In her mind now, she had never left. She had her baby Kitty, and that's where she lived and perhaps would for the remainder of her life.

What a mercy.

But what about me? What did I have? As I watched her hands move shakily across the wall, searching for unhung pictures, I saw that this tiny sliver of a mother was still my mother. And this was my opportunity to face a lifetime worth of reverberating pain. I thought of the way she'd robbed Dad of the optimism she'd described him as having, how she'd stolen his time away from me.

But my dad was his own person, too, responsible for his actions and behavior. Being a grandfather to my children made him express how he regretted squandering away my youth. I didn't hold it against him forever, though. Couldn't. Otherwise, I would have been no better than him. But could I hold it against my mother forever?

This was all we had.

But was it enough?

"I have so many questions that she can't answer," Joy whispered beside me.

This news rocked Joy's world as much as my own. And to be honest, it felt good to not be facing it alone. Although we lived in different worlds and knew this woman pacing down the hall in entirely different capacities, we were entwined forever, and each had to deal with this separately and yet together.

"I know. I wish I could just walk up to her and tell her who I am."

Claude, standing on my other side, squeezed my hand. "You can."

I could, I realized. Whether she understood the words or not. Whether she recognized me or not. Whether she accepted me or not. I still had the opportunity.

I dropped Claude's hand and moved down the hall.

"Hi, Magnolia," I said softly.

She looked at me with an upturned face.

I pointed to the baby doll she held. "What's your baby's name?"

She smiled down at the doll then looked back at me. "Kitty."

She regarded me with such sincerity I felt my chest crack, and in the way she looked at me, I could see it too. What Joy saw. Save for a few features and the markings of age, I saw myself in her.

"That's a beautiful name," I said. I knew these words wouldn't fall on receptive ears, but I drew in a breath and, through strength I couldn't claim as mine, said, "My name is Kitty, too. I'm actually *your* Kitty. I'm . . . your daughter."

Maggy watched tears gather in my eyes, though no miraculous breakthrough happened on her end. But still, she understood empathy and reached out to comfort me with a silent touch. Footsteps fell behind me, and Claude stopped at my side.

"And this is my husband, Claude."

She followed my gesture toward him and said hello as though she were meeting any random person in the world. He held out his hand, and she gently shook it.

"Nice to finally meet you, Maggy."

"Mom," Joy said, joining us.

The word jostled me, and I mulled it over in my mouth, letting my lips part and silently come back together. How would it feel to say it out loud? To call someone the name I'd only heard myself called by my own four children.

Whether Maggy recognized Joy or not, she gave Joy her attention.

"Do you remember a man named"—her eyes caught mine—"Jeb Ralph?"

Maggy absently shook her head, and Joy sighed.

"I don't want to ask her a zillion questions. I think it will only frustrate all of us."

"That's fine," I said. I wasn't expecting any answers. We already knew the truth, could feel it in our bones, in the very DNA that we both shared.

"But let's see if the locket breaks a memory loose." Joy

dangled the necklace before Maggy, instantly catching her eye. She reached for it and cradled the locket in her palm.

"This is very pretty," she said. Her eyes softened with admiration. She looked up at Joy. "Is this yours?"

Joy's smile faltered. The memories were gone. "No, not mine."

My mother's eyes shifted to mine, staring for a moment. I longed to call her by her title. But the word wouldn't quite come.

"Is it yours?" she asked.

"Not mine, either."

"Oh, you're back!" Abbi's voice rang from the top of the hall. I turned to see her standing behind her walker, her fiery red hair glowing in Thimbleberry's soft light. It looked even brighter than the last time I saw her.

"Of course I am. I couldn't leave without saying goodbye. I also have some news for you." I glanced at Joy.

"News? What news?" Abbi said.

"Go ahead and tell her," Joy said. "I don't think I can talk through it all again yet."

Claude handed me the manila envelope he'd been holding for me and went to find the twins while I followed Abbi to her room. Before sitting in one of her chairs that threatened to swallow me whole again, I asked for access to Abbi's drawer. I pulled out the last remaining pieces to the puzzle.

"Don't tell me you've solved this mystery?" Her red lips parted in wonder as I laid the items on the bed.

"I need to thank you, Abbi."

"Whatever for?"

Her knee jiggled as I handed her the photo from her stash, the one of the sleeping baby. I opened the manila envelope and took out the matching photograph from Maggy's house.

"They're identical." She looked at me with poorly lined eyebrows pitched to her hairline. "Where did you get this? And why are they the same?"

"Apparently, the owner had more than one copy. One she squirreled away and carried with her, and one she left behind for someone else to find."

"My old brain can't keep up with your riddles. Whose was this? Someone here?"

"It was my . . . mom's."

Abbi's face twisted. "What did I just tell you about riddles?"

I smiled and plunged into the story. When I finished, she stared, slack-jawed and eyes starry.

"So Maggy is . . . Oh, have mercy." Her hands moved over the letters and the photographs as though she could feel them speak. A minute ticked by. "This is unbelievable."

I still couldn't believe it myself and wondered if I ever would.

"These are the types of situations that will give you gray hair. Thank goodness for hair dye. Not that I would know anything about that," she muttered, and it made me smile. She passed my items back to me and patted my leg. "This is more than you bargained for, I'd imagine."

My head swam. I sharply inhaled. "Much more."

"I hope you treasure the answers you have." Her eyes gleamed with a sadness unreachable.

"What about you, Abbi?"

She leaned back a little, like her sadness needed space to grow. "Like I said before, I wasted it all away."

"Did you ever marry?"

She nodded. "I did. My first husband left me for someone a little younger, a little looser. My second husband was a franchise owner of a major league team dand had a heart attack five years into our marriage. He left me well taken care of, but I was lonely.

"After he passed, I grew a bone of bravery and went home, tail tucked. But my family no longer lived in my childhood home. The little girl living there was a sweetheart, though, and offered me a few things she'd found that the previous owners had mistakenly left behind: my sister's barrette and my mother's broach."

I felt a twinge of fear. "Did you find your family?"

"No. But I did learn that they'd hit hard times and folded on the house. Meanwhile, I'd been living lavishly, all the money I could want at my fingertips."

All traces of Abbi's whimsy were snuffed out. It broke my heart.

"And the barrette and broach?"

"I still have them in my drawer. I always thought that maybe if I held onto them, our paths would cross one day, and I could return them as an olive branch of sorts. But I know my folks are a long time gone. Maybe my sister by now too."

"Is that why these little mysteries matter so much to you?"

She let out a soft sigh. "I suppose that's why I hold onto these things I find and try to locate their owners. I always think of what reconciliation they could bring to someone . . . The kind I've hoped for all my life."

Her brokenness spilled over and filled the room.

"I'm glad someone was able to make amends," Abbi said quietly. "To think that all of this was borne from grief."

"Grief is fascinating in the way it both tears apart and unites us all."

Abbi looked at her window. A shadow of sadness passed over her drawn face. "Well, thank you for making me feel useful again."

"I can't take the credit. That's owed to God."

She let a puff of air escape through her lips.

"What? You don't have any faith?"

"Faith in my own ability to mess things up." She laughed. "If you're about to give me a sales pitch on some religious junk, I should have you know there's a no soliciting sign on my door.

You just can't see it."

"Because it's not actually there."

"It's invisible," she argued with a scowl. "God doesn't want anything to do with me. I've squandered away most of the gifts He gave me in order to follow my own selfish whims instead."

"Heaven isn't full of people who deserve to be there. It's full of broken people who've accepted His grace."

Abbi folded her hands in her lap and stared at me. "So, you think that by knowing Him, I might feel the fulfillment I've always desired?" There was a prickliness to her voice.

"Has anything else been able to sustain your heart for all your life and beyond?"

It took a moment for her to answer. "No." Her voice was small.

There was no way of knowing whether she would be receptive to my testimony, but I had no other choice. This was my only chance.

"I can only tell you what I know," I started. "I believed for a long time that I was unworthy and unlovable. But then I learned that a man—not just any man, mind you, but God in the flesh—was mocked, spat on, broken, and accused; humiliated and forced to physically carry the cross to which He would be mounted and murdered. And He did it . . . for me. He rose from the dead . . . for me. He sacrificed everything to give me life, to bridge the chasm between my broken self and the One who created me. That is how worthy I am. And that's how worthy you are, too.

"Once I accepted that, all the lies were silenced, the clogs of debris and sin washed away. I could finally take a real breath, knowing how loved I was and am. And the more I walk with Him, the more of Him my heart wants. And it's that way for everyone who drinks from His living waters. Even my own mother."

The ticking wall clock filled the space as I allowed her room to respond. When she said nothing and stared at her lap, I went on.

"You can't change the past, Abbi. What's done is done. But you can repent, and you can rest in His forgiveness and provision."

Her eyes remained fixated, but I saw the tremble of her chin. Maybe one day, I prayed, Abbi would feel the freedom of submission, of letting go and entrusting herself to her Maker.

I scooted closer to her on the bed and wrapped my arm around her. "Thank you for helping me find my mother. Maybe I'll find myself in your neck of the woods again one day. Now that I know I have family in the area."

A smile finally broke though like a piece clicked into place. She looked at me. "Joy's your sister, isn't she?"

"Half-sister, yes. And apparently, there are two more half-siblings that go along with her. Though, I don't think I'll be meeting them this trip. Perhaps one day. It's a lot for everyone to process for the time being."

She looked back at her hands. Guilt nibbled in my gut. I was living the reunion she'd dreamed of most her life. I didn't know what to do other than to hug her once again.

48

1962
Glenwood Springs, CO

ALAN HOPPED ONTO Jeb's back, his skinny arms wrapping around his grandpa's neck. Jeb roared and swung his body to the left, then to the right, until Alan swooped around into Jeb's arms. Lorraine squealed from the couch, where she jumped up and down alongside her little sister. Jeb gently tossed Al onto the cushions and scooped up Lorraine and Gloria in one go. He swung them around until their infectious giggles made him laugh so hard he had to stop.

"Dad!" Kitty gripped her pregnant belly as she laughed too. "You're going to make them pee their pants." *Or me,* she thought, the constant pressure on her bladder always on her mind.

He set the girls down then plopped onto the couch. Alan jumped onto his lap, still ready to fight. "Okay, okay, give your ol' grandpa a break for a minute." Jeb panted for breath.

Alan sprang to his feet and batted Gloria with a pillow,

which sent her crying. Jeb reached out and dragged him back, giving him a playful noogie. The phone rang, and Kitty struggled to her feet.

"Sit down," Jeb said, Alan squirming in his arms. "I'll get it."

"It's fine, Dad. I need to use the restroom anyway." She crossed the room and lifted the receiver. "Hello?" She pressed a finger to her other ear to drown out her noisy children and roaring father.

It was Maisy. "Do I have a niece or nephew yet?"

"Not yet."

"You're really *still* pregnant?"

Kitty looked down at her giant bump. "That, or I swallowed far too many watermelon seeds. How's that trip shaping up?"

"Cliff got the greenlight, so we'll be there next week. If I don't have a baby to snuggle by then, I won't be happy. Just warning ya."

The kids screamed louder, and Kitty heard one of them yell, "Dad!" She looked up in time to see Claude come through the door. It took less than a second for him to join in on the wrestling. Kitty pressed the phone harder into her ear and tugged the cord around the corner.

"If this baby hasn't come by then, I'm going to take him or her out myself."

Maisy's laughter rang through the commotion. "What on earth is going on over there? Are you having a party?"

"Chaos. Pure chaos."

"Cliff can only manage four days of leave. Are you still sure you don't mind me and the boys staying longer?"

"Are you kidding? We miss you all so much, and can't you hear that I need desperate help over here?"

"I think you need more than help." She laughed again. "Well, you'd best tell Fly to call as soon as you go into labor, okay? I want to know."

"At this rate you might be here when I do."

The volume in the living room continued to rise to the point Kitty could barely hear her sister-in-law anymore. "I've gotta go," she shouted into the phone. "If you can hear me, I love you and can't wait to see you soon."

She caught the tail end of Maisy saying she loved her, too, before she hung up the phone. Back around the corner, the room had transformed into a full wrestling arena. Claude was on his knees with Gloria pounding on his back with her small fists. Alan was on Jeb's shoulders, yanking him by the ears. And Lorraine was screaming at the top of her lungs as she danced on the coffee table.

Yes, it was chaos. But as her dad looked up and caught her eye, a look passed between them, and she couldn't imagine it any other way.

49

AS JOY HUGGED me outside of Thimbleberry, it made sense that she'd always felt like a sister. When she pulled away, she wiped her eyes. "I can't believe you've been part of our story all this time without us ever knowing until now."

The words stretched my heart with the impact of a tidal wave. As impossible as anything in life had ever seemed, it had become abundantly clear that impossible meant nothing with God. How many lives were we all connected to without even being aware? How long was the common thread that connected us all?

I locked eyes with my sister. "So, what now?"

"We're having a family meeting with Connie and Jason this weekend," she said softly.

"How do you think that will go?"

She took a small breath. "It's hard to say. But Kitty . . . I want you to know that just because you're leaving doesn't mean I want to lose contact with you. I'd love to stay in touch and make up for lost time. If you want to as well, that is."

To be chosen was all I'd ever wanted.

"I would love that too." My eyes darted to Thimbleberry's eccentric facade. Behind those walls, my mother wandered with a lifeless version of me in tow. As much as I was ready to return to Colorado, I hoped to visit Oregon again. Sooner rather than later.

Joy lit up, but after a moment, her face fell. "Look, I wanted to say I'm sorry."

"For?"

She hesitated a moment, then said, "What you had to go through with Mom. Well, without her, I guess I should say."

"I learned long ago not to apologize for our parents' mistakes. It's none of our fault."

Joy nodded and seemed to accept my words. "Maybe once Connie and Jason know and have a chance to digest the news, we can have you back. I mean, regardless of their feelings, I'd love to host you. You're welcome anytime."

"Thank you. Same to you." I glanced at Claude. "You can consider Glenwood Springs a second home now."

Claude opened his arms to hug Joy. "Anytime. We really mean that."

"How many times can a person cry in one day?" She laughed and brushed a tear away.

"Like you said, we have a lot of lost time to make up for. Tears and all. You have our number and address, right?"

Joy nodded resolutely.

"Please let me know if something changes with . . . Mom." The name finally left my mouth. A tad clumsily, but it felt better than I expected.

"I will. Absolutely."

Claude and I moved toward our car, and Joy to hers. With a final wave, we both got in, and silence permeated the air.

"Kitty. Are you okay?"

The way he spoke my name told me he already knew the answer. Claude slid a hand onto my knee as we drove away from Thimbleberry. I wiped my tears, feeling like I was saying goodbye to a part of myself. And I supposed I was.

Yet this trip had not been filled only with goodbyes but with unexpected hellos.

"She was so close," I whispered. The trees flew by, and I felt as though they were suffocating me. "She'll never know that her prayer to be reunited with me was answered."

"Come on, honey. You and I both know that she'll know one day."

God promised to one day wipe away all disease, to wipe away every tear of sorrow and pain. To make all things new. I leaned back against the headrest and closed my eyes to block out the zipping pines. "I can't wait to get home to our family."

"It's a good life we have, isn't it?"

I let my head lazily roll to the side to gaze at his profile as his eyes remained on the curving road. "All things considered, it's an exceptional life."

"Are you ready to go home tomorrow?"

I knew what he meant without him having to say it. My sole purpose for embarking on this trip had yet to be completed, as my father's ashes still remained in our hotel room.

Are you ready to let him go?

"It's okay if you need more time, sweetheart. If you're not ready, we can stay another day if you need."

I swallowed the lump in my throat. "I don't know what I need. But I don't think I can stand any more time away from home."

He nodded. "So, we'll still leave tomorrow? Or shall I ask the front desk to extend our stay?"

I couldn't hide out in Galia forever. I wanted to be in the Rockies, where a draft came through our front windows, and foxes stored their kits under the front porch, where a loving embrace could be found around every corner, and the mountains stretched tall like my faith.

"No," I answered. "I want to go home."

—

In the middle of the night, we moved by the light of the stars, the moon, and borrowed hotel flashlights. Our tires spun, and night hummed its song around us, but time itself stood still. My father's urn bumbled in the bicycle's basket as we traveled over the hard packed sand of midnight's low tide. The breeze kept us perked up and awake, not that a moment of this magnitude could put one to sleep.

The only other chance for low tide's permission to the sea cave would be at midday when we'd already be well on our way out of town. I lagged behind Claude, following his tire marks. Night stretched on for what felt like forever, and finally he slowed. We got off our bikes, and I could already feel a dull ache in my knee. I'd pay for all this biking later, but it didn't matter. We continued the rest of the way on foot, over the exposed rocky ground to the cave's entrance.

"Would you like me to carry that for you?" Claude shone his flashlight on the urn tucked under my arm.

Granted, it might have been safer in his arms than mine, but I shook my head. "I've got it."

He stayed close to me, gripping my elbow as we stepped over the rocks and algae. Our flashlights only did so much when we reached the cave, its darkness reaching another shade of black. But we moved together, one step at a time, across the jagged floor until we reached the narrow door that led to the sea.

Claude slipped through first, his body almost too wide for

the opening. He grabbed my hand and guided me through next. The rocks spread out before us, and we continued our journey, Claude patiently waiting for my cue to stop. I wanted to reach the farthest point, but soon, he squeezed my hand and said, "I think this is far enough."

I shone my light ahead and saw how the ocean swallowed our trail just ahead. We stopped. The ocean's spray reached us, and its chill took my breath away. I gasped as my knees were soaked with the mist, and in spite of myself, a laugh burst forth.

I knelt to the ground and set down the urn. In contrast to the laughter that had just left my mouth, tears came, heavy and full and unabashed. They were tears of loss and tears of gain, and the breeze hungrily licked them from my cheeks.

I felt the sting of a lifetime of goodbyes. Vern, a sparkling golden light, snuffed out at the young age of seventeen. Cliff, a stoic and determined sailor, swept into Heaven on the wings of an enemy's blasts at thirty-five. And now my father, a man put back together by the grace of God, killed on a country back road at seventy.

But the sting of death itself could not be felt.

For that was already conquered. The grave had no victory.

I twisted the lid to the urn and set it aside.

"For dust you are, and to dust you will return." My whisper got lost in the wind. "But you, Dad, are seated in the Heavenlies now."

As the grave could not hold Jesus, neither could it hold my father. I turned the urn upside down and let the contents join with the sea. I braced myself on the rock, my hand grasping over wet moss, and though my eyes couldn't see into the deep, dark waves, I knew they carried a million pieces of my heart. But his soul was not in these waters but with Christ in His victory. Stray hairs stuck to my face, plastered wet against my cheeks, but my mouth trembled into some semblance of a smile. Though the night darkened around me, it felt like the sun was shining down.

Claude gripped my shoulder and leaned down, his breath warm and sweet on my neck.

"He was a good man."

Those five words built a sob in my throat. Claude held out his hand for me to take. I rose to my feet, unsteady from kneeling.

"Thank you for learning to love him too," I whispered. He kissed my forehead. "I don't ever want to lose you."

"Hey." He rubbed my arms. "Don't worry about that, okay?"

"We're getting older, Claude. Like it or not."

His features pulled toward the earth. A moment later, he stepped away from me and moved the empty urn aside to prop his flashlight on a rock so that it shone toward us.

"I know you've been afraid of aging. But tonight, sweetheart, we're young," he said, his eyes gleaming in the light. "Tonight, it's only us. Not the could-haves and should-haves of the past, not the what-ifs of the future. We're here right now. Just a couple of young kids, as in love as we've ever been, as thankful for this life as we ever were."

I wanted to bottle it up. The way he made me feel. The sincerity with which he loved me.

We danced, under the witness of the stars, held in tune to the ebb and flow of the tide that carried pieces of my father. We drifted on the waves of memory under the shining lamp of Heaven, my cheeks crusted with tears. Our bodies pressed together, and the sob finally broke free. It was a cry wrapped in a thousand emotions, but of them all, gratitude led the way.

Author's Note & Acknowledgments

Friends,

If you take one thing away from this story, I hope that it's this: You matter. In fact, you matter so much that Jesus suffered the unimaginable for you. Yes, you. No matter the weight of your sins, no matter what darkness you keep locked away and hidden from others, He knows it all and loves you without end.

I never understood my true worth until I met Christ. When I learned who He is, what He did, and why He did it, everything in my life changed. No longer was my identity found in who I thought myself to be. It wasn't found in my deeds or my sins, in job titles or declarations made by others. It was and is found instead in Him and what He calls me: chosen, forgiven, redeemed, beloved.

Like Kitty, who believed herself unworthy of love because of her upbringing, or like Lia, who made decisions that she deemed unforgiveable, no matter your story, Jesus' love is big enough for you. I pray with all my heart that you can rest in that truth and that you can surrender your heart to Him.

—

My heart overflows with gratitude to all who have joined me on this writing journey. First, to my readers, thank you. To think that my words have reached people of all walks of life in countries all over the world boggles my mind. Every time you purchase a book, request it from your local library, share it with a friend, post a review online, or shout me out on social media, you are supporting my dream and helping me reach others for the glory of God. From the bottom of my heart, thank you.

A special thank you to Alissa Zavalianos and Britt Howard for reading the early version of this story and encouraging me to stay the course. Both of your friendships mean so much to me. Thank you to Britt for also being my editor and cover designer. It's truly a blessing to work with and do life with you!

To all my family, near and far, I love each of you so much. Your support keeps me going. Thank you for cheering me on and inspiring me every day. God sure blessed me with the greatest family around. Mom and Dad, thank you for instilling in me a special love for the elderly and showing me how precious life is at every stage.

Patrick, to whom this book is dedicated, you are more than my husband. You are my best friend. I praise God every day that He brought us together. Thank you for chasing this dream with me and working laborious hours to build me a writing studio and a library, for facilitating my writing time, and for always providing an epic dad joke right when I need one.

My children, Leo and Nora. You are such bright lights in my life. Thank you for teaching me something new every day. I'm so glad I get to be your mommy.

To my grandparents, my dear friends in Heaven, you are tucked within every word I write. It pains me still to not be able to share this with you, but I feel you with me every step of the way. One day, we will be reunited, and what a glorious day that will be.

To Jesus, who gives me hope and fights my battles. I don't like to even think of where I'd be without You. Thank You for being trustworthy with the details, even when they don't make sense at the time, for being my guiding light every day, and for Your precious blood You spilled for me and the world. Thank You for setting me free.